Bangs and Whimpers: Stories About the End of the World

EDITED BY
JAMES FRENKEL

ROXBURY PARK

LOWELL HOUSE
LOS ANGELES

NTC/Contemporary Publishing Group

ISBN: 0-7373-0271-2
Library of Congress Catalog Number: 99-73648

Roxbury Park is a division of NTC/Contemporary Publishing Group, Inc.

Managing Director and Publisher: Jack Artenstein
Editor in Chief, Roxbury Park Books: Michael Artenstein
Director of Publishing Services: Rena Copperman
Editorial Assistant: Nicole Monastirsky
Assistant Editors: Seth Johnson, Kristopher O'Higgins
Series Editor: Mark Robert Waldman
Interior Designer: Susan H. Hartman
Cover Artwork: Ron Walotsky

Printed and bound in the United States of America
99 00 01 VP 10 9 8 7 6 5 4 3 2 1

Contents

Acknowledgments

Any anthology takes a lot of work and the cooperation of many people. This one is no exception, and I'd like to thank Mark Waldman, my editor at Lowell House, Michael Artenstein, and all the rest of the Lowell House crew. Also, my assistant editors, Seth Johnson and Kristopher O'Higgins, contributed mightily to making this the book it's finally become. They were an integral part of the editorial process in putting *Bangs and Whimpers* together.

—JF

Introduction

This is the way the world ends / not with a bang
but a whimper.

T. S. Eliot, *The Hollow Men*

Who really cares about the end of the world?
We do.
Since the beginning of time, we have pondered our ultimate
fate: in our epic tales, our creation myths, our folk stories, fantasies,
and dreams. In virtually every culture and tribe, there is a story about
the end of the world.

Some suggest that life on earth will end in fiery cataclysm; others in icy stillness; still others in catastrophic floods. Sometimes with
a whimper, sometimes with a bang.

As we have advanced technologically and increased our ability to
perceive the world on both microscopic and macroscopic levels, so
have our ideas about the end of the world advanced and become more
fantastic, more varied and more technically complex. But whether one
looks at ancient epics or at the modern stories within this book, all
these tales have one thing in common: Life for humanity ends.

Why are we so fascinated by the end of human life? Perhaps
because it poses such a challenge. How better to test the mettle of an
individual than to pit him or her against some force or circumstance

that threatens to end that person's existence? Could there be a more stern testing of someone's courage than this?

Yet the question of bravery is moot, for regardless of the protagonist's personal abilities or attitude about impending doom, the world still comes to an end. Whether the man or woman in the street quails in the face of the ultimate sacrifice or stands firm against the inevitable is really not at issue.

But how things end, by what means, for what reason, and with what possibility of anything further after the supposed end—these are all items of intense interest to most people. For we are mortal, and the prospect of annihilation has always fascinated us. Many religions speculate on the nature of death, the process, the consequences, and the possibility of something . . . more.

Yet it's not the question of what lies beyond death that mostly interests the writers in this anthology. As the title suggests, these stories offer a variety of different ways the world might end.

From the terminal increase in chaos of Robert A. Heinlein's "Year of the Jackpot," to the eerie silence at the conclusion of Arthur C. Clarke's "The Nine Billion Names of God," our stellar cast of contributors have clearly had great fun with the ways the world might end.

Do I believe that aliens will come and try to rescue us, as Robert Sheckley suggests in his mordantly funny "Emissary from a Green and Yellow World"? No, but I love the way he spins out his tale. He and the other writers in this anthology capture the human element in their stories. Each is a gem of a tale, leaving us with a single image that still will be memorable years after its reading.

It's no coincidence that science fiction has been a burgeoning field in the twentieth century, a time when the most intense development of technology has taken place. Science fiction has always, since its earliest examples, been a literature of ideas. H. G. Wells, one of the greatest writers of our age, is considered by many to be the first modern science fiction writer, and some of his most famous works deal with the end of human life, or its possibility. Wells himself might have been furious to hear his work so categorized, but his influence on the field is undeniable. Ultimately concerned with the effects of society and technology on the individual, Wells would recognize such issues in the works of most of the writers here. He led the way to the twentieth century. For evidence of his science fictional vision, look no further than at his eerie scenario of mankind's doom in his short novel, *The Time Machine.*

SF writers love to play, to experiment, and to attempt to top themselves with stories that they haven't done or seen before. So as our ability to destroy the world has increased—with nuclear war, pollution, germ warfare, or other modern techno-threats—it's only sensible that scenarios for the end of the world should abound. When Wells wrote, he could only imagine the horrors that scientific advances could wreak on the rest of the century. Writers since then have witnessed far greater atrocities, infusing their work with the temper of their time.

From our turbulent century, one would expect writers to respond with a kaleidoscope of possibilities, and they do. *Bangs and Whimpers* includes the wonder-filled tales of Arthur C. Clarke, Robert A. Heinlein, and Isaac Asimov, the gods of the golden age of science fiction (the late 1930s). Frederik Pohl, Robert Sheckley, Philip K. Dick, J. G. Ballard and Robert Silverberg created extraordinarily different and wildly new visions of imagination in the 1950s and 1960s, and are well represented here.

John Varley, Connie Willis, and James Tiptree, Jr. belong to a younger generation that got its start in the 1970s, and their stories reflect the changes that occurred in the world during those years. Neil Gaiman, Robert Reed, and Richard Kadrey are among the brightest, most creative writers of the past few years. I also have included works by James Thurber, Walter Van Tilburg Clark, C. C. Shackleton, Frank Pollack, and Howard Fast, writers usually not associated with science fiction but who have contributed stories that complement the rest of the volume.

Collectively, the authors herein offer up a kaleidoscope of dooms, some funny, some sad. Some will make you gasp in wonder and delight; others will bring a tear to your eye. Our intention is to entertain you, first and foremost, but I know that each of these authors wants to make us stop and think about what we might do to prevent some of these scenarios from coming horribly true. They make us care, about their stories, about ourselves, and about the world.

The Nine Billion Names of God

ARTHUR C. CLARKE

Arthur C. Clarke is unquestionably the best-known science fiction writer in the world today. Apart from his fine stories and novels and the kudos he's received within the field, his fame dates to a scientific paper he wrote in 1947, in which he postulated the communications satellite. It would be nearly two decades until the first one was actually launched, but it established Clarke as a science fiction writer with distinguished scientific credentials.

"The Nine Billion Names of God," which first appeared in 1951, is a classic Clarke piece. It combines timely scientific information with rational speculation and that metaphysical sense of wonder that infuses Clarke's finest works.

It's not giving anything away to say that this powerful story is partly about religion, for speculation on ultimate causation in the universe is a common science fiction theme. Clarke simply does it better, and more eloquently, than just about anyone else.

This is a slightly unusual request," said Dr. Wagner, with what he hoped was commendable restraint. "As far as I know, it's the first time anyone's been asked to supply a Tibetan monastery with an Automatic Sequence Computer. I don't wish to be inquisitive, but I should hardly have thought that your—ah—establishment had much use for such a machine. Could you explain just what you intend to do with it?"

"Gladly," replied the lama, readjusting his silk robes and carefully putting away the slide rule he had been using for currency conversions. "Your Mark V Computer can carry out any routine mathematical operation involving up to ten digits. However, for our work we are interested in *letters*, not numbers. As we wish you to modify the output circuits, the machine will be printing words, not columns of figures."

"I don't quite understand. . . ."

"This is a project on which we have been working for the last three centuries—since the lamasery was founded, in fact. It is somewhat alien to our way of thought, so I hope you will listen with an open mind while I explain it."

"Naturally."

"It is really quite simple. We have been compiling a list which shall contain all the possible names of God."

"I beg your pardon?"

"We have reason to believe," continued the lama imperturbably, "that all such names can be written with not more than nine letters in an alphabet we have devised."

"And you have been doing this for three centuries?"

"Yes: we expected it would take us about fifteen thousand years to complete the task."

"Oh," Dr. Wagner looked a little dazed. "Now I see why you wanted to hire one of our machines. But exactly what is the *purpose* of this project?"

The lama hesitated for a fraction of a second, and Wagner wondered if he had offended him. If so, there was no trace of annoyance in the reply.

"Call it ritual, if you like, but it's a fundamental part of our belief. All the many names of the Supreme Being—God, Jehovah, Allah, and so on—they are only man-made labels. There is a philosophical problem of some difficulty here, which I do not propose to discuss, but somewhere among all the possible combinations of letters that can occur are what one may call the *real* names of God. By systematic permutation of letters, we have been trying to list them all."

"I see. You've been starting at AAAAAAA . . . and working up to ZZZZZZZZ. . . ."

"Exactly—though we use a special alphabet of our own. Modifying the electromatic typewriters to deal with this is, of course, trivial.

A rather more interesting problem is that of devising suitable circuits to eliminate ridiculous combinations. For example, no letter must occur more than three times in succession."

"Three? Surely you mean two."

"Three is correct: I am afraid it would take too long to explain why, even if you understood our language." .

"I'm sure it would," said Wagner hastily. "Go on."

"Luckily, it will be a simple matter to adapt your Automatic Sequence Computer for this work, since once it has been programmed properly it will permute each letter in turn and print the result. What would have taken us fifteen thousand years it will be able to do in a hundred days."

Dr. Wagner was scarcely conscious of the faint sounds from the Manhattan streets far below. He was in a different world, a world of natural, not man-made, mountains. High up in their remote aeries these monks had been patiently at work, generation after generation, compiling their lists of meaningless words. Was there any limit to the follies of mankind? Still, he must give no hint of his inner thoughts. The customer was always right. . . .

"There's no doubt," replied the doctor, "that we can modify the Mark V to print lists of this nature. I'm much more worried about the problem of installation and maintenance. Getting out to Tibet, in these days, is not going to be easy."

"We can arrange that. The components are small enough to travel by air—that is one reason why we chose your machine. If you can get them to India, we will provide transport from there."

"And you want to hire two of our engineers?"

"Yes, for the three months that the project should occupy."

"I've no doubt that Personnel can manage that." Dr. Wagner scribbled a note on his desk pad. "There are just two other points—"

Before he could finish the sentence the lama had produced a small slip of paper.

"This is my certified credit balance at the Asiatic Bank."

"Thank you. It appears to be—ah—adequate. The second matter is so trivial that I hesitate to mention it—but it's surprising how often the obvious gets overlooked. What source of electrical energy have you?"

"A diesel generator providing fifty kilowatts at a hundred and ten volts. It was installed about five years ago and is quite reliable. It's made life at the lamasery much more comfortable, but of course it was really installed to provide power for the motors driving the prayer wheels."

"Of course," echoed Dr. Wagner. "I should have thought of that."

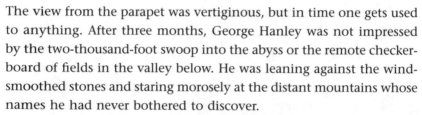

The view from the parapet was vertiginous, but in time one gets used to anything. After three months, George Hanley was not impressed by the two-thousand-foot swoop into the abyss or the remote checkerboard of fields in the valley below. He was leaning against the wind-smoothed stones and staring morosely at the distant mountains whose names he had never bothered to discover.

This, thought George, was the craziest thing that had ever happened to him. "Project Shangri-La," some wit back at the labs had christened it. For weeks now the Mark V had been churning out acres of sheets covered with gibberish. Patiently, inexorably, the computer had been rearranging letters in all their possible combinations, exhausting each class before going on to the next. As the sheets had emerged from the electromatic typewriters, the monks had carefully cut them up and pasted them into enormous books. In another week, heaven be praised, they would have finished. Just what obscure calculations had convinced the monks that they needn't bother to go on to words of ten, twenty, or a hundred letters, George didn't know. One of his recurring nightmares was that there would be some change of plan, and that the high lama (whom they'd naturally called Sam Jaffe, though he didn't look a bit like him) would suddenly announce that the project would be extended to approximately A.D. 2060. They were quite capable of it.

George heard the heavy wooden door slam in the wind as Chuck came out onto the parapet beside him. As usual, Chuck was smoking one of the cigars that made him so popular with the monks—who, it seemed, were quite willing to embrace all the minor and most of the major pleasures of life. That was one thing in their favor: they might be crazy, but they weren't bluenoses. Those frequent trips they took down to the village, for instance . . .

"Listen, George," said Chuck urgently. "I've learned something that means trouble."

"What's wrong? Isn't the machine behaving?" That was the worst contingency George could imagine. It might delay his return, and nothing could be more horrible. The way he felt now, even the sight of a TV commercial would seem like manna from heaven. At least it would be some link with home.

"No—it's nothing like that." Chuck settled himself on the parapet, which was unusual because normally he was scared of the drop. "I've just found what all this is about."

"What d'ya mean? I thought we knew."

"Sure—we know what the monks are trying to do. But we didn't know *why*. It's the craziest thing—"

"Tell me something new," growled George.

"—but old Sam's just come clean with me. You know the way he drops in every afternoon to watch the sheets roll out. Well, this time he seemed rather excited, or at least as near as he'll ever get to it. When I told him that we were on the last cycle he asked me, in that cute English accent of his, if I'd ever wondered what they were trying to do. I said, 'Sure'—and he told me."

"Go on: I'll buy it."

"Well, they believe that when they have listed all His names—and they reckon that there are about nine billion of them—God's purpose will be achieved. The human race will have finished what it was created to do, and there won't be any point in carrying on. Indeed, the very idea is something like blasphemy."

"Then what do they expect us to do? Commit suicide?"

"There's no need for that. When the list's completed, God steps in and simply winds things up . . . bingo!"

"Oh, I get it. When we finish our job, it will be the end of the world."

Chuck gave a nervous little laugh.

"That's just what I said to Sam. And do you know what happened? He looked at me in a very queer way, like I'd been stupid in class, and said, 'It's nothing as trivial as *that*.'"

George thought this over for a moment.

"That's what I call taking the Wide View," he said presently. "But what d'you suppose we should do about it? I don't see that it makes the slightest difference to us. After all, we already knew that they were crazy."

"Yes—but don't you see what may happen? When the list's complete and the Last Trump doesn't blow—or whatever it is they expect—*we* may get the blame. It's our machine they've been using. I don't like the situation one little bit."

"I see," said George slowly. "You've got a point there. But this sort of thing's happened before, you know. When I was a kid down in Louisiana we had a crackpot preacher who once said the world was going to end next Sunday. Hundreds of people believed him—even sold their homes. Yet when nothing happened, they didn't turn nasty, as you'd expect. They just decided that he's made a mistake in his calculations and went right on believing. I guess some of them still do."

"Well, this isn't Louisiana, in case you hadn't noticed. There are just two of us and hundreds of these monks. I like them, and I'll be sorry for old Sam when his lifework backfires on him. But all the same, I wish I was somewhere else."

"I've been wishing that for weeks. But there's nothing we can do until the contract's finished and the transport arrives to fly us out."

"Of course," said Chuck thoughtfully, "we could always try a bit of sabotage."

"Like hell we could! That would make things worse."

"Not the way I meant. Look at it like this. The machine will finish its run four days from now, on the present twenty-hours-a-day basis. The transport calls in a week. O.K.—then all we need to do is to find something that will hold up the works for a couple of days. We'll fix it, of course, but not too quickly. If we time matters properly, we can be down at the airfield when the last name pops out of the register. They won't be able to catch us then."

"I don't like it," said George. "It will be the first time I ever walked out on a job. Besides, it would make them suspicious. No, I'll sit tight and take what comes."

▼

"I *still* don't like it," he said, seven days later, as the tough little mountain ponies carried them down the winding road. "And don't you think I'm running away because I'm afraid. I'm just sorry for those poor old guys up there, and I don't want to be around when they find what suckers they've been. Wonder how Sam will take it?"

"It's funny," replied Chuck, "but when I said good-by I got the idea he knew we were walking out on him—and that he didn't care because he knew the machine was running smoothly and that the job would soon be finished. After that—well, of course, for him there just isn't any After That. . . ."

George turned in his saddle and stared back up the mountain road. This was the last place from which one could get a clear view of the lamasery. The squat, angular buildings were silhouetted against the afterglow of the sunset: here and there, lights gleamed like portholes in the side of an ocean liner. Electric lights, of course, sharing the same circuit as the Mark V. How much longer would they share it? wondered George. Would the monks smash up the computer in their rage and disappointment? Or would they just sit down quietly and begin their calculations all over again?

He knew exactly what was happening up on the mountain at this very moment. The high lama and his assistants would be sitting in their silk robes, inspecting the sheets as the junior monks carried them away from the typewriters and pasted them into the great volumes. No one would be saying anything. The only sound would be the incessant patter, the never-ending rainstorm of the keys hitting the paper, for the Mark V itself was utterly silent as it flashed through its thousands of calculations a second. Three months of this, thought George, was enough to start anyone climbing up the wall.

"There she is!" called Chuck, pointing down into the valley. "Ain't she beautiful!"

She certainly was, thought George. The battered old DC3 lay at the end of the runway like a tiny silver cross. In two hours she would be bearing them away to freedom and sanity. It was a thought worth savoring like a fine liqueur. George let it roll round his mind as the pony trudged patiently down the slope.

The swift night of the high Himalayas was now almost upon them. Fortunately, the road was very good, as roads went in that region, and they were both carrying torches. There was not the slightest danger, only a certain discomfort from the bitter cold. The sky overhead was perfectly clear, and ablaze with the familiar, friendly stars. At least there would be no risk, thought George, of the pilot being unable to take off because of weather conditions. That had been his only remaining worry.

He began to sing, but gave it up after a while. This vast arena of mountains, gleaming like whitely hooded ghosts on every side, did not encourage such ebullience. Presently George glanced at his watch.

"Should be there in an hour," he called back over his shoulder to Chuck. Then he added, in an afterthought: "Wonder if the computer's finished its run. It was due about now."

Chuck didn't reply, so George swung round in his saddle. He could just see Chuck's face, a white oval turned toward the sky.

"Look," whispered Chuck, and George lifted his eyes to heaven. (There is always a last time for everything.)

Overhead, without any fuss, the stars were going out.

Killing
the Morrow

ROBERT REED

There are many ways the world can end. The obvious ones are forms of physical catastrophe, but there are more subtle ways to end the world. Our proprietary attitude about our world has been known to get us in trouble, as when we've polluted the environment in the process of selfishly pursuing particular human needs.

The shortsightedness of self-interest has allowed us to foul our nest with pesticides and an appalling variety of other poisons. But sometimes the human trait of claiming the world as our own also can work in positive ways, as the following story demonstrates.

Robert Reed, an author who at this writing seems just on the verge of being acknowledged as one of the finest in the field, has published numerous short stories and more than a half-dozen novels, including the recent *Beneath the Gated Sky* and *An Exaltation of Larks*. He burst onto the scene in the mid-1980s, when he was named the first Grand Prize Winner of the L. Ron Hubbard Writers of the Future contest. Since then he's been nominated for the Hugo Award and won the *Asimov's Science Fiction* readers poll for best novella. "Killing the Morrow," first published in 1996, is one of his most fascinating stories: with endings, and beginnings as well . . .

You know, I've heard my share of disembodied voices. I'm accustomed to their fickle, sometimes bizarre demands. But tonight's voice is different, clear as gin and utterly compelling. I must listen. Sitting inside my old packing crate, my worldly possessions at arm's length, I am fed instructions that erase everything familiar and prosaic. Yet I cannot resist, can't offer even a token resistance, now crawling out of my little house and rising, my heart pounding as the last shreds of sanity are lost to me.

I've lived in this alleyway for eight months, yet I don't look back. I'm in poor physical condition and my shoes are worn through, but I walk several miles without rest, without complaint. And there are others, too: the streets are full of silent walkers. They exhibit a calmness, a liquid orderliness, that would disturb the healthy observer. Yet I barely notice the others. I want a specific street, which I find, turning right and following it for another mile. The tall buildings fall away into trim working-class houses. Another street beckons. I start to read the numbers on mailboxes. The house I want is on a corner, lit up and its front door left open. I step inside without ringing the bell, thinking that the place looks familiar . . . as if I've been here before, or maybe seen it in dreams. . . .

My new life begins.

More than most people, I have experience with radical change, with the vagaries of existence. Tonight's change is simply more sudden and more tightly orchestrated than those of the past. I'm here for a reason, no doubt about it. There's some grand cause that will be explained in due time. And meanwhile, there's pleasure: for the first time in years, existence has a palatable purpose, authority, and as astonishing as it seems, a genuine beauty.

An opened can of warming beer is set on the coffee table. I pick it up and sniff, then set it down again, which is uncharacteristic for me. An enormous television is in the corner, the all-sports channel still broadcasting, nothing to see but an empty court and arena. The game was canceled without fuss. Somehow I know that nobody will ever again play that particular sport, that it was rendered extinct in an instant. Yet any sense of loss is cushioned by the Voice. It makes me crumble onto a lumpy sofa, listening and nodding, eyes fixed on nothing.

Tools are in the garage, I'm told. I carry them into the living room, arranging them according to their use. Then armed with a short rusty crowbar I head upstairs, finding the bathroom and a big steel bathtub, and with the crowbar I start to batter the mildewed tile and plaster, startled cockroaches fleeing the light.

After a little while the front door opens, closes.

I go downstairs, part of me curious. A handsome woman is waiting for me, offering a thin smile. She's dressed in quality clothes, and she's my age but with much less mileage. That smile of hers is hopeful, even enthusiastic, but beneath it is a much-hidden sense of terror.

What's her name? I wonder. But I won't ask.

Nor does she ask about me.

With two backs available, we start to clear the living room of furniture and the dusty old carpeting. By now the television has gone blank. I unplug it, and together we carry it to the curb. Electronics are an important resource. Our neighbors—mismatched couples like ourselves—are doing the same job, stereos and microwave ovens and televisions stacked and covered carefully with plastic. Firearms make smaller, secondary piles. Then around midnight a large truck arrives. I'm dragging out the last of the carpeting, pausing long enough to watch a crew of burly men loading everything into the long trailer. One of them seems familiar. He was a police officer, wasn't he? I remember him. He bullied me on several occasions, for the fun of it. And now we are equals, animosity nothing but a luxury. I manage to wave at him. No response. Then I return to the house, never hurrying. Rain begins to fall, fat cold drops striking the back of my neck, and with them comes a fatigue, sudden and profound, that leaves my legs shaking and my breath coming in little wet gulps.

The Voice has already told us to sleep when it's needed. The woman and I move upstairs, climbing into the same bed without undressing. Nudity is permitted. Many things are permitted, we've been told. But I can't help thinking of the woman's terror as I lie beside her, looking as I do, unshaved and filthy, wearing sores and months of grime. It's better to do nothing, I decide. Just to sleep.

"Good night," I whisper.

She isn't crying, but when she says, "Sleep well," I hear her working not to cry, the words tight and slow. Was she married in her former life? She doesn't wear any rings, yet she seems like a person who would enjoy, even demand marriage. She's awake for more than an hour, lying as motionless as possible, her ordinary old parts struggling to find some reason for the bizarre things that are happening now.

I feel pity.

Yet for the most part, I like these changes. The bed is soft, the sheets almost clean. I lie awake out of contentment, listening to the rain on the roof and thinking about my packing crate in the alley-way—feeling no fondness at all for that dead past.

I dream of grass, astonishing as that seems.

Of an apeman.

No, that's a lousy term. *Hominid* is more appropriate. The creature walks under a bright tropical sky, minding its own narrow business. A male, I realize. I'm sitting in the future, watching it from ground level and feeling waves of excitement. Here is an ancestor of the human species, naked and lovely, and it doesn't even notice me, strolling past and out of sight. I have seen through time, changing nothing. Aren't I a clever ape? I ask myself.

Not clever enough, a voice warns me.

A quiet, almost whispered voice.

We divide our jobs according to ability. Being somewhat stronger than the woman, I work to dislodge the bathtub from the wall, then lever it into the hallway and shove it down the splintering wooden stairs. And meanwhile the woman has cleaned the living room a dozen times, at least, the windows covered with foil and the air heavy with chlorine.

Vans and small trucks begin to deliver equipment. Thermostats and filters have been adapted from local stocks, I suppose. More sophisticated machinery arrives later. Jugs of thick clear fluid are stacked in the darkest corner. Perfect cleanliness isn't mandatory, yet the woman struggles to keep the room surgically clean, hoping that the Voice will applaud her efforts.

She's first to say, "The Voice comes from the future."

Obviously, yes.

"From the distant future," she adds.

I can't guess dates, but it seems likely.

"And this is a womb," she remarks, pointing at the old bathtub. "Here is where the future will be born."

The Voice speaks differently to different people, it seems. I assumed that the tub was an elaborate growth chamber, but how exactly does one grow the future?

Taking me by the waist, she says, "It'll be like our own child."

I make affirmative sounds, but something feels wrong.

"I love you," she assures me.

"I love you," I lie. Nothing is as vital to her as her illusions of the loving family.

Does the Voice know that?

In the night, between work and sleep, she invites me to her side of the bed. It's been a long time. My performance is less than sterling, but at least the experience is pleasant, building new bonds. Then afterward we cuddle under the sheets, whisper in secret tones, then drift off into a fine deep sleep, dreams coming from the darkness.

▼

Rain falls in my dreams.

Motion, I learn, is matter shaped by the hand of Chaos. Tiny variations in wind and moisture will conspire to ignite or extinguish entire storms. And no conceivable machine or mind can know every fluctuation, every inspiration. It's not even possible to predict which minuscule event will produce the perfect day, leaving millions of lives changed, the fundamental shape of everything warped ever so slightly. . . .

Suppose you can reach back in time, says my dream voice. Suppose you're aware of the dangers in changing what was, but you have ego enough to accept the risks. Channeling vast energies, you create your windows entirely from local materials. It is thermally identical to the surrounding ground. You limit your study to a few useful moments. All you allow yourself is a camera and transmitter, intricate but indistinguishable from the local sand and grit. The hominid can stare at the window. He can stomp on it. He can fling it, eat it, or simply ignore it. But nothing, nothing, nothing he can do will make it behave as anything but the perfect grain of dirty quartz.

And yet, says the dream voice.

Despite your hard work and cleverness, there is some telling impact. Perhaps heat leaked from the mechanism, atoms jostled by their touch. Or perhaps its optical energies were imperfectly balanced, excess photons added to or taken away from the local environment. There would be no way to know what went wrong. But the consequences will spread, becoming apparent, growing from nothing until they encompass everything.

The universe, I'm learning, is incomprehensibly fragile.

How can any person, any intelligence, hope to put *everything* back where it belongs?

------------▼------------

A young man delivers foodstuffs and other general supplies, coming twice a week, and sometimes he lingers on the porch, telling me what he has seen around town. Factories and warehouses have been refurbished, he says. Old people and eerily patient children work and live inside them. Some of the factories make the machines that fill my living room/nursery. But the majority of the products are stranger. He grins, describing brilliant lights and tiny power plants, robots, and more robots. Isn't it all amazing? Wondrous? And fun?

I nod. Astonishment does seem like the day's most abundant product.

The woman dislikes my chatting with the young man. She feels that he's a poor worker, obviously not paying ample attention to the Voice. For the first time, for just an instant, I wonder if the Voice doesn't touch people with equal force. For instance, the woman claims to hear it all of the time, her initial terror replaced with energy and commitment, or at least the nervous desire to please it. But for me there are long periods of silence, of relative peace. It's the woman who wakes first in the morning. It's the woman who loses track of time and hunger, scrubbing the floor until her hands bleed. And she's the one who snaps at the delivery boy, telling him:

"You're not helping us at all!"

To which he says, "Except I am." At once, without hesitation, he says, "Part of my job is to tell others what I see, to keep them aware of what's being done. How else can you know? You can't go anywhere. Your job is to stay put, and you're doing that perfectly."

The logic has its impact. She retreats with a growl, her anger helping her to polish the bathtub for the umpteenth time.

I wonder, in secret, if the delivery boy is telling the truth.

Or is he a clever liar?

And how can I wonder about such things? Just considering the possibility of subterfuge is a kind of subterfuge. Particularly when I find myself admiring the boy's courage.

In secret.

The past has been changed, I learn in my sleep.

Small events have evolved into mammoth ones.

Perhaps an excess heat caused an instability that altered the precise pattern of raindrops in a summer shower. Hominids made love in the rain. It's not that they wouldn't have had rain, but it's the delicate impact of thousands of raindrops that matter. Eggs and sperm are extraordinarily sensitive, I'm learning. Change any parameter—the instant of ejaculation; the angle of thrust; the simplest groan of thanks—and a different sperm will find its target. Even the drumming of raindrops will jostle the testicles enough, now and again, and produce different offspring. Which in turn means a different human evolution.

The species isn't altered appreciably. People remain people, good or not. Nor is the character of history changed. Humankind will master the same tools, then warfare and the intricacies of nation-states. What matters is that the specific faces will change, and the names, every historical figure erased along with every anonymous one, an enormous wavelike disruption racing out through time.

In order to kill myself, I don't have to kill my grandpa.

I just have to tickle his hairy balls.

They bring the embryo in, of all things, an old florist's van.

Each house on our street gets its own embryo, and the Voice fills everyone with a sense of honor and duty. We've sealed the bathtub's drain, then filled it with the heavy fluids. Tubes pump in oxygen. The workers connect the embryo to a plastic umbilical, then I help the woman check every dial and sensor, making certain that the tiny smear of living tissue is healthy.

It doubles in size, that day and every day, hands and feet showing before the end of the week. It's not growing like any human, but maybe that's a consequence of the fluids. Or synthetic genes. Or maybe all the generations of evolution between him and me.

The woman shivers, weeps. Holding herself, she announces, "At least one of us has to stay with it now. Always."

In case of some unlikely, unforeseen problem, yes. We can pick up the telephone, emergency services waiting to troubleshoot.

"Night and day," she says, with a thrill.

I'll give her the night shift, I decide.

"This is our child," she claims, repeating what the Voice tells her. Her own voice is stiff and dry. Unabashedly fanatical. "Don't you think he's lovely, darling?"

But he's not my child, or my grandchild, either. For an instant, I consider mentioning my dreams of Africa and the vagaries of time . . . but then I think again, some piece of me guessing that this woman has had no such dreams.

"Isn't he lovely?" she asks again.

I say, "Lovely," without feeling.

Yet the word itself is enough for her. She nods and smiles, her face lit up with the injected joy.

▼

The past is a sea, I dream. A great flat mirror of a sea. Standing on the present, on a low shoreline, I carelessly throw a grain of sand over my shoulder. Its impact is tiny, too tiny to observe, but the resulting wave is growing, a small ripple becoming a mountainous wall rushing straight at me.

What can I do? Flee into the future? But with each step the future becomes the present, and I can never run so far that the wave won't catch me, utterly and forever dissolving my existence.

But there is one answer. Pack a bag, bend at the knees, and wait. Wait, then leap. With care and a certain desperate fearlessness, I can launch myself over the wave, evading it entirely. Then I'll fall again, tumbling onto the calm past, creating a second obliterating wave but my own life saved regardless.

Fuck the costs.

Our "child" is less childlike with each passing day.

Even the woman is having difficulty sounding like the proud parent.

Curled in a fetal position, this citizen from the future resembles a middle-aged man, comfortably plump and shockingly hairy, lost in sleep while his memories are placed inside his newly minted mind.

I can't help but notice, his brain is huge.

I sit alone with him in the morning and again in the early evening, nothing to do but watch his slumber as well as the humming and clicking machines. It's ironic that this creature, having his existence threatened by the most trivial event, is now employing the coarsest tomfoolery to save his ass. The entire Earth must be involved. Every human and every resource is being marshaled to meet some rigorous schedule. This is an invasion; and like any invasion, success hinges on the beachhead.

The future is attempting to leap over its extinction, very little room for error.

And I'm beginning to notice how the Voice, busy speaking to this superman's mind, speaks less and less to me.

The Voice has its limits, of course.

Yet at night my dreams persist, that different voice showing me wonders as fascinating as anything in my waking life.

The delivery boy begins to arrive at irregular intervals, but never as often as before.

"To save gas," he claims, always smiling. But that smile has a satirical bite to it. "And from now on, sorry. There's no more meat or eggs."

For health reasons, perhaps. Or the invaders could be vegetarians.

"Let me look at yours," says the boy, stepping indoors for the first time. He doesn't wait for approval, walking up to the bathtub and staring at the sleeping shape. "I wonder what he's like. When he's finished, I mean."

I have no idea. And that bothers me.

"Of course he'll be grateful for your help. I'm sure of that."

I'm nervous. It's against every rule to have visitors. What if the woman wakes early and finds the boy here? What if a neighbor reports me? Touching a shoulder, I try easing him toward the door, asking in a whisper, "What have you seen lately?"

He mentions giant machines that have rolled to the north. Bright lights show at night, and there's rumbling that might mean construction. A new city is being built, he hears. From others.

I ask about the people who built those rolling machines. Where have they gone?

"They've been reassigned, of course. There's always work to be done somewhere. Always, always."

He smiled at me, the message in his eyes.

Then we reach the door, and again he stands on the porch, telling me, "Once a week, and I don't know which day. No meat, no eggs. And that's a lovely boy you've got there. A real darling."

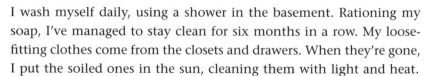

I wash myself daily, using a shower in the basement. Rationing my soap, I've managed to stay clean for six months in a row. My loose-fitting clothes come from the closets and drawers. When they're gone, I put the soiled ones in the sun, cleaning them with light and heat.

I wanted to seem more attractive to the woman, and for a little while she was responding.

But now she has doubts about sex, always distracted, needing to be in some position that leaves her able to monitor the dials. More and more she complains about being tired or disinterested. The man-child's presence makes her edgy. I wish she'd become pregnant, except of course a pregnancy would be a problem. A division of allegiances. But then I realize that if the Voice can speak to a mind, interfacing with its network of interlocking neurons, then shouldn't it be able to speak to glands as well? Couldn't it put all of our bothersome sperm and eggs to sleep?

One night, waking alone in bed, I feel a powerful desire to make love to a woman. I come downstairs and ask permission, and the woman's response is a sharp "Not here, no!" Which leads me to suggest that she abandon her post for a few minutes. I promise to hurry, and where's the harm?

She gasps, moans, and nearly collapses. "I can't do *that*."

We'll never couple again. I know it, and it both saddens and relieves me. Alone, I feel free. An old reflex lets me wonder where I could find someone else. A lady more amiable, someone that I've selected for myself.

Beginning tomorrow morning, the woman sleeps in the living room, on sheets and pillows spread over the clean hard floor.

She won't leave me alone at my post.

She has a bucket next to the door where she pisses and shits. And when she looks at me, in those rare moments, nothing can hide her total scorn.

This is my last lucid dream.

I'm standing on the beach, sand without color and a wall of radiant ocean water roaring toward me. And a woman appears. Like the man in my bathtub, she has an elongated skull and a superior intellect, but her face is completely human, showing a mixture of fear and empathy, as well as a sturdy strength born of convictions.

"We think they are wrong," she begins. "Please remember this. Not all of us are like *them*."

I nod, trying to describe my appreciation.

But she interrupts, telling me, "This is all we can do for you."

I can't recognize her language, yet I understand every word.

"Best wishes," she says.

Then she begins to cry.

I try to embrace her. I step forward and open my arms . . . but then the water is on me, the beach and her dissolving into atoms . . . and my hands struggle to reassemble her from memory, the task impossible for every good reason. . . .

▼

A new delivery boy arrives.

Perhaps ten years old, he needs to make two trips from his station wagon, carrying the minimal groceries to the porch and no farther. I'm standing on my porch waiting for the second load. Fresh air feels pleasant. The lawn has grown shaggy and seedy, the old furniture and carpeting rotting without complaint amidst the greenness. A quick calculation tells me that this is late autumn, early winter. The trees should have changed and lost their leaves by now. Yet the world smells and tastes like spring, both climate and vegetation under some kind of powerful control.

The boy struggles with a numbered sack. Not only is he small, he looks malnourished. But he brings my food with a fanatical sense of purpose, and when I ask about the other boy, the older boy, he merely replies:

"He's done."

What does that mean?

"Done," he repeats, angry not to be understood.

Hearing our voices, the woman wakes and comes to the door. "Get back in here," she snaps. "I'm warning you!"

One last look at the improved world, then I retreat, taking both sacks with me. Meanwhile the boy fires up the station wagon, black smoke dispersing in all directions. He looks silly, that fierce little head peering through the steering wheel. He pulls into the next driveway, and I wonder who lives in that house. And what do they dream about?

The woman is complaining about my attitudes, my carelessness. Everything. I'm a safer subject than the lousy quality of today's barley and rice.

"Come here," she tells me.

Perhaps I will, perhaps I won't.

"Or I'll pick up the phone and complain," she threatens.

She won't. First of all, I terrify her. What if I exacted some kind of vengeance in response? And secondly, the thought of being entirely alone must disturb her. I know it whenever I stare at her, making her shrink away. As much as she hates me, without my presence she might forget that she's genuinely alive.

The future doomed itself.

Then it packed its bags, intending to save itself.

But like a weather system, the future is too large and chaotic to be of one mind, holding to a single outcome. Some of its citizens argued that they didn't have the right to intrude on the past. "Why should we supplant these primitive people?" they asked. "We screwed up, and if we were any sort of hominids, we would accept our fate and be done with it."

But most of their species felt otherwise. And by concentrating the energies of two earths, present and past, they felt there was a better than good chance of success.

Unaware of the secret movement in their midst.

Never guessing that there was a second surreptitious Voice.

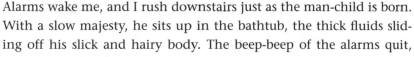

Alarms wake me, and I rush downstairs just as the man-child is born. With a slow majesty, he sits up in the bathtub, the thick fluids sliding off his slick and hairy body. The beep-beep of the alarms quit, replaced with a scream from the woman. "Look at you," she says. "Oh, look at you!"

The man couldn't look more pissed, coughing until his lungs clear, then screwing up his face, saying something in that future language. A nearby machine activates itself, translating his words. "I want water. Cold water. Get me water."

"I'll get it," I say.

The woman is too busy grinning and applauding herself. "You're a darling lovely man, sir. And I took care of you. Almost entirely by myself, I did."

The man-child speaks again.

"I'm still thirsty," the machine reports, both voices impatient.

In the kitchen, propped next to the back door, is the same crowbar that I used on the bathtub. That's what I bring him. A useful sense of rage has been building, probably from the beginning: this stranger and his ilk have destroyed my world. It's only fair, only just, to take the steel bar in my hands and swing, striking him before he has the strength or coordination to fight me.

The woman wails and moans, too stunned to move.

That elongated skull is paper-thin, demolished with the first blow and its jellylike contents scattered around the room.

Too late, she grabs at me, trying to wrestle the crowbar from my hands. I throw her to the floor, considering a double homicide. But that wouldn't be right. Even when she picks up the phone and begs for help, I can't bring myself to kill her. Instead I demolish the wall above her head, startling her, and when she crawls away I lift the receiver, grinning as I calmly tell whoever is listening, "You're next, friend. Your time is just about done."

▼

Outdoors is the smell of sweet chemicals and smoke. Strange robotic craft streak overhead, probably heading for crisis points. They ignore me. Maybe too much is happening; maybe their mechanisms were sabotaged at the factory. Either way, I'm left to move up the street, entering each house and killing the just-born invaders where I find them. It's messy, violent work, but in one living room I find the "parents" slain, presumably by their thankless "child." The ceiling creaks above their bodies. I climb the stairs on my toes, catching the murderer as she tries on spare clothes, pants around her knees and no chance for her to grab her bloody softball bat.

From then on I'm a demon, focused and confident and very nearly tireless.

Finishing my block, I start for the next one. Rounding the corner of a house, I come face to face with a stout woman wielding a fire axe. The two of us pause, then smile knowingly. Then we join forces. Toward dawn, taking a break from our gruesome work, I think to ask:

"What's your name?"

"Laverne," she replies, with a lifelong embarrassment. "And yours?"

"Harold," I confess, pleased that I can remember it after so long. "Good to meet you, and Laverne is a lovely name."

Later that day, she and I and twenty other new friends find the invaders barricaded inside a once-gorgeous mansion. Once it's burned to the ground, the city is liberated.

Where now?

Laverne suggests, "How about north? I once heard that they were building something in that direction."

I hug her, no words needed just now.

We name our daughter Unique.

The three of us are living in a city meant for the extinct future, in a shelter made from scraps and set between empty buildings. The buildings themselves are tall and clean, yet somehow very lonely edifices. They won't admit us, but they won't fight us either. And the climate remains ideal. Gardens thrive wherever the earth shows, and our neighbors are scarce and uniformly pleasant.

One night I speak to my infant daughter, telling her that perhaps someday she'll learn how to enter the buildings. Or better, tear them down and use their best parts.

She acts agreeable, babbling something in her baby language.

Laverne stretches out before me, naked and agreeable in a different sense. With a sly grin, she asks:

"Care to ride the chaos, darling?"

Always and gladly, thank you. And together, with every little motion, we change the universe in ways we happily cannot predict.

We Can Get Them
for You Wholesale

NEIL GAIMAN

Science fiction has always been a rather inclusive field, embracing writers whose work may defy easy classification. Neil Gaiman is a perfect case in point. If his name sounds familiar, it might be because of his enormously popular comic, *The Sandman*. He has written and had produced the television series *Neverwhere* for BBC TV and continues to write in a variety of literary forms ranging from fairy tales to poetry, from fantasy and horror to science fiction.

"We Can Get Them for You Wholesale" starts out not innocently, but certainly on a small scale. Just goes to show you what can happen when you get a really good idea. First published in 1984, this is one of Gaiman's hard-to-classify stories. I don't know what you would call it, but I would say it's chilling.

P eter Pinter had never heard of Aristippus of the Cyrenaics, a lesser-known follower of Socrates, who maintained that the avoidance of trouble was the highest attainable good; however, he had lived his uneventful life according to this precept. In all respects except one (an inability to pass up a bargain, and which of us is entirely free from that?) he was a very moderate man. He did not go to extremes. His speech was proper and reserved; he rarely overate; he drank enough to be sociable and no more; he was far from rich, and in no wise poor. He liked people and people liked him. Bearing all that in mind, would you expect to find him in a lowlife pub on the seamier side of London's East End, taking out what is colloquially known as a "contract" on someone he hardly knew? You would not. You would not even expect to find him in the pub.

And until a certain Friday afternoon, you would have been right. But the love of a woman can do strange things to a man, even one so colorless as Peter Pinter, and the discovery that Miss Gwendolyn Thorpe, twenty-three years of age, of 9, Oaktree Terrace, Purley, was messing about (as the vulgar would put it) with a smooth young gentleman from the accounting department—*after*, mark you, she had consented to wear an engagement ring, composed of real ruby chips, nine-carat gold, and something that might well have been a diamond (£37.50) that it had taken Peter almost an entire lunch-hour to choose—can do very strange things to a man indeed.

After he made this shocking discovery Peter spent a sleepless Friday night, tossing and turning, with visions of Gwendolyn and Archie Gibbons (the Don Juan of Clamages Accounting Department) dancing and swimming before his eyes—performing acts that even Peter, if he were pressed, would have to admit were most improbable. But the bile of jealousy had risen up within him, and by the morning Peter had resolved that his rival should be done away with.

Saturday morning was spent wondering how one contacted an assassin, for, to the best of Peter's knowledge, none were employed by Clamages (the department store that employed all three of the members of our eternal triangle, and, incidentally, furnished the ring), and he was wary of asking anyone outright for fear of attracting attention to himself.

Thus it was that Saturday afternoon found him hunting through the Yellow Pages.

Assassins, he found, was not between *Asphalt Contractors* and *Assessors (Quantity)*; *Killers* was not between *Kennels* and *Kindergartens*; *Murderers* was not between *Mowers* and *Museums*. *Pest Control* looked promising; however closer investigation of the Pest Control advertisements showed them to be almost solely concerned with "rats, mice, fleas, cockroaches, rabbits, moles, and rats" (to quote from one that Peter felt was rather hard on rats), and not really what he had in mind. Even so, being of a careful nature, he dutifully inspected the entries in that category, and at the bottom of the second page, in small print, he found a firm that looked promising.

"*Complete discreet disposal of irksome and unwanted mammals, etc.*" went the entry, "*Ketch, Hare, Burke and Ketch. The Old Firm.*" It went on, to give no address, but only a telephone number.

Peter dialled the number, surprising himself by so doing. His heart pounded in his chest, and he tried to look nonchalant. The telephone rang once, twice, three times. Peter was just starting to hope that it would not be answered and he could forget the whole thing, when there was a click and a brisk young female voice said, "Ketch Hare Burke Ketch, can I help you?"

Carefully not giving his name Peter said, "Er, how big—I mean, what size mammals do you go up to? To, uh, dispose of?"

"Well, that would depend on what size sir requires."

He plucked up all his courage. "A person?"

Her voice remained brisk and unruffled. "Of course, sir. Do you have a pen and paper handy? Good. Be at the Dirty Donkey pub, off Little Courtney Street, E3, tonight at eight o'clock. Carry a rolled-up copy of the *Financial Times*—that's the pink one, sir—and our operative will approach you there." Then she put down the phone.

Peter was elated. It had been far easier than he had imagined. He went down to the newsagent's and bought a copy of the *Financial Times*, found Little Courtney Street in his *A–Z of London*, and spent the rest of the afternoon watching football on the television and imagining the smooth young gentleman from accounting's funeral.

▼

It took Peter a while to find the pub. Eventually he spotted the pub sign, which showed a donkey, and was indeed remarkably dirty.

The Dirty Donkey was a small and more-or-less filthy pub, poorly lit, in which knots of unshaven people wearing dusty donkey jackets stood around eyeing each other suspiciously, eating crisps and drinking pints of Guinness, a drink that Peter had never cared for. Peter held his *Financial Times* under one arm, as conspicuously as he could, but no one approached him, so he bought a half of shandy and retreated to a corner table. Unable to think of anything else to do while waiting he tried to read the paper, but, lost and confused by a maze of grain futures, and a rubber company that was selling something or other short (quite what the short somethings were he could not tell), he gave it up and stared at the door.

He had waited almost ten minutes when a small, busy man hustled in, looked quickly around him, then came straight over to Peter's table and sat down.

He stuck out his hand. "Kemble. Burton Kemble, of Ketch Hare Burke Ketch. I hear you have a job for us."

He didn't look like a killer, Peter said so.

"Oh lor' bless us no. I'm not actually part of our workforce, sir. I'm in sales."

Peter nodded. That certainly made sense. "Can we—er—talk freely here?"

"Sure. Nobody's interested. Now then, how many people would you like disposed of?"

"Only one. His name's Archibald Gibbons and he works in Clamages accounting department. His address is . . ."

Kemble interrupted. "We can go into all that later, sir, if you don't mind. Let's just quickly go over the financial side. First of all, the contract will cost you £500 . . ."

Peter nodded. He could afford that, and in fact had expected to have to pay a little more.

". . . although there's always the special offer," Kemble concluded smoothly.

Peter's eyes shone. As I mentioned earlier, he loved a bargain, and often bought things he had no imaginable use for in sales or on special offers. Apart from this one failing (one that so many of us share), he was a most moderate young man. "Special offer?"

"Two for the price of one, sir."

Mmm. Peter thought about it. That worked out at only £250 each, which couldn't be bad no matter how you looked at it. There was only one snag. "I'm afraid I don't *have* anyone else I want killed."

Kemble looked disappointed. "That's a pity, sir. For two we could probably have even knocked the price down to, well, say £450 the both of them."

"Really?"

"Well, it gives our operatives something to do, sir. If you must know," and here he dropped his voice, "there really isn't enough work in this particular line to keep them occupied. Not like the old days. Isn't there just *one* other person you'd like to see dead?"

Peter pondered. He hated to pass up a bargain, but couldn't for the life of him think of anyone else. He liked people. Still, a bargain was a bargain . . .

"Look," said Peter. "Could I think about it, and see you here tomorrow night?"

The salesman looked pleased. "Of course, sir," he said. "I'm sure you'll be able to think of someone."

The answer—the obvious answer—came to Peter as he was drifting off to sleep that night. He sat straight up in bed, fumbled the bedside light on and wrote a name down on the back of an envelope, in case he forgot it. To tell the truth he didn't think that he could forget it, for it was painfully obvious, but you can never tell with these late-night thoughts.

The name that he had written down on the back of the envelope was this: Gwendolyn Thorpe.

He turned the light off, rolled over and was soon asleep, dreaming peaceful and remarkably un-murderous dreams.

▼

Kemble was waiting for him when he arrived in the Dirty Donkey on Sunday night. Peter bought a drink and sat down beside him.

"I'm taking you up on the special offer," he said, by way of introduction.

Kemble nodded vigorously. "A very wise decision, if you don't mind me saying so, sir."

Peter Pinter smiled modestly, in the manner of one who read the *Financial Times* and made wise business decisions. "That will be £450, I believe?"

"Did I say £450, sir? Good gracious me, I do apologize. I beg your pardon, I was thinking of our bulk rate. It would be £475 for two people."

Disappointment mingled with cupidity on Peter's bland and youthful face. That was an extra twenty-five pounds. However, something that Kemble had said caught his attention.

"Bulk rate?"

"Of course, but I doubt that sir would be interested in that."

"No, no I am. Tell me about it."

"Very well, sir. Bulk rate, £450, would be for a large job. Ten people."

Peter wondered if he had heard correctly. "Ten people? But that's only £45 each."

"Yes, sir. It's the large order that makes it profitable."

"I see," said Peter, and "Hmm," said Peter and "Could you be here the same time tomorrow night?"

"Of course, sir."

Upon arriving home Peter got out a scrap of paper and a pen. He wrote the numbers one to ten down one side and then filled it in as follows:

1) . . . Archie G.

2) . . . Gwennie.

3) . . .

and so forth.

Having filled in the first two he sat sucking his pen, hunting for wrongs done to him and people the world would be better off without.

He smoked a cigarette. He strolled around the room.

Aha! There was a physics teacher at a school he had attended who had delighted in making his life a misery. What was the man's name again? And for that matter, was he still alive? Peter wasn't sure, but he wrote *The Physics Teacher, Abbot Street Secondary School* next to the number three. The next came more easily—his department head had refused to raise his salary a couple of months back; that the raise had eventually come was immaterial. *Mr. Hunterson* was number four.

When he was five a boy name Simon Ellis had poured paint on his head, while another boy named James somebody-or-other had held him down and a girl named Sharon Hartsharpe had laughed. They were numbers five through seven respectively.

Who else?

There was the man on television with the annoying snicker who read the news. He went down the list. And what about the woman in the flat next door, with the little yappy dog that shat in the hall? He put her and the dog down on nine. Ten was the hardest. He scratched his head and went into the kitchen for a cup of coffee, then dashed back and wrote *My Great Uncle Mervyn* down in the tenth place. The old man was rumored to be quite affluent and there was a possibility (albeit rather slim) that he could leave Peter some money.

With the satisfaction of an evening's work well done he went off to bed.

Monday at Clamages was routine; Peter was a senior sales assistant in the books department, a job that actually entailed very little. He clutched his list tightly in his hand, deep in his pocket, rejoicing in the feeling of power that it gave him. He spent a most enjoyable lunch hour in the canteen with young Gwendolyn (who did not know that he had seen her and Archie enter the stockroom together), and even smiled at the smooth young man from the accounting department when he passed him in the corridor.

He proudly displayed his list to Kemble that evening.

The little salesman's face fell.

"I'm afraid this isn't ten people, Mr. Pinter," he explained. "You've counted the woman in the next-door flat *and* her dog as one person. That brings it to eleven, which would be an extra. . . ." his pocket calculator was rapidly deployed, ". . . an extra seventy pounds. How about if we forget the dog?"

Peter shook his head. "The dog's as bad as the woman. Or worse."

"Then I'm afraid we have a slight problem. Unless . . ."

"What?"

"Unless you'd like to take advantage of our wholesale rate. But of course sir wouldn't be . . ."

There are words that do things to people; words that make people's faces flush with joy, excitement, or passion. *Environmental* can be one, *occult* is another. *Wholesale* was Peter's. He leaned back in his chair. "Tell me about it," he said, with the practiced assurance of an experienced shopper.

"Well, sir," said Kemble, allowing himself a little chuckle, "We can, uh, *get* them for you, wholesale. £17.50 each, for every quarry after the first fifty, or a tenner each for every one over two hundred."

"I suppose you'd go down to a fiver if I wanted a thousand people knocked off?"

"Oh no, sir," Kemble looked shocked. "If you're talking those sorts of figures we can do them for a quid each."

"One *pound*?"

"That's right, sir. There's not a big profit margin on it, but the high turnover and productivity more than justifies it."

Kemble got up. "Same time tomorrow, sir?"

Peter nodded.

One thousand pounds. One thousand people. Peter Pinter didn't even *know* a thousand people. Even so . . . there were the Houses of Parliament. He didn't like politicians, they squabbled and argued and carried on so.

And for that matter . . .

An idea, shocking in its audacity. Bold. Daring. Still, the idea was there and it wouldn't go away. A distant cousin of his had married the younger brother of an earl or a baron or something . . .

On the way home from work that afternoon he stopped off at a little shop that he had passed a thousand times without entering. It had a large sign in the window—guaranteeing to trace your lineage for you, and even draw up a coat of arms if you happened to have mislaid your own—and an impressive heraldic map.

They were very helpful and phoned him up just after seven to give him their news.

If approximately fourteen million, seventy-two thousand, eight hundred and eleven people died, he, Peter Pinter, would be *King of England*.

He didn't have fourteen million, seventy-two thousand, eight hundred and eleven pounds: but he suspected that when you were talking in those figures, Mr. Kemble would have one of his special discounts.

▼

Mr. Kemble did.

He didn't even raise an eyebrow.

"Actually," he explained, "it works out quite cheaply; you see we wouldn't have to do them all individually. Small-scale nuclear weapons, some judicious bombing, gassing, plague, dropping radios in swimming pools and then mopping up the stragglers. Say four thousand pounds."

"Four thou—? That's in*cred*ible!"

The salesman looked pleased with himself. "Our operatives will be glad of the work, sir." He grinned. "We pride ourselves on servicing our wholesale customers."

The wind blew cold as Peter left the pub, setting the old sign swinging. It didn't look much like a dirty donkey, thought Peter; more like a pale horse.

Peter was drifting off to sleep that night, mentally rehearsing his Coronation Speech, when a thought drifted into his head and hung around. It would not go away. Could he—could he *possibly* be passing up an even larger saving than he already had? Could he be missing out on a bargain?

Peter climbed out of bed and walked over to the phone. It was almost three a.m., but even so . . .

His Yellow Pages lay open, where he had left it the previous Saturday, and he dialled the number.

The phone seemed to ring forever. There was a click and a bored voice said "Burke Hare Ketch, can I help you?"

"I hope I'm not phoning too late . . ." he began.

"Of course not, sir."

"I was wondering if I could speak to Mr. Kemble."

"Can you hold? I'll see if he's available."

Peter waited for a couple of minutes, listening to the ghostly crackles and whispers that always echo down empty phone lines.

"Are you there, caller?"

"Yes, I'm here."

"Putting you through." There was a buzz, then "Kemble speaking."

"Ah, Mr. Kemble. Hello. Sorry if I got you out of bed or anything. This is, um, Peter Pinter."

"Yes, Mr. Pinter?"

"Well, I'm sorry it's so late, only I was wondering . . . How much would it cost to kill everybody? Everybody in the world?"

"Everybody? All the people?"

"Yes. How much? I mean for an order like that you'd have to have some kind of a big discount. How much would it be? For everyone?"

"Nothing at all, Mr. Pinter."

"You mean you wouldn't do it?"

"I mean we'd do it for nothing, Mr. Pinter. We only have to be asked, you see. We always have to be asked."

Peter was puzzled. "But—when would you start?"

"Start? Right away. Now. We've been ready for a long time. But we had to be asked, Mr. Pinter. Goodnight. It *has* been a *pleasure* doing business with you."

The line went dead.

Peter felt strange. Everything seemed very distant. He wanted to sit down. What on earth had the man meant? *We always have to be asked.* It was definitely strange. Nobody does anything for nothing in this world; he had a good mind to phone Kemble back, and call the whole thing off. Perhaps he had overreacted; perhaps there was a perfectly innocent reason why Archie and Gwendolyn had entered the stock room together. He would talk to her; that's what he'd do. He'd talk to Gwennie first thing tomorrow morning . . .

That was when the noises started.

Odd cries from across the street. A cat fight? Foxes probably. He hoped someone would throw a shoe at them. Then, from the corridor outside his flat, he heard a muffled clumping, as if someone were dragging something very heavy along the floor. It stopped. Someone knocked on his door, twice, very softly.

Outside his window the cries were getting louder. Peter sat in his chair, knowing that somehow, somewhere, he had missed something. Something important. The knocking redoubled. He was thankful that he always locked and chained his door at night.

They'd been ready for a long time, but they had to be asked . . .

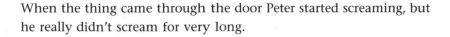

When the thing came through the door Peter started screaming, but he really didn't scream for very long.

Fire Catcher

RICHARD KADREY

Some science fiction involves scenarios set in the far distant future. When published in 1986, Richard Kadrey's story was set in a time that is occasionally referred to as "the day after tomorrow." Kadrey, known as much for his non-fiction as for his fiction, knows about a lot of underground things—gonzo literary movements and wildly visionary magazines—and some of what he imparts in "Fire Catcher" may be closer to the truth than you really want to know.

When reading this frighteningly realistic yet surreal piece, I was reminded of *Dr. Strangelove*. The tone in Kadrey's fiction is not the wicked satire of Kubrick's black-comic masterpiece, but each has a character who does something that he shouldn't be able to do, and with enormous consequences. "Fire Catcher" may be read as science fiction, but it also should be considered a cautionary tale.

Preston promises himself that when this bottle is empty, he will stop taking the pills.

The black market barbiturates are strong, much more potent than the sleeping pills he used to get from the Army infirmary in town. (But why call a dozen T-shacks, barracks, and a million tons of rubble a town?)

Even so, without the booze to wash the pills down, Preston knows he would never get to sleep.

Once, Preston took some of the pills to an Army lab and had them analyzed. It turned out that each pill was completely different, a crazy-quilt combination of whatever the manufacturers had lying around: Thorazine, MDA, Megaludes, Nembutal. Sometimes Preston purchases small amounts of raw opium. This he mixes with vodka to produce his own crude version of laudanum. At times all of this effort strikes him as amusing. He is well aware that any of the drugs combined with all the alcohol he drinks could kill him. And what would General Bower say then? How would he explain to the European high command that he had let the best assassin in the American Occupation Army drug himself to death?

Within a half hour it becomes clear that the pills are not working. The blinking cursors on a dozen computer terminals are about to drive him crazy. Preston takes two more pills and gulps them down with vodka from a plastic cup. He goes to the bedroom to get his coat but pauses to close the door of his wife's empty closet.

▼

Four A.M., Berlin time. Outside the computer bunker a metallic-smelling fog drifts through the city. Preston needs a drink. Six pills to the wind, and he isn't even drowsy yet. The beam of his flashlight plays over the unlit ruins. Each day the Army busies itself clearing the street, pushing pulverized buildings back onto the blasted foundations from which they have fallen.

Jumbled concrete blocks and twisted wires abut each other in long rows until the residential blocks begin to resemble one vast and continuous block.

Preston moves the beam of his flashlight over the empty buildings, hoping for some romantic sense of connection with the ruins, as if among the shattered stones might lie the antidote to all his unnamed fears. He finds a pair of sunglasses, some sheets of scorched piano music, and the acid fog.

It has only been a few days since she left, but already he has forgotten her face, what he said to her, what she said to him. She is gone; that is the only truth. He watched her cross the tarmac; watched her board the military transport for New York.

He had tamed the most complex computer systems in the world, yet he could not stop his wife from leaving.

When she was walking up the boarding ramp to the plane and Preston was standing on the other side of a barbed-wire fence, he screamed out her name. Just once. Everybody on the airstrip turned to stare at him. Preston hurried back to his bunker and got drunk. Later, when he was sober, he discovered gashes on his hands where he had gripped the barbed wire.

▼

Back in the computer bunker, Preston turned his attention to the monitor where the pharmacy codes for the state hospital in Leningrad are displayed. He begins typing, changing a number here, a number there. A white wave of interference shimmers across the screen, washing out the display. A bad connection? Preston gets up and checks his fiberoptic leads. He cracked the pharmacy system just a few minutes before and is anxious not to call attention to his presence.

Reflexively his hands move over the cables, testing connections and solder points. He pours himself some vodka and drains the cup. As the interference subsides, he begins to work quickly.

Finding the room number is easy. High Party officials are always given special accommodations and kept well away from the general hospital population. Locating the proper drugs, however, is another matter. In the state hospitals, paranoia reigns. All of the drugs are listed either by complex chemical codes or by obscure euphemisms that mean virtually nothing to Preston, an outsider. He works his way through the drug catalog, a page at a time, occasionally shifting to another system when his LED alarm flashes, indicating that someone at the hospital is trying to access the pharmacy listings.

Finally Preston finds the chemical symbols he is looking for. After that, it is a matter of a few seconds to reprogram the nursing drones and change the Party official's daily vitamin B shot to a lethal dose of succinylcholine.

Before he exits the system, Preston dumps the contents of a slave disk throughout the hospital's patient records. The disk contains approximately a million words of English pornography (with pictures) and ten digitized hours of American rock music.

The Army told him to dump the porn. The music Preston added himself.

▼

He takes two more hits of speed. From his seat at the console, Preston can see the unmade bed across the hall. He has not slept in the bed since his wife left. He has not slept at all. He is, in fact, afraid of the room. The contours of the rumpled sheets, the stark geometry of the empty closet imply an end a thousand times more terrifying than all the rubble overhead.

▼

They call him the Fire Catcher because he once held the nuclear blaze in his hands, and he snuffed it out.

1996: Alone, Preston hacked his way into the nexus of the Soviet nuclear-missile system. He sliced through the data web; boiled through 3-D grids; smashed the vectors, system checks, fail-safes. Preston the Visigoth, the madman, the cybernetic assassin, had breached the Russian program, and it had yielded up its prize.

On the eve of World War III, Preston had locked the Soviet missiles in their silos. A day later American and French paratroopers landed in Vladivostok and began shooting their way west. A Soviet submarine, *The People's Victorious Liberator*, torpedoed the British naval base at Gibraltar.

Preston returned to the United States. There the President gave him a medal, calling Preston a great humanitarian.

Preston married an anthropologist named Nina Abreu, and they settled in New York. Preston continued his research on developing intelligent security programs for computer systems.

Fought with conventional weapons, the war Preston had helped shape seethed back and forth across Europe for twelve years without a winner.

National boundaries were liquid, flowing in and around interregnum war states. New countries appeared and disappeared overnight. In the first two years of the war, twenty million people died.

▼

Preston sips some of his homemade laudanum while he completes his report on the Party official's death. When the report is done, he queues it into General Bower's private security file. Above the console a bank of red and green LEDs flash a warning. Preston checks out his lines. The CIA is monitoring him again. He switches on the slave disk and jams the Agency lines with the same porn he dumped on the Soviets.

Taped to the side of the slave drive is a wallet-size hologram of Preston's wife. He rips the rectangle of plastic from the drive and holds his lighter to it. In the wedge of flame the hologram melts, his wife's face twisting, turning in on itself, liquefying, and finally fading completely as the hologram drips away.

Later Preston goes to the base infirmary and stares through blue-gray bulletproof glass at the Soviet flier who had been shot down a few days earlier. There he reflects on the nature of sweet circumstance. Over forty million dead, and the small woman with the Red Star and serial number tattooed on her forearm is only the second war casualty Preston has ever seen. The first was his wife.

Preston wonders if the flier is awake, if she is aware of the burns that have blackened her skin, if she can sense that the interrogations will soon begin.

Looking at the soot the burning hologram left on his fingertips, Preston begins to cry. In a few minutes an embarrassed guard asks him to leave.

They gave Preston a long list of names when he was recalled to Europe. To the base he was the Fire Catcher, but officially he became known as Project Earwig. An earwig is an insect that will sometimes burrow into the body of an animal, lay its eggs, and then continue through the animal's body, eating its way out. When the earwig's young are born they repeat the pattern, often destroying the host animal.

Preston carried out his first assassination a week before he cracked the Soviet database. His victim was a key official in the Transportation Ministry. Preston simply entered the Party records and erased all traces of the man. After that the man's official State Access Card would no longer function. He could not enter his home, retrieve his car, buy food. His comrades refused his panicked calls; assuming a new purge was under way, they avoided him.

The man was found a few weeks later, frozen stiff to a bench at a bus stop in his hometown of Gorki.

Preston was a methodical worker. He made backup disks of all his work. He had records of every system he had ever cracked, from his high-school records code (he had manipulated other students' files for a fee) to the Soviet missile system. It was easier than recracking the system each time he went in.

He kept the disks in a lead-lined floor safe under his bed. Besides the disks, the safe contained a .45 caliber pistol, sleeping pills, and an emergency bottle of vodka.

▼

His system clear again, Preston enters a military override code into the lines for the United States and clears a data path straight to New York. Then he enters the phone company's lines and accesses his wife's phone, transmitting a playback signal to the CIA tap he had discovered there months before.

His wife's voice, thin and shot through with static, crackles out of a tiny speaker over his console.

Her conversation is nothing; it is ordinary. She is speaking with a friend whose name Preston remembers as being something like Judy or Julie. He fast-forwards the tape. The conversation is the same. The mundane life of the city. The price of eggs, the refugees from Europe who crowd the subways, a day on the beach at Coney Island. Preston listens for his name, but no one mentions him. He plays the whole thing through again before shutting down the override. Something burns in Preston's throat. A sudden wave of drowsiness engulfs him, but it's too late. He does not want the pills to work. Preston stumbles to his dresser, pulls out a bottle of amphetamines, downs a handful. In a few minutes he vomits the whole thing back up, but he is no longer sleepy.

When he is alone, Preston goes through his papers, emptying his desk and collecting reams of printouts. Spreading the papers around himself, he sits on the floor and reads, reconstructing his past with hard data. He keeps lists—things like his mother's maiden name, computers he has owned, and the color of his first car—which he tapes to the walls of the bunker. When he is working and can't concentrate, the lists form a sort of mantra for him: Boyle, IBM, NEC, red Riviera, and Nina's eyes.

Love is a dangerous concept. People do strange things for love, but Preston is well aware of this. Love of a spouse, love of a country, an ideology. Love as strength, as power, as fear.

"Murder," Preston once told his wife, "is the American moral equivalent of enlightenment. The ultimate expression of the *self.*"

In the first two years of World War III, twenty million people died. The President once gave Preston a medal. Preston was well aware of the symbol implicit in the decoration: He was a hero, he was loved. Preston's wife married him for love. A victim of circumstance, he knew that she had left him for love, too. In the next eleven years of World War III, forty million people died, all victims of circumstance.

There are terrifying mathematical possibilities in the dimensions of empty closets and vacant dresser drawers. The sheets of an unmade bed reveal clues to a whole landscape of conflict; the crease in a blanket, the trajectory of shadows on a pillow imply the flow of armies in the shapes left by two bodies moving together.

All of this, Preston is aware, has something to do with the price of eggs and the feel of wind at the beach, but he has trouble making the connections.

▼

Preston touches the rigid face of the Soviet pilot. Her skin is dry and coarse, delicate as rice paper. She stirs for a moment and opens her eyes. Preston has never seen such fear on a human face before.

Her eyes are wide and gray, sunk deep in the immobile black mask of her ruined face. Lightly Preston touches his fingers to her lips. "Don't be afraid," he says. "Everything is going to be alright."

A dying guard stares at Preston from the floor; on the guard's chest, a red orchid of blood widens, seeping through his knotted fingers. Preston sets his pistol on the bedside table. From his pocket he pulls a remote trigger switch. Before he left the bunker, Preston went to his safe and removed one of the backup disks. Sitting next to the flier on the bed, he punches in a code that loads the program.

A thousand miles away, Klaxon horns sound. Underground doors, rusted and full of grit, slide, screaming and groaning, open to the night.

The Fire Catcher opens his hands, and flame takes the sky.

▼

Preston offers the dying guard a glass of water. "Don't worry," he tells the guard, "I'm supposed to be here."

Turning to the pilot, Preston almost tells her he loves her, but he knows that is not true. He loves what she might have been, what she could have been, under different circumstances. But none of that matters now. Preston thinks of unmade beds and empty closets. The foolish icons of love. It occurs to Preston vaguely, for the first time, that he, too, might be a victim. He thinks of this and can almost smell his wife's body but they are all burned away before he can recall her face.

Not with a Bang

HOWARD FAST

Howard Fast has had a long and illustrious career spanning more than
a half century. His *oeuvre* has included historical fiction, family sagas,
and other works that include collections of fantasy and science fiction
stories.

"Not with a Bang," first published in 1975, is based on a simple
premise that one can either accept or reject. What makes this tale so
effective is its marvelously narrow focus on Alfred Collins, an ordinary
man who must deal with an extraordinary event. The simple clarity of
the narrative leaves no room for argument; one is first mesmerized, then
stunned by the matter-of-fact way he copes.

O n the evening of the third of April, standing at the window of
his pleasant three-bedroom, split-level house and admiring the
sunset, Alfred Collins saw a hand rise above the horizon, spread
thumb and forefinger, and snuff out the sun. It was the moment of
soft twilight, and it ended as abruptly as if someone had flicked an
electric switch.

Which is precisely what his wife did. She put on lights all over
the house. "My goodness, Al," she said, "it did get dark quickly,
didn't it?"

"That's because someone snuffed out the sun."

"What on earth are you talking about?" she asked. "And by the
way, the Bensons are coming for dinner and bridge tonight, so you'd
better get dressed."

"All right. You weren't watching the sunset, were you?"

"I have other things to do."

"Yes. Well, what I mean is that if you were watching, you would have seen this hand come up behind the horizon, and then the thumb and forefinger just spread out, and then they came together and snuffed out the sun."

"Really. Now for heaven's sake, Al, don't redouble tonight. If you are doubled, have faith in your bad bidding. Do you promise me?"

"Funniest damn thing about the hand. It brought back all my childhood memories of anthropomorphism."

"And just what does that mean?"

"Nothing. Nothing at all. I'm going to take a shower."

"Don't be all evening about it."

At dinner, Al Collins asked Steve Benson whether he had been watching the sunset that evening.

"No—no, I was showering."

"And you, Sophie?" Collins asked of Benson's wife.

"No way. I was changing a hem. What does women's lib intend to do about hems? There's the essence of the status of women, the nitty-gritty of our servitude."

"It's one of Al's jokes," Mrs. Collins explained. "He was standing at the window and he saw this hand come over the horizon and snuff out the sun."

"Did you, Al?"

"Scout's honor. The thumb and forefinger parted, then came together. Poof. Out went the sun."

"That's absolutely delicious," Sophie said. "You have such delicious imagination."

"Especially in his bidding," his wife remarked.

"She'll never forget that slam bid doubled and redoubled," Sophie said. It was evident that she would never forget it either.

"Interesting but impractical," said Steve Benson, who was an engineer at IBM. "You're dealing with a body that is almost a million miles in diameter. The internal temperature is over ten million degrees centigrade, and at its core the hydrogen atoms are reduced to helium ash. So all you have is poetic symbolism. The sun will be here for a long time."

After the second rubber, Sophie Benson remarked that either it was chilly in the Collins house or she was catching something.

"Al, turn up the thermostat," said Mrs. Collins.

The Collins team won the third and fourth rubbers, and Mrs. Collins had all the calm superiority of a winner as she bid her guests good night. Al Collins went out to the car with them, thinking that, after all, suburban living was a strange process of isolation and alienation. In the city, a million people must have watched the thing happen; here, Steve Benson was taking a shower and his wife was changing a hem.

It was a very cold night for April. Puddles of water left over from a recent rain had frozen solid, and the star-drenched sky had the icy look of midwinter. Both of the Bensons had arrived without coats, and as they hurried into their car, Benson laughingly remarked that Al was probably right about the sun. Benson had difficulty starting the car, and Al Collins stood shivering until they had driven away. Then he looked at the outside thermometer. It was down to sixteen degrees.

"Well, we beat them loud and clear," his wife observed when he came back to the house. He helped her clean up, and while they were at it, she asked him just what he meant by anthropomorphism or whatever it was.

"It's sort of a primitive notion. You know, the Bible says that God made man in His own image."

"Oh? You know, I absolutely believed it when I was a child. What are you doing?"

He was at the fireplace, and he said that he thought he'd build a fire.

"In April? You must be out of your mind. Anyway, I cleaned the hearth."

"I'll clean it tomorrow."

"Well, I'm going to bed. I think you're crazy to start a fire at this time of the night, but I'm not going to argue with you. This is the first time you did not overbid, and thank heavens for small favors."

The wood was dry, and the fire was warm and pleasant to watch. Collins had never lost his pleasure at watching the flames of a fire, and he mixed himself a long scotch and water, and sat in front of the flames, sipping the drink and recalling his own small scientific knowledge. The green plants would die within a week, and after that the oxygen would go. How long? he wondered. Two days—ten days—he couldn't remember and he had no inclination to go to the encyclopedia and find out. It would get very cold, terribly cold. It surprised him that instead of being afraid, he was only mildly curious.

He looked at the thermometer again before he went to bed. It was down to zero now. In the bedroom, his wife was already asleep, and he undressed quietly and put an extra comforter on the bed before he crawled in next to her. She moved toward him, and feeling her warm body next to him, he fell asleep.

Lost and Found

CONNIE WILLIS

In the 1970s, a crop of talented young writers came into the science fiction field, and none was more gifted than Connie Willis. Winner of numerous Hugo and Nebula awards for science fiction novels and short stories, Willis is notable for the range of her stories, both in tone and in subject.

"Lost and Found," like many of Willis's tales, uses organized religious institutions as a background. This 1982 work is full of the anger and irony that mark her fiercest, most deeply felt creations. Set in the near future, it may seem to be a bleak prediction for our world, but as is often true in Willis's work, the human spirit shines through this tale of people left to cope in a world that has become a nightmare of chaos and paranoia.

Is it the end of the world?" Megan asked. "Losing your cup, I mean?" Finney had come up to the Reverend Mr. Davidson's study to see if he might have left it there and found Megan at her father's desk, pasting bits of cotton wool to a sheet of blue paper.

"No, of course not," Finney said. "It's only annoying. It's the third time this week I've lost it." He pulled the desk drawers open one by one. The top two were empty. The bottom was full of construction paper. He limped around the desk to a chair and dropped down onto it.

He watched Megan. The top two buttons of her blouse were unbuttoned, and she was leaning forward over the paper, so Finney had a nice view of her bosom, though she was unaware of it. She was making a botch of the pasting, daubing the brown glue onto the cotton instead of the paper. The glue leaked through the cotton wool when she pounded it down with the flat of her hand, and sticky bits of it clung to her palm. The face of an angel and the body of a woman and she could not paste as well as her nursery church school class. It was her father the Reverend Mr. Davidson's voice one heard when she spoke, his learned speech patterns and quotations of scripture, but the effect was strong enough that one forgot she recited them without understanding. Finney constantly had to remind himself that she was only a child, even if she was eighteen, that her words were children's words with children's meanings, inspired though they might sound.

"Why did you ask if it were the end of the world?" Finney said.

"Because then you might find your cup. 'Of all which he hath given me I should lose nothing, but should raise it up again at the last day,' When is Daddy coming home?"

Finney's foot began to throb. "When he's finished with his business."

"I hope he comes soon," Megan said. "There are only the three of us till he comes."

"Yes," Finney said, thinking of the other teacher, Mrs. Andover. A fine threesome to hold down the fort: a middle-aged spinster, an eighteen-year-old child, and a thirty-year-old . . . what? Church school teacher, he told himself firmly. His foot began to ache worse than ever. Lame church school teacher.

"I hope he comes soon," Megan said again.

"So do I. What are you making?"

"Sheep," Megan said. She held up the paper. White bits of the cotton wool were struck randomly to the blue paper. They looked like clouds in a blue sky. "My class is going to make them after tea."

"Where are your children then?" Finney said, trying to keep his voice casual.

She looked at him with round blue eyes. "We were playing a game outside before. About sheep. So I came in to make some."

St. John's at End sat on a round island in the middle of the River End. The river on both sides was so shallow one could walk across it, but it was possible to drown in only a foot of water, wasn't it? Finney nearly had.

"I'll find them," he said.

"'The lost shall be found,'" Megan said, and patted a bit of wool with her hand.

▼

He collided with Mrs. Andover on the stairs. "Megan's let her class out with no one to watch them," he said rapidly. "She's in there pasting and the children are God knows where. My boys are out, but they won't think to watch out for them."

Mrs. Andover turned and walked slowly down the stairs ahead of him, as if she were purposely impeding his progress. "The children are perfectly all right," she said calmly. She stopped at the foot of the stairs and faced Finney, her arms folded across her matronly bosom. "I set one of the older girls to watch them," she said. "She has been spying for me all week, seeing that nothing happens to them."

Finney was a little taken aback. Mrs. Andover was so much the Oxford tour guide, prim blue skirt and sturdy walking shoes. He would have thought a word like "spying" beneath her.

"You needn't worry," she said, mistaking Finney's surprise for concern. "I'm paying her. Two pounds the week. Money's the root of all loyalty, isn't it, then?"

"Sometimes," Finney said, even more surprised. "At any rate I think I'll go make sure of them."

Mrs. Andover lifted an eyebrow and said, "Whatever you think best." She turned at the landing and went into the sanctuary. Finney started out the side door and then stopped, wondering what Mrs. Andover could possibly be doing in there. She had not had a pocket torch with her, and the sanctuary was nearly pitch-black. He hesitated, then turned painfully around, using the stone lintel for support, and followed her into the sanctuary.

At first he could not see her. The spaces where the stained glass windows had been were boarded up with sheets of plywood. Only the little arch at the top was left open to let in light. The windows had been the first to go, of course, even before the government had decided that a state church should by definition help support the state. The windows had been sold because the cults could afford to buy them and the churches needed the money. The government had seen at once that the churches could be a source of income as well as grace, and the systematic sacking had begun. The great cathedrals, like Ely and Salisbury, were long since stripped bare, and it would not be long before the looting reached St. John's.

St. John's will be crammed with spies, Finney thought. The Reverend Mr. Davidson, Mrs. Andover's girl, the government spies, and myself, all working undercover in one way or another. We shall have to sell the pews to make room for everyone. He stood perfectly still, balancing on his good foot. He let his eyes adjust, waiting to get his bearings from the marble angel that always shone dimly near the doors. The little curved triangles of sky were thick with gray clouds that absorbed the light like Megan's cotton wool absorbed the brown glue.

He caught a glimpse of white to the left, but it was not the angel. It was Mrs. Andover's white blouse. She was bending over one of the pews. "I say," he called out cheerfully, "this would make a good hiding place, wouldn't it?"

She straightened abruptly.

"What are you looking for?" Finney said, making his way toward her with the pew backs for awkward crutches.

"Your cup," Mrs. Andover said nervously. "I heard you tell Megan you'd lost it again. I thought one of the children might have hidden it."

Mrs. Andover was full of surprises today. Finney did not really know her at all, had not really thought about her presence though she had come after he did. Finney had ticketed her from the start as a schoolmistress spinster and not thought any more about her. Now he was not certain he should have dismissed her so easily. "What are you doing here?" he said aloud.

"I was not aware the sanctuary was off-limits," she snapped. Finney was amazed. She looked as properly guilty as one of his upper form boys.

"I didn't mean to be rude," he said. "I was only wondering how you came to be here at St. John's."

She looked even guiltier, which was ridiculous. What had she been doing in here?

"One might wonder the same thing about you, Mr. Finney." She looked coldly at his stub of a foot. "You apparently came here through violent means."

Very good, thought Finney. "A shark bit it off," he said. "In the River End. I was wading."

"It is no wonder you are so concerned about the children then. Perhaps you'd better go see to them." She started past him. He put out his hand to stop her, not even sure what he wanted to say. She stopped stock-still. "I shouldn't question other people's fitness to teach, Mr. Finney," she said. "A lame man and a half-witted girl. The Reverend Mr. Davidson is apparently not in a position to pick and choose who represents his church."

Finney thought of Reverend Davidson bending over him, his shoes wet and his trousers splattered with water and Finney's blood. He had propped Finney's arm around his neck, and then, as if Finney were one of his children, picked him up and carried him out of the water. "Either that," Finney said, "or he has Jesus's unfortunate affinity for idiots and cripples. Which are you, Mrs. Andover?"

She shook off his hand and brushed angrily past him.

"What were you looking for, Mrs. Andover?" Finney said. "What exactly did you expect to find?"

"Hullo," Megan said as if on cue. "Look what I've just found."

She was holding a heavy leather notebook full of yellowing pages. "I was looking for some nice black construction paper to make shadows with," she said. "'Yea, though I walk through the valley of the shadow of death.' I thought how nice it would be if each of the sheep had a nice black shadow and I looked in the bottom drawer of Daddy's desk, where he always keeps the paper, and this is all that was in there. Not any green at all." She handed the notebook to Finney.

"Green shadows?" he said absently, thinking of the drawer he had pulled out, full of colored paper.

"Of course not," Megan said. "Green pastures. 'He maketh me to lie down in green pastures.'"

He wasn't really listening to her. He was looking at the notebook. It was made of a soft, dark brown leather, now stiffening at the edges and even peeling off in curling layers at one corner. He started to open the cover. Mrs. Andover made a sound. Finney looked over Megan's bright blond head at her. Her face was lined with triumph.

"Is it Daddy's?" Megan said.

"I don't know," Finney said. Megan's sticky fingers had marked the cover with bits of cotton and stuck the first two pages to the cover. Finney looked at the close handwriting on the pages, written in faded blue ink. He gently pried the glued pages from the cover.

"Is it?" Megan said insistently.

"No," Finney said finally. "It appears to belong to T. E. Lawrence. How did it get in your father's desk?"

"Megan," Mrs. Andover said, "it's time for the children to come in. Go and fetch them."

"Is it time for tea, then?" Megan said.

Finney looked at his watch. "Not yet," he said. "It's only three."

"We'll have it early today," Mrs. Andover said. "Tell them to come in for their tea."

Megan ran out. Mrs. Andover came over to stand beside Finney. "It looks like a rough draft of a book or something," Finney said. "Like a manuscript. What do you think?"

"I don't need to think," Mrs. Andover said. "I know what it is. It's the manuscript copy of Lawrence's book *The Seven Pillars of Wisdom*. He wrote it after he became famous as Lawrence of Arabia, before he—succumbed to his unhappiness. It was lost in Reading Railroad Station in 1919."

"How did it get here?"

"Why don't you tell me?" Mrs. Andover said.

Finney looked at her, amazed. She was staring at him as if he might actually know something about it. "I wasn't even born in 1919. I've never even been in Reading Station."

"It wasn't in the desk this morning when I searched it."

"Oh, really," Finney said, "and what were you looking for in Reverend Davidson's desk? Green construction paper?"

"I've set the tea out," Megan said from the doorway, "only I can't find any cups."

"I forgot," Finney said. "Jesus was fond of tax collectors, too, wasn't he?"

▼

Finney went into the kitchen on the excuse of looking for something better than a paper cup for his tea. Instead, he stood at the sink and stared at the wall. If the brown leather notebook were truly a lost manuscript of Lawrence's book, and if Mrs. Andover was one of the state's spies, as he was almost certain she was, Reverend Davidson would lose his church for withholding treasures from the state. That was not the worst of it. His name and picture would be in all the papers, and that would mean an end to the undercover rescue work getting the children out of the cults, and an end to the children.

"Take care of her, Finney," he had said before he left. "'Into thy hands I commend my spirit.'" And he had let a government spy loose in the church, had let her roam about taking inventory. Finney gripped the linoleum drainboard.

Perhaps she was not from the government. Even if she was, she might be here for a totally different reason. Finney was a reporter, but he was hardly here for a good story. He was here because he had nearly bled to death in the End and Davidson had pulled him out. Perhaps Reverend Davidson had rescued Mrs. Andover, too, had brought her into the fold like all the rest of his lost lambs.

Finney was not even sure why he was here. He told himself he was staying until his foot healed, until Davidson found another teacher for the upper form boys, until Davidson got safely back from the north. He did not think it was because he was afraid, although of course he was afraid. They would know he was a reporter by now, they would know he had been working undercover investigating the cults. There would be no question of cutting off a foot for attempting to escape this time. They would murder him, and they would find a scripture to say over him as they did it. 'If thy right hand offend, cut it off.' He had thought he never wanted to hear scripture again. Perhaps that was why he stayed. To hear Megan prattling her sweet and senseless scriptures was like a balm. And what was St. John's to Mrs. Andover? A balm? A refuge? Or an enemy to be conquered and then sacked?

Megan came in, knelt down beside the cupboard below the sink, and began banging about.

"What are you looking for?" Finney said.

"Your cup, of course. Mrs. Andover found some others, but not yours."

"Megan," he said seriously, kneeling beside her, "what do you know about Mrs. Andover?"

"She's a spy," Megan said from inside the cupboard.

"Why do you think that?"

"Daddy said so. He gave her all the treasures. The marble angel and the choir screen and all the candlesticks. 'Render unto Caesar that which is Caesar's.' It isn't there," she said, pulling her head out of the cupboard. "Only pots." She handed Finney a rusted iron skillet and two banged-about aluminum pots. Finney put them carefully back into the empty cupboard, trying to think how best to ask Megan why she thought Mrs. Andover had stayed on. Her answer might be nonsense, of course, or it might be inspired. It might be scripture.

"She thinks we didn't give her all the treasures," Megan volunteered suddenly, on her knees beside him. "She asks me all the time where Daddy hid them."

"And what do you tell her?"

"'Lay not up for yourselves treasures on earth, where moths corrupt and thieves break in and steal.'"

"Good girl," Finney said, and lifted her up. "What's an old cup? We'll find it later." He took her hand and led her into tea.

▼

Mrs. Andover was already being mother, pouring out hot milk and tea into a styrofoam cup with a half circle bitten out of it. She handed it to Finney. "Did you and Megan find your cup?" she asked.

"No," Finney said. "But then we aren't experts like you, are we?"

Mrs. Andover did not answer him. She poured Megan's tea. "When is your father coming back, Megan?" she said.

"Not soon enough," Finney snapped. "Are you that eager to arrest him? Or is it hanging you're after, for treasonable offenses?" He thought of Davidson, crouched by a gate somewhere, waiting for the child to be bundled out to him. "If the cults don't murder him, the government will, is that the game then? How can he possibly win a game like that?"

"The game's not finished yet," Megan said.

"What?" Finney slopped tea all over his trousers.

"Go and finish your game," Mrs. Andover said. "Take the children with you. You needn't come in till it's ended." Now that Finney was looking for it, he saw her nod to a tall girl with a large bosom. The girl nodded back and went out after the children. What else had he missed because he wasn't looking for it?

"It's a game of Megan's," Mrs. Andover said to Finney. "One child's the shepherd, and he must get all the sheep into the fold by putting them inside a ring drawn on the ground. When he's got them all inside the ring, then it's bang! the end, and all adjourn for tea and cake."

"Bang! the end," said Finney. "Tea and cakes for everyone. I wish it were as simple as that."

"Perhaps you should join one of the cults," Mrs. Andover said.

Finney looked up sharply from his tea.

"They are always preaching the end, aren't they? When it is coming and to whom. Lists of who's to be saved and who's to be left to his own devices. Dates and places and timetables."

"They're wrong," Finney said. "It's supposed to come like a thief in the night so no one will see it coming."

"I doubt there's a thief could get past me without my knowing it."

"Yes, I forgot," said Finney. "'It takes a thief to catch a thief.' Isn't that one of Megan's scriptures?"

She looked thoughtful. "Aren't the lost supposed to be safely gathered into the fold before the end can come?"

"Ah, yes," said Finney, "but the good shepherd never does spec-ify just who those lost ones are he's so bent on finding. Perhaps he has a list of his own, and when all the people on it are safely inside some circle he's drawn on the ground—"

"Or perhaps we don't understand at all," Mrs. Andover said dreamily. "Perhaps the lost are not people at all, but things. Perhaps it's they that are being gathered in before the end. T. E. Lawrence was a lost soul, wasn't he?"

"I'd hardly call Lawrence of Arabia lost," Finney said. "He seemed to know his way round the Middle East rather well."

"He hired a man to flog him, did you know that? He would have had to be well and truly lost to have done that." She looked up sud-denly at Finney. "If something else turned up, something valuable, that would prove the end was coming, wouldn't it?"

"It would prove something," Finney said. "I'm not certain what."

"Where exactly is your Reverend Mr. Davidson?" she asked, almost offhand, as if she could catch him by changing the subject.

He is out rescuing the lost, dear lady, while you sit here seducing admissions out of me. A thief can't sneak past me either. "In London, of course," Finney said. "Pawning the crown jewels and hiding the money in Swiss bank accounts."

"Quite possibly," Mrs. Andover said. "Perhaps he should think about returning to St. John's. He is in a good deal of trouble."

▼

Finney pulled his class in and sat them down in the crypt. "Tisn't fair," one of the taller boys said. "The game was still going. It wasn't very nice of you to pull us in like that." He kicked at the gilded toe of a fifteenth-century wool merchant.

"I quite agree," Finney said, which remark caused all of them sit up and look at him, even the kicker. "It was not fair. Neither was it fair for me to have had to drink my tea from a paper cup."

"It isn't our bloody fault you lost the cup," the boy said sulkily.

"That would be quite true, if indeed the cup were lost. The Holy Grail has been lost for centuries and never found, and that is certainly no one's bloody fault. But my cup is not lost forever, and you are going to find it." He tried to sound angry, so they would look and not play. "I want you to search every nook and cranny of this church, and if you find the cup"—here was the tricky bit, just the right casual tone— "or anything else interesting, bring it straightaway to me." He paused and then said, as if he had just thought of it, "I'll give fifty pence for every treasure."

The children scattered like players in a game. Finney hobbled up the stairs after them and stood in the side door. The younger children were down by the water and Mrs. Andover was standing near them.

Two of the boys plummeted past Finney and up the stairs to the study. "Don't . . ." Finney said, but they were already past him. By the time he had managed the stairs, the boys had strewn open every drawer of the desk. They were tumbling colored paper out of the bottom drawer, trying to see what was under it.

"It isn't there," one of the boys said, and Finney's heart caught.

"What isn't?"

"Your cup. This is where we hid it. This morning."

"You must be mistaken," he said, and led them firmly down the stairs. Halfway down, Mrs. Andover's girl burst in at them.

"She says you are to come at once," she said breathlessly.

Finney released the boys. "You two can redeem yourselves by finding my cup," and then as they escaped down the stairs to the crypt, he shouted, "and stay out of the study."

▼

Mrs. Andover was standing by the End, watching the children and Megan wade knee-deep in the clear water. The sun had come out. Finney could see the flash of sunlight off Megan's hair.

"They're playing a game," Mrs. Andover said without looking at him. "It's an old nursery rhyme about how bad King John lost his clothes in the Wash. The children stand in a circle, and when the rhyme's done, they fall down in the water. Megan stepped on something when she went down. She cut her foot."

Water and blood and Davidson reaching out for Finney's hand. "No!" Finney had cried, "not my hand, too!" Davidson had started to say something and Finney had flailed away from him like a landed fish, afraid it would be holy scripture. But he had said, "The cults did this to you, didn't they?" in a voice that had no holiness in it at all, and Finney had collapsed gratefully into his arms.

"Is she hurt?" he said, blinded by the sun and the memory.

"It was just a scratch," Mrs. Andover said. "King John did lose his clothes. In a battle in 1215. His army was fighting in a muddy estuary of the Wash when a tide came in and knocked everyone under. He lost his crown, too."

"And it was never found," Finney said, knowing what was coming.

"Not until now."

"Megan!" Finney shouted. "Come here right now!"

She ran up out of the water, her bare legs dripping wet. On her head was a rusty circle that looked more like a tin lid than a crown. He did not have the slightest doubt that it was what Mrs. Andover said, the crown of a king dead eight hundred years.

"Give me the crown, Megan," Finney said.

"'Behold I come quickly. Hold that fast which thou hast, that no man take thy crown,'" she said, handing it to Finney.

Finney scratched through the encrusted minerals to the definite scrape of metal. It was thinner in several spots. Finney poked his little finger into one of the indentations and through it, making a round hole.

"Those are for the jewels," Megan said.

"What makes you think that?" Mrs. Andover said. "Have you seen any jewels?"

"All crowns have jewels," Megan said. Finney handed the crown back to her and she put it on. Finney looked at the sky behind Megan's head. The clouds had pulled back from a little circlet of blue over the church. "Can I go back now?" Megan said. "The game's almost done."

"This is the End," Finney said, watching her walk fearlessly into the water. "Not the Wash."

"Nor is it Reading Railway Station," Mrs. Andover said. "Nevertheless."

"The water's perfectly clear. I would have seen it. Someone would have seen it. It can't have lain there since 1215."

"It could have been put there," Mrs. Andover said. "After the jewels had been removed."

"So could the colored paper," he said without thinking, "after the book was taken out."

"What about the paper?" Mrs. Andover said.

"It's back in the drawer where Megan found the book. I saw it."

"You might have put it back."

"But I didn't."

"Perhaps," she said thoughtfully, "the pious Reverend Davidson has come back without telling us."

"For what purpose?" Finney said, losing his temper altogether. "To play some incredible game of hide-and-seek? To race about his church scattering priceless manuscripts and ancient crowns like prizes for us to find? What would we have to find to convince you he's innocent? The Holy Grail?"

"Yes," Mrs. Andover said coldly, and started back toward the church.

"Where are you going?" Finney shouted.

"To see for myself this miracle of the colored paper."

"King John was a pretty lost soul, too," he shouted at her back. "Perhaps he's the last on the list. Perhaps it'll all go bang before you even get to the church."

But she made it safely to the vestry door and inside, and Finney hobbled after her, suddenly afraid of what his boys might have found now.

Mrs. Andover was staring bleakly into the open drawer as Finney had done, as if it held some answer. Finney felt a pang of pity for her, standing there in her sturdy shoes, believing in no one, alone in the enemy camp. He put his hand out to her shoulder, but she flinched away from his touch. There was a sudden clatter on the stairs, and the two boys exploded into the room with Finney's cup.

"Look what we found!" one of them said.

"And you'll never guess what else," the other said, tumbling his words out. "After you said we shouldn't look in here, we went down to the sanctuary, only it was too dark to see properly. So then we went into where we all have tea and there were no good hiding places at all, so we said to ourselves where would a cup logically be and the answer of course was in the kitchen." He stopped to take a breath. "We pulled everything out of the cupboard, but it was just pots."

"And an iron skillet," Finney said.

"So we were putting them all back when we saw something else, a big old metal sort of thing rather like a cup, and your cup was inside it!" He handed the china cup triumphantly to Finney.

"Where is it?" Mrs. Andover said, as if it were an effort to speak. "This big old metal cup?"

"In the kitchen. We'll fetch it if you like."

"Please do."

The boys dashed out. Finney turned to look at her. "It wasn't there. Megan and I looked. You know what it is, don't you?" Finney said, his heart beating sickeningly fast. It was the way he had felt before he lost his foot, when he saw the ax coming down.

"Yes," she said.

"It's what you've been waiting for," he said accusingly. "It's the proof you said you wanted."

"Yes," she said, her lip trembling. "Only I didn't know what it would mean."

The boys were already racketing up the stairs. They burst in the door with it. For one awful endless moment, the steel blade falling against the sound of his own heart, louder than the drone of scripture, Finney prayed that it was an old metal cup.

The boys set it on the desk. It was badly dented from endless hidings and secretings and journeys. Tarnished like an old spoon. It shone like the cup of the sky.

"Is it a treasure?" the boy who had stolen Finney's cup said, looking at their faces. "Do we get the fifty pence?"

"It is the Holy Grail," Mrs. Andover said, putting her hands on it like a benediction.

"I thought it was lost forever."

"It was," she said. "'I should lose nothing, but should raise it up again at the last day.'"

Finney rubbed the back of his hand across his dry mouth. "I think we'd better get the children inside," he said.

He sent the boys downstairs to put the kettle on for tea. Mrs. Andover stood by the desk, holding onto the Grail as if she were afraid of what would happen if she let go.

"It isn't so bad once it's over," Finney said kindly. "What you think is the end isn't always, and it turns out better than you dreamed."

She set the Grail down gently and turned to him.

"It is only the last moment before the blade falls that is hard to bear," he said.

"I have never told you," Mrs. Andover said, her eyes filling with tears, "how sorry I am about your foot." She fumbled for a handkerchief.

"It doesn't matter," Finney said. "At any rate, the way things seem to be going, it might just turn up."

She smiled at that, dabbing at her eyes with the handkerchief, but when they went down the stairs, she clung to Finney's arm as if she were the one who was lame. Finney sent her into the kitchen to set out the tea things and then went down to the edge of the End to bring the children in.

"Is Daddy here?" Megan said, dancing along beside him with one hand on her crown to keep it from falling off. "Is that why we're having tea again?"

"No," Finney said. "But he's coming. He'll be here soon."

"'Surely I come quickly,'" Megan said, and ran inside.

Finney looked at the sky. Above the church the clouds peeled back from the blue like the edges of a scroll. Finney shut and barred the double doors to the sanctuary. He bolted the side door on the stairs and wedged a folding chair under the lock. Then he went into tea.

The Wind and
the Rain

ROBERT SILVERBERG

Many of the other bright young talents of the 1950s have long since left the scene, but Robert Silverberg continues to write fine short stories and well-crafted novels. He has edited an impressive array of excellent anthologies, including the recent volumes *Legends* and *Far Horizons*.

He has always been a bold, ambitious writer, especially in his short fiction. "The Wind and the Rain," first published in 1982, is an unusual piece of work, even for him. Looking back from a great distance of time, this sober, sad tale tells a damning story of nothing more than the way the human race has lived in the twentieth century.

Because of its lack of fancy or artifice, this tale is more horrifying than any other end-of-the-world chronicle. One can only hope that we will change the ending of the story before it's too late.

The planet cleanses itself. That is the important thing to remember, at moments when we become too pleased with ourselves. The healing process is a natural and inevitable one. The action of the wind and the rain, the ebbing and flowing of the tides, the vigorous rivers flushing out the choked and stinking lakes—these are all natural rhythms, all healthy manifestations of universal harmony. Of course, we are here too. We do our best to hurry the process along. But we are only auxiliaries, and we know it. We must not exaggerate the value of our work. False pride is worse than a sin: it is a foolishness. We do not deceive ourselves into thinking we are important. If we were not here at all, the planet would repair itself anyway within 20 to 50 million years. It is estimated that our presence cuts that time down by somewhat more than half.

————▼————

The uncontrolled release of methane into the atmosphere was one of the most serious problems. Methane is a colorless, odorless gas, sometimes known as "swamp gas." Its components are carbon and hydrogen. Much of the atmosphere of Jupiter and Saturn consists of methane. (Jupiter and Saturn have never been habitable by human beings.) A small amount of methane was always normally present in the atmosphere of Earth. However, the growth of human population produced a consequent increase in the supply of methane. Much of the methane released into the atmosphere came from swamps and coal mines. A great deal of it came from Asian rice-fields fertilized with human or animal waste; methane is a byproduct of the digestive process.

The surplus methane escaped into the lower stratosphere, from 10 to 30 miles above the surface of the planet, where a layer of ozone molecules once existed. Ozone, formed of three oxygen atoms, absorbs the harmful ultraviolet radiation that the sun emits. By reacting with free oxygen atoms in the stratosphere, the intrusive methane reduced the quantity available for ozone formation. Moreover, methane reactions in the stratosphere yielded water vapor that further depleted the ozone. This methane-induced exhaustion of the ozone content of the stratosphere permitted the unchecked ultraviolet bombardment of the Earth, with a consequent rise in the incidence of skin cancer.

A major contributor to the methane increase was the flatulence of domesticated cattle. According to the U.S. Department of Agriculture, domesticated ruminants in the late twentieth century were generating more than 85 million tons of methane a year. Yet nothing was done to check the activities of these dangerous creatures. Are you amused by the idea of a world destroyed by herds of farting cows? It must not have been amusing to the people of the late twentieth century. However, the extinction of domesticated ruminants shortly helped to reduce the impact of this process.

————▼————

Today we must inject colored fluids into a major river. Edith, Bruce, Paul, Elaine, Oliver, Ronald, and I have been assigned to this task. Most members of the team believe the river is the Mississippi, although there is some evidence that it may be the Nile. Oliver, Bruce, and Edith believe it is more likely to be the Nile than the Mississippi, but they defer to the opinion of the majority. The river is wide and deep and its color is black in some places and dark green in others. The fluids are computer-mixed on the east bank of the river in a large factory erected by a previous reclamation team. We supervise their passage into the river. First we inject the red fluid, then the blue, then the yellow; they have different densities and form parallel stripes running for many hundreds of kilometers in the water. We are not certain whether these fluids are active healing agents—that is, substances which dissolve the solid pollutants lining the riverbed—or merely serve as markers permitting further chemical analysis of the river by the orbiting satellite system. It is not necessary for us to understand what we are doing, so long as we follow instructions explicitly. Elaine jokes about going swimming. Bruce says, "How absurd. This river is famous for deadly fish that will strip the flesh from your bones." We all laugh at that. *Fish?* Here? What fish could be as deadly as the river itself? This water would consume our flesh if we entered it, and probably dissolve our bones as well. I scribbled a poem yesterday and dropped it in, and the paper vanished instantly.

---▼---

In the evenings we walk along the beach and have philosophical discussions. The sunsets on this coast are embellished by rich tones of purple, green, crimson, and yellow. Sometimes we cheer when a particularly beautiful combination of atmospheric gases transforms the sunlight. Our mood is always optimistic and gay. We are never depressed by the things we find on this planet. Even devastation can be an art-form, can it not? Perhaps it is one of the greatest of all art-forms, since an art of destruction *consumes* its medium, it *devours* its own epistemological foundations, and in this sublimely nullifying doubling-back upon its origins it far exceeds in moral complexity those forms which are merely productive. That is, I place a higher value on transformative art than on generative art. Is my meaning clear? In any event, since art ennobles and exalts the spirits of those who perceive it, we are exalted and ennobled by the conditions on Earth. We envy those who collaborated to create those extraordinary conditions. We know ourselves to be small-souled folk of a minor latter-day epoch; we lace the dynamic grandeur of energy that enabled our ancestors to commit such depredations. This world is a symphony. Naturally you might argue that to restore a planet takes more energy than to destroy it, but you would be wrong. Nevertheless, though our daily tasks leave us weary and drained, we also feel stimulated and excited, because by restoring this world, the mother-world of mankind, we are in a sense participating in the original splendid process of its destruction. I mean in the sense that the resolution of a dissonant chord participates in the dissonance of that chord.

———————▼———————

Now we have come to Tokyo, the capital of the island empire of Japan. See how small the skeletons of the citizens are? That is one way we have of identifying this place as Japan. The Japanese are known to have been people of small stature. Edward's ancestors are Japanese. He is of small stature. (Edith says his skin should be yellow as well. His skin is just like ours. Why is his skin not yellow?) "See?" Edward cries. "There is Mount Fuji!" It is an extraordinarily beautiful mountain, mantled in white snow. On its slopes one of our archaeological teams is at work, tunneling under the snow to collect samples from the twentieth-century strata of chemical residues, dust, and ashes. "Once there were over 75,000 industrial smokestacks around Tokyo," says Edward proudly, "from which were released hundreds of tons of sulfur, nitrous oxides, ammonia, and carbon gases every day. We should not forget that this city had more than 1,500,000 automobiles as well." Many of the automobiles are still visible, but they are very fragile, worn to threads by the action of the atmosphere. When we touch them they collapse in puffs of gray smoke. Edward, who has studied his heritage well, tells us, "It was not uncommon for the density of carbon monoxide in the air here to exceed the permissible levels by factors of 250% on mild summer days. Owing to atmospheric conditions, Mount Fuji was visible only one day of every nine. Yet no one showed dismay." He conjures up for us a picture of his small, industrious yellow ancestors toiling cheerfully and unremittingly in their poisonous environment. The Japanese, he insists, were able to maintain and even increase their gross national product at a time when other nationalities had already begun to lose ground in the global economic struggle because of diminished population owing to unfavorable ecological factors. And so on and so on. After a time we grow bored with Edward's incessant boasting. "Stop boasting," Oliver tells him, "or we will expose you to the atmosphere." We have much dreary work to do here. Paul and I guide the huge trenching machines; Oliver and Ronald follow, planting seeds. Almost immediately, strange angular shrubs spring up. They have shiny bluish leaves and long crooked branches. One of them seized Elaine by the throat yesterday and might have hurt her seriously had Bruce not uprooted it. We were not upset. This is merely one phase in the long, slow process of repair. There will be many such incidents. Some day cherry trees will blossom in this place.

▼

This is the poem that the river ate:

DESTRUCTION

I. *Nouns.* Destruction, desolation, wreck, wreckage, ruin, ruination, rack and ruin, smash, smashup, demolition, demolishment, ravagement, havoc, ravage, dilapidation, decimation, blight, breakdown, consumption, dissolution, obliteration, overthrow, spoilage; mutilation, disintegration, undoing, pulverization; sabotage, vandalism; annulment, damnation, extinguishment, extinction, invalidation, nullification, shatterment, shipwreck; annihilation, disannulment, discreation, extermination, extirpation, obliteration, perdition, subversion.

II. *Verbs*. Destroy, wreck, ruin, ruinate, smash, demolish, raze, ravage, gut, dilapidate, decimate, blast, blight, break down, consume, dissolve, overthrow; mutilate, disintegrate, unmake, pulverize; sabotage, vandalize; annul, blast, blight, damn, dash, extinguish, invalidate, nullify, quell, quench, scuttle, shatter, shipwreck, torpedo, smash, spoil, undo, void; annihilate, devour, disannul, discreate, exterminate, obliterate, extirpate, subvert; corrode, erode, sap, undermine, waste, waste away, whittle away (*or* down); eat away, canker, gnaw; wear away, abrade, batter, excoriate, rust.

III. *Adjectives*. Destructive, ruinous, vandalistic, baneful, cutthroat, fell, lethiferous, pernicious, slaughterous, predatory, sinistrous, nihilistic; corrosive, erosive, cankerous, caustic, abrasive.

"I validate," says Ethel.

"I unravage," says Oliver.

"I integrate," says Paul.

"I devandalize," says Elaine.

"I unshatter," says Bruce.

"I unscuttle," says Edward.

"I discorrode," says Ronald.

"I undesolate," says Edith.

"I create," say I.

We reconstitute. We renew. We repair. We reclaim. We refurbish. We restore. We renovate. We rebuild. We reproduce. We redeem. We reintegrate. We replace. We reconstruct. We retrieve. We revivify. We resurrect. We fix, overhaul, mend, put in repair, retouch, tinker, cobble, patch, darn, staunch, calk, splice. We celebrate our successes by energetic and lusty singing. Some of us copulate.

▼

Here is an outstanding example of the dark humor of the ancients. At a place called Richland, Washington, there was an installation that manufactured plutonium for use in nuclear weapons. This was done in the name of "national security," that is, to enhance and strengthen the safety of the United States of America and render its inhabitants carefree and hopeful. In a relatively short span of time these activities produced approximately 55 million gallons of concentrated radioactive waste. This material was so intensely hot that it would boil spontaneously for decades, and would retain a virulently toxic character for many thousands of years. The presence of so much dangerous waste posed a severe environmental threat to a large area of the United States. How, then, to dispose of this waste? An appropriately comic solution was devised. The plutonium installation was situated in a seismically unstable area located along the earthquake belt that rings the Pacific Ocean. A storage site was chosen nearby, directly above a fault line that had produced a violent earthquake half a century earlier. Here 140 steel and concrete tanks were constructed just below the surface of the ground and some 240 feet above the water table of the Columbia River, from which a densely populated region derived its water supply. Into these tanks the boiling radioactive wastes were poured: a magnificent gift to future generations. Within a few years the true subtlety of the jest became apparent when the first small leaks were detected in the tanks. Some observers predicted that no more than 10 to 20 years would pass before the great heat caused the seams of the tanks to burst, releasing radioactive gases into the atmosphere or permitting radioactive fluids to escape into the river. The designers of the tanks maintained, though, that they were sturdy enough to last at least a century. It will be noted that this was something less than 1% of the known half-life of the materials placed in the tanks. Because of discontinuities in the records, we are unable to determine which estimate was more nearly correct. It should be possible for our decontamination squads to enter the affected regions in 800 to 1300 years. This episode arouses tremendous admiration in me. How much gusto, how much robust wit, those old ones must have had!

------▼------

We are granted a holiday so we may go to the mountains of Uruguay to visit the site of one of the last human settlements, perhaps the very last. It was discovered by a reclamation team several hundred years ago and has been set aside, in its original state, as a museum for the tourists who one day will wish to view the mother-world. One enters through a lengthy tunnel of glossy pink brick. A series of airlocks prevents the outside air from penetrating. The village itself, nestling between two craggy spires, is shielded by a clear shining dome. Automatic controls maintain its temperature at a constant mild level. There were a thousand inhabitants. We can view them in the spacious plazas, in the taverns, and in places of recreation. Family groups remain together, often with their pets. A few carry umbrellas. Everyone is in an unusually fine state of preservation. Many of them are smiling. It is not yet known why these people perished. Some died in the act of speaking, and scholars have devoted much effort, so far without success, to the task of determining and translating the last words still frozen on their lips. We are not allowed to touch anyone, but we may enter their homes and inspect their possessions and toilet furnishings. I am moved almost to tears, as are several of the others. "Perhaps these are our very ancestors," Ronald exclaims. But Bruce declares scornfully, "You say ridiculous things. Our ancestors must have escaped from here long before the time these people lived." Just outside the settlement I find a tiny glistening bone, possibly the shinbone of a child, possibly part of a dog's tail. "May I keep it?" I ask our leader. But he compels me to donate it to the museum.

------------▼------------

The archives yield much that is fascinating. For example, this fine example of ironic distance in ecological management. In the ocean off a place named California were tremendous forests of a giant seaweed called kelp, housing a vast and intricate community of maritime creatures. Sea urchins lived on the ocean floor, 100 feet down, amid the holdfasts that anchored the kelp. Furry aquatic mammals known as sea otters fed on the urchins. The Earth people removed the otters because they had some use for their fur. Later, the kelp began to die. Forests many square miles in diameter vanished. This had serious commercial consequences, for the kelp was valuable and so were many of the animal forms that lived in it. Investigation of the ocean floor showed a great increase in sea urchins. Not only had their natural enemies, the otters, been removed, but the urchins were taking nourishment from the immense quantities of organic matter in the sewage discharges dumped into the ocean by the Earth people. Millions of urchins were nibbling at the holdfasts of the kelp, uprooting the huge plants and killing them. When an oil tanker accidentally released its cargo into the sea, many urchins were killed and the kelp began to re-establish itself. But this proved to be an impractical means of controlling the urchins. Encouraging the otters to return was suggested; but there was not a sufficient supply of living otters. The kelp foresters of California solved their problem by dumping quicklime into the sea from barges. This was fatal to the urchins; once they were dead, healthy kelp plants were brought from other parts of the sea and embedded to become the nucleus of a new forest. After a while the urchins returned and began to eat the kelp again. More quicklime was dumped. The urchins died and new kelp was planted. Later, it was discovered that the quicklime was having harmful effects on the ocean floor itself, and other chemicals were dumped to counteract those effects. All of this required great ingenuity and a considerable outlay of energy and resources. Edward thinks there was something very Japanese about these maneuvers. Ethel points out that the kelp trouble would never have happened if the Earth people had not originally removed the otters. How naive Ethel is! She has no understanding of the principles of irony. Poetry bewilders her also. Edward refuses to sleep with Ethel now.

▼

In the final centuries of their era the people of Earth succeeded in paving the surface of their planet almost entirely with a skin of concrete and metal. We must pry much of this up so that the planet may start to breathe again. It would be easy and efficient to use explosives or acids, but we are not overly concerned with ease and efficiency; besides there is great concern that explosives or acids may do further ecological harm here. Therefore we employ large machines that insert prongs in the great cracks that have developed in the concrete. Once we have lifted the paved slabs they usually crumble quickly. Clouds

of concrete dust blow freely through the streets of these cities, cov-
ering the stumps of the buildings with a fine, pure coating of gray-
ish-white powder. The effect is delicate and refreshing. Paul suggested
yesterday that we may be doing ecological harm by setting free this
dust. I became frightened at the idea and reported him to the leader
of our team. Paul will be transferred to another group.

▼

Toward the end here they all wore breathing-suits, similar to ours but
even more comprehensive. We find these suits lying around everywhere like the discarded shells of giant insects. The most advanced
models were complete individual housing units. Apparently it was not
necessary to leave one's suit except to perform such vital functions
as sexual intercourse and childbirth. We understand that the reluc-
tance of the Earth people to leave their suits even for those functions,
near the close, immensely hastened the decrease in population.

▼

Our philosophical discussions. God created this planet. We all agree
on that, in a manner of speaking, ignoring for the moment defini-
tions of such concepts as "God" and "created." Why did He go to so
much trouble to bring Earth into being, if it was His intention merely
to have it rendered uninhabitable? Did He create mankind especially
for this purpose, or did they exercise free will in doing what they did
here? Was mankind God's way of taking vengeance against His own
creation? Why would He want to take vengeance against his own creation? Perhaps it is a mistake to approach the destruction of Earth
from the moral or ethical standpoint. I think we must see it in purely
esthetic terms, i.e., a self-contained artistic achievement, like a *fou-
etté en tournant* or an *entrechat-dix*, performed for its own sake and
requiring no explanations. Only in this way can we understand how
the Earth people were able to collaborate so joyfully in their own
asphyxiation.

▼

My tour of duty is almost over. It has been an overwhelming experience; I will never be the same. I must express my gratitude for this

opportunity to have seen Earth almost as its people knew it. Its rusted streams, its corroded meadows, its purpled skies, its bluish puddles. The debris, the barren hillsides, the blazing rivers. Soon, thanks to the dedicated work of reclamation teams such as ours, these superficial but beautiful emblems of death will have disappeared. This will be just another world for tourists, of sentimental curiosity but no unique value to the sensibility. How dull that will be: a green and pleasant Earth once more, why, why? The universe has enough habitable planets; at present it has only one Earth. Has all our labor here been an error, then? I sometimes do think it was misguided of us to have undertaken this project. But on the other hand I remind myself of our fundamental irrelevance. The healing process is a natural and inevitable one. With us or without us, the planet cleanses itself. The wind, the rain, the tides. We merely help things along.

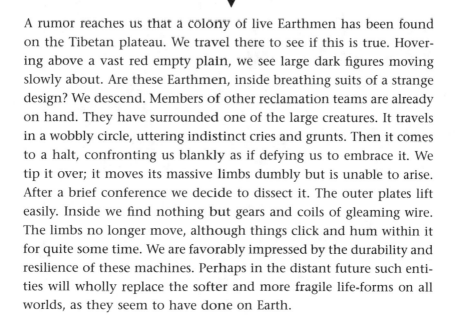

A rumor reaches us that a colony of live Earthmen has been found on the Tibetan plateau. We travel there to see if this is true. Hovering above a vast red empty plain, we see large dark figures moving slowly about. Are these Earthmen, inside breathing suits of a strange design? We descend. Members of other reclamation teams are already on hand. They have surrounded one of the large creatures. It travels in a wobbly circle, uttering indistinct cries and grunts. Then it comes to a halt, confronting us blankly as if defying us to embrace it. We tip it over; it moves its massive limbs dumbly but is unable to arise. After a brief conference we decide to dissect it. The outer plates lift easily. Inside we find nothing but gears and coils of gleaming wire. The limbs no longer move, although things click and hum within it for quite some time. We are favorably impressed by the durability and resilience of these machines. Perhaps in the distant future such entities will wholly replace the softer and more fragile life-forms on all worlds, as they seem to have done on Earth.

The wind. The rain. The tides. All sadnesses flow to the sea.

The Year of the Jackpot

ROBERT A. HEINLEIN

There are many who consider Robert A. Heinlein to be the single most important writer in the history of the genre, and I wouldn't argue. In addition to his best-selling novels, Heinlein wrote dozens of terrific short stories. His output was so prodigious that his editor, John W. Campbell Jr., had to tack pseudonyms on various stories so that readers wouldn't know Heinlein was contributing multiple stories each month to Campbell's SF magazine *Astounding Stories*.

"Year of the Jackpot" is one of Heinlein's latest stories, written in 1952, and in it he uses statistics in a terribly inexorable way. Hard science or not, the ending of the world in Heinlein's scenario makes this a powerfully affecting tale.

At first Potiphar Breen did not notice the girl who was undressing. She was standing at a bus stop only ten feet away. He was indoors but that would not have kept him from noticing; he was seated in a drugstore booth adjacent to the bus stop; there was nothing between Potiphar and the young lady but plate glass and an occasional pedestrian.

Nevertheless he did not look up when she began to peel. Propped up in front of him was a Los Angeles *Times*; beside it, still unopened, were the *Herald-Express* and the *Daily News*. He was scanning the newspaper carefully but the headline stories got only a passing glance. He noted the maximum and minimum temperatures in Brownsville, Texas and entered them in a neat black notebook; he did the same with the closing prices of three blue chips and two dogs on the New York Exchange, as well as the total number of shares. He then began a rapid sifting of minor news stories, from time to time entering briefs of them in his little book; the items he recorded seemed randomly unrelated—among them a publicity release in which Miss National Cottage Cheese Week announced that she intended to marry and have twelve children by a man who could prove that he had been a life-long vegetarian, a circumstantial but wildly unlikely flying saucer report, and a call for prayers for rain throughout Southern California.

Potiphar had just written down the names and addresses of three residents of Watts, California who had been miraculously healed at a tent meeting of the God-is-All First Truth Brethren by the Reverend Dickie Bottomley, the eight-year-old evangelist, and was preparing to tackle the *Herald-Express*, when he glanced over his reading glasses and saw the amateur ecdysiast on the street corner outside. He stood up, placed his glasses in their case, folded the newspapers and put them carefully in his right coat pocket, counted out the exact amount of his check and added twenty-five cents. He then took his raincoat from a hook, placed it over his arm, and went outside.

By now the girl was practically down to the buff. It seemed to Potiphar Breen that she had quite a lot of buff. Nevertheless she had not pulled much of a house. The corner newsboy had stopped hawking his disasters and was grinning at her, and a mixed pair of transvestites who were apparently waiting for the bus had their eyes on her. None of the passers-by stopped. They glanced at her, then with the self-conscious indifference to the unusual of the true Southern Californian, they went on their various ways. The transvestites were frankly staring. The male member of the team wore a frilly feminine blouse but his skirt was a conservative Scottish kilt—his female companion wore a business suit and Homburg hat; she stared with lively interest.

As Breen approached the girl hung a scrap of nylon on the bus stop bench, then reached for her shoes. A police officer, looking hot and unhappy, crossed with the lights and came up to them. "Okay," he said in a tired voice, "that'll be all, lady. Get them duds back on and clear out of here."

The female transvestite took a cigar out of her mouth. "Just," she said, "what business is it of yours, officer?"

The cop turned to her. "Keep out of this!" He ran his eyes over her get up, that of her companion. "I ought to run both of you in, too."

The transvestite raised her eyebrows. "Arrest us for being clothed, arrest her for not being. I think I'm going to like this." She turned to the girl, who was standing still and saying nothing, as if she were puzzled by what was going on. "I'm a lawyer, dear." She pulled a card from her vest pocket. "If this uniformed Neanderthal persists in annoying you, I'll be delighted to handle him."

The man in the kilt said, "Grace! Please!"

She shook him off. "Quiet, Norman—this *is* our business." She went on to the policeman, "Well? Call the wagon. In the meantime my client will answer no questions."

The officer looked unhappy enough to cry and his face was getting dangerously red. Breen quietly stepped forward and slipped his raincoat around the shoulders of the girl. She looked startled and spoke for the first time. "Uh—thanks." She pulled the coat about her, cape fashion.

The female attorney glanced at Breen then back to the cop. "Well, officer? Ready to arrest us?"

He shoved his face close to hers. "I ain't going to give you the satisfaction!" He sighed and added, "Thanks, Mr. Breen—you know this lady?"

"I'll take care of her. You can forget it, Kawonski."

"I sure hope so. If she's with you, I'll do just that. But get her out of here, Mr. Breen—please!"

The lawyer interrupted. "Just a moment—you're interfering with my client."

Kawonski said, "Shut up, you! You heard Mr. Breen—she's with him. Right, Mr. Breen?"

"Well—yes. I'm a friend. I'll take care of her."

The transvestite said suspiciously, "I didn't hear *her* say that."

Her companion said, "Grace—please! There's our bus."

"And I didn't hear her say she was your client," the cop retorted. "You look like a—" His words were drowned out by the bus's brakes. "—and besides that, if you don't climb on that bus and get off my territory, I'll . . . I'll . . ."

"You'll what?"

"Grace! We'll miss our bus."

"Just a moment, Norman. Dear, is this man really a friend of yours? Are you with him?"

The girl looked uncertainly at Breen, then said in a low voice, "Uh, yes. That's right."

"Well . . ." The lawyer's companion pulled at her arm. She shoved her card into Breen's hand and got on the bus; it pulled away.

Breen pocketed the card. Kawonski wiped his forehead. "Why did you do it, lady?" he said peevishly.

The girl looked puzzled. "I . . . I don't know."

"You hear that, Mr. Breen? That's what they all say. And if you pull 'em in, there's six more the next day. The Chief said—" He sighed. "The Chief said—well, if I had arrested her like that female shyster wanted me to, I'd be out at a hundred and ninety-sixth and Ploughed Ground tomorrow morning, thinking about retirement. So get her out of here, will you?"

The girl said, "But—"

"No 'buts,' lady. Just be glad a real gentleman like Mr. Breen is willing to help you." He gathered up her clothes, handed them to her. When she reached for them she again exposed an uncustomary amount of skin; Kawonski hastily gave them to Breen instead, who crowded them into his coat pockets.

She let Breen lead her to where his car was parked, got in and tucked the raincoat around her so that she was rather more dressed than a girl usually is. She looked at him.

She saw a medium-sized and undistinguished man who was slipping down the wrong side of thirty-five and looked older. His eyes had that mild and slightly naked look of the habitual spectacles wearer who is not at the moment with glasses; his hair was gray at the temples and thin on top. His herringbone suit, black shoes, white shirt, and neat tie smacked more of the East than of California.

He saw a face which he classified as "pretty" and "wholesome" rather than "beautiful" and "glamorous." It was topped by a healthy mop of light brown hair. He set her age at twenty-five, give or take eighteen months. He smiled gently, climbed in without speaking and started his car.

He turned up Doheny Drive and east on Sunset. Near La Cienega he slowed down. "Feeling better?"

"Uh, I guess so Mr.—'Breen'?"

"Call me Potiphar. What's your name? Don't tell me if you don't want to."

"Me? I'm . . . I'm Meade Barstow."

"Thank you, Meade. Where do you want to go? Home?"

"I suppose so. I—Oh my no! I can't go home like *this*." She clutched the coat tightly to her.

"Parents?"

"No. My landlady. She'd be shocked to death."

"Where, then?"

She thought. "Maybe we could stop at a filling station and I could sneak into the ladies' room."

"Mmm . . . maybe. See here, Meade—my house is six blocks from here and has a garage entrance. You could get inside without being seen." He looked at her.

She stared back. "Potiphar—you don't *look* like a wolf?"

"Oh, but I am! The worst sort." He whistled and gnashed his teeth. "See? But Wednesday is my day off from it."

She looked at him and dimpled. "Oh, well! I'd rather wrestle with you than with Mrs. Megeath. Let's go."

He turned up into the hills. His bachelor diggings were one of the many little frame houses clinging like fungus to the brown slopes of the Santa Monica Mountains. The garage was notched into this hill; the house sat on it. He drove in, cut the ignition, and led her up a teetery inside stairway into the living room. "In there," he said, pointing. "Help yourself." He pulled her clothes out of his pockets and handed them to her.

She blushed and took them, disappeared into his bedroom. He heard her turn the key in the lock. He settled down in his easy chair, took out his notebook, and opened the *Herald-Express*.

He was finishing the *Daily News* and had added several notes to his collection when she came out. Her hair was neatly rolled; her face was restored; she had brushed most of the wrinkles out of her skirt. Her sweater was neither too tight nor deep cut, but it was pleasantly filled. She reminded him of well water and farm breakfasts.

He took his raincoat from her, hung it up, and said, "Sit down, Meade."

She said uncertainly, "I had better go."

"Go if you must—but I had hoped to talk with you."

"Well—" She sat down on the edge of his couch and looked around. The room was small but as neat as his necktie, clean as his collar. The fireplace was swept; the floor was bare and polished. Books crowded bookshelves in every possible space. One corner was filled by an elderly flat-top desk; the papers on it were neatly in order. Near it, on its own stand, was a small electric calculator. To her right, French windows gave out on a tiny porch over the garage. Beyond it she could see the sprawling city; a few neon signs were already blinking.

She sat back a little. "This is a nice room—Potiphar. It looks like you."

"I take that as a compliment. Thank you." She did not answer; he went on, "Would you like a drink?"

"Oh, would I!" She shivered. "I guess I've got the jitters."

He got up. "Not surprising. What'll it be?"

She took Scotch and water, no ice; he was a Bourbon-and-ginger-ale man. She had soaked up half her highball in silence, then put it down, squared her shoulders and said, "Potiphar?"

"Yes, Meade?"

"Look—if you brought me here to make a pass, I wish you'd go ahead and make it. It won't do you a bit of good, but it makes me nervous to wait for it."

He said nothing and did not change his expression. She went on uneasily, "Not that I'd blame you for trying—under the circumstances. And I *am* grateful. But . . . well—it's just that I don't—"

He came over and took both her hands. "My dear, I haven't the slightest thought of making a pass at you. Nor need you feel grateful. I butted in because I was interested in your case."

"My case? Are you a doctor? A psychiatrist?"

He shook his head. "I'm a mathematician. A statistician, to be precise."

"Huh? I don't get it."

"Don't worry about it. But I would like to ask some questions. May I?"

"Uh, sure, sure! I owe you that much—and then some."

"You owe me nothing. Want your drink sweetened?"

She gulped it and handed him her glass, then followed him out into the kitchen. He did an exact job of measuring and gave it back. "Now tell me why you took your clothes off?"

She frowned. "I don't know. I *don't* know. I don't *know*. I guess I just went crazy." She added round-eyed, "But I don't feel crazy. Could I go off my rocker and not know it?"

"You're not crazy . . . not more so than the rest of us," he amended. "Tell me—where did you see someone else do this?"

"Huh? But I never have."

"Where did you read about it?"

"But I haven't. Wait a minute—those people up in Canada. Dooka-somethings."

"Doukhobors. That's all? No bareskin swimming parties? No strip poker?"

She shook her head. "No. You may not believe it but I was the kind of a little girl who undressed under her nightie." She colored and added, "I still do—unless I remember to tell myself it's silly."

"I believe it. No news stories?"

"No. Yes, there was too! About two weeks ago, I think it was. Some girl in a theater, in the audience, I mean. But I thought it was just publicity. You know the stunts they pull here."

He shook his head. "It wasn't. February 3rd, the Grand Theater, Mrs. Alvin Copley. Charges dismissed."

"Huh? How did *you* know?"

"Excuse me." He went to his desk, dialed the City News Bureau. "Alf? This is Pot Breen. They still sitting on that story? . . . yes, yes, the Gypsy Rose file. Any new ones today?" He waited; Meade thought that she could make out swearing. "Take it easy, Alf—this hot weather

can't last forever. Nine, eh? Well, add another—Santa Monica Boulevard, late this afternoon. No arrest." He added, "Nope, nobody got her
name—a middle-aged woman with a cast in one eye. I happened to
see it . . . who, me? Why would I want to get mixed up? But it's rounding up into a very, very interesting picture." He put the phone down.

Meade said, "Cast in one eye, indeed!"

"Shall I call him back and give him your name?"

"Oh, no!"

"Very well. Now, Meade, we seemed to have located the point of
contagion in your case—Mrs. Copley. What I'd like to know next is
how you felt, what you were thinking about, when you did it?"

She was frowning intently. "Wait a minute, Potiphar—do I understand that *nine other* girls have pulled the stunt I pulled?"

"Oh, no—nine others *today*. You are—" He paused briefly. "The
three hundred and nineteenth case in Los Angeles county since the
first of the year. I don't have figures on the rest of the country, but
the suggestion to clamp down on the stories came from the eastern
news services when the papers here put our first cases on the wire.
That proves that it's a problem elsewhere, too."

"You mean that women all over the country are peeling off their
clothes in public? Why, how shocking!"

He said nothing. She blushed again and insisted, "Well, it is
shocking, even if it was me, this time."

"No, Meade. One case is shocking; over three hundred makes it
scientifically interesting. That's why I want to know how it felt. Tell
me about it."

"But—All right, I'll try. I told you I don't know why I did it; I still
don't. I—"

"You remember it?"

"Oh, yes! I remember getting up off the bench and pulling up my
sweater. I remember unzipping my skirt. I remember thinking I would
have to hurry as I could see my bus stopped two blocks down the
street. I remember how *good* it felt when I finally, uh—" She paused
and looked puzzled. "But I still don't know why."

"What were you thinking about just before you stood up?"

"I don't remember."

"Visualize the street. What was passing by? Where were your hands? Were your legs crossed or uncrossed? Was there anybody near you? What were you thinking about?"

"Uh . . . nobody was on the bench with me. I had my hands in my lap. Those characters in the mixed-up clothes were standing near by, but I wasn't paying attention. I wasn't thinking much except that my feet hurt and I wanted to get home—and how unbearably hot and sultry it was. Then—" Her eyes became distant. "—suddenly I knew what I had to do and it was very urgent that I do it. So I stood up and I . . . and I—" Her voice became shrill.

"Take it easy!" he said. "Don't do it again."

"Huh? Why, Mr. Breen! I wouldn't do anything like that."

"Of course not. Then what?"

"Why, you put your raincoat around me and you know the rest." She faced him. "Say, Potiphar, what were you doing with a raincoat? It hasn't rained in weeks—this is the driest, hottest rainy season in years."

"In sixty-eight years, to be exact."

"Huh?"

"I carry a raincoat anyhow. Uh, just a notion of mine, but I feel that when it does rain, it's going to rain awfully hard." He added, "Forty days and forty nights, maybe."

She decided that he was being humorous and laughed. He went on, "Can you remember how you got the idea?"

She swirled her glass and thought. "I simply don't know."

He nodded. "That's what I expected."

"I don't understand you—unless you think I'm crazy. Do you?"

"No. I think you had to do it and could not help it and don't know why and can't know why."

"But *you* know." She said it accusingly.

"Maybe. At least I have some figures. Ever take any interest in statistics, Meade?"

She shook her head. "Figures confuse me. Never mind statistics—
I want to know why I did what I did!"

He looked at her very soberly. "I think we're lemmings, Meade."

▼

She looked puzzled, then horrified. "You mean those little furry
mouselike creatures? The ones that—"

"Yes. The ones that periodically make a death migration, until millions, hundreds of millions of them drown themselves in the sea. Ask
a lemming why he does it. If you could get him to slow up his rush
toward death, even money says he would rationalize his answer as
well as any college graduate. But he does it because he has to—and
so do we."

"That's a horrid idea, Potiphar."

"Maybe. Come here, Meade. I'll show you figures that confuse me,
too." He went to his desk and opened a drawer, took out a packet of
cards. "Here's one. Two weeks ago—a man sues an entire state legis-
lature for alienation of his wife's affection—and the judge lets the suit
be tried. Or this one—a patent application for a device to lay the globe
over on its side and warm up the arctic regions. Patent denied, but
the inventor took in over three hundred thousand dollars in down
payments on South Pole real estate before the postal authorities
stepped in. Now he's fighting the case and it looks as if he might win.
And here—prominent bishop proposes applied courses in the so-
called facts of life in high schools." He put the card away hastily.
"Here's a dilly: a bill introduced in the Alabama lower house to repeal
the laws of atomic energy—not the present statutes, but the natural
laws concerning nuclear physics; the wording makes that plain." He
shrugged. "How silly can you get?"

"They're crazy."

"No, Meade. One such is crazy; a lot of them is a lemming death
march. No, don't object—I've plotted them on a curve. The last time
we had anything like this was the so-called Era of Wonderful Nonsense. But this one is much worse." He delved into a lower drawer,
hauled out a graph. "The amplitude is more than twice as great and

we haven't reached peak. What the peak will be I don't dare guess—three separate rhythms, reinforcing."

She peered at the curves. "You mean that the laddy with the arctic real estate deal is somewhere on this line?"

"He adds to it. And back here on the last crest are the flag-pole sitters and the goldfish swallowers and the Ponzi hoax and the marathon dancers and the man who pushed a peanut up Pikes Peak with his nose. You're on the new crest—or you will be when I add you in."

She made a face. "I don't like it."

"Neither do I. But it's as clear as a bank statement. This year the human race is letting down its hair, flipping its lip with a finger, and saying, '*Wubba, wubba, wubba.*'"

She shivered. "Do you suppose I could have another drink? Then I'll go."

"I have a better idea. I owe you a dinner for answering questions. Pick a place and we'll have a cocktail before."

She chewed her lip. "You don't owe me anything. And I don't feel up to facing a restaurant crowd. I might . . . I might—"

"No, you wouldn't," he said sharply. "It doesn't hit twice."

"You're sure? Anyhow, I don't want to face a crowd." She glanced at his kitchen door. "Have you anything to eat in there? I can cook."

"Um, breakfast things. And there's a pound of ground round in the freezer compartment and some rolls. I sometimes make hamburgers when I don't want to go out."

She headed for the kitchen. "Drunk or sober, fully dressed or—or naked, I can cook. You'll see."

He did see. Open-faced sandwiches with the meat married to toasted buns and the flavor garnished rather than suppressed by scraped Bermuda onion and thin-sliced dill, a salad made from things she had scrounged out of his refrigerator, potatoes crisp but not vulcanized. They ate it on the tiny balcony, sopping it down with cold beer.

He sighed and wiped his mouth. "Yes, Meade, you can cook."

"Some day I'll arrive with proper materials and pay you back. Then I'll prove it."

"You've already proved it. Nevertheless I accept. But I tell you three times, you owe me nothing."

"No? If you hadn't been a Boy Scout, I'd be in jail."

Breen shook his head. "The police have orders to keep it quiet at all costs—to keep it from growing. You saw that. And, my dear, you weren't a person to me at the time. I didn't even see your face; I—"

"You saw plenty else!"

"Truthfully, I didn't look. You were just a—a statistic."

She toyed with her knife and said slowly, "I'm not sure, but I think I've just been insulted. In all the twenty-five years that I've fought men off, more or less successfully, I've been called a lot of names—but a 'statistic'—why I ought to take your slide rule and beat you to death with it."

"My dear young lady—"

"I'm not a lady, that's for sure. But I'm *not* a statistic."

"My dear Meade, then. I wanted to tell you, before you did anything hasty, that in college I wrestled varsity middle-weight."

She grinned and dimpled. "That's more the talk a girl likes to hear. I was beginning to be afraid you had been assembled in an adding machine factory. Potty, you're rather a dear."

"If that is a diminutive of my given name, I like it. But if it refers to my waist line, I resent it."

She reached across and patted his stomach. "I like your waist line; lean and hungry men are difficult. If I were cooking for you regularly, I'd really pad it."

"Is that a proposal?"

"Let it lie, let it lie—Potty, do you really think the whole country is losing its buttons?"

He sobered at once. "It's worse than that."

"Huh?"

"Come inside. I'll show you." They gathered up dishes and dumped them in the sink, Breen talking all the while. "As a kid I was fascinated by numbers. Numbers are pretty things and they combine in such interesting configurations. I took my degree in math, of course, and got a job as a junior actuary with Midwestern

Mutual—the insurance outfit. That was fun—no way on earth to tell when a particular man is going to die, but an absolute certainty that so many men of a certain age group would die before a certain date. The curves were so lovely—and they always worked out. Always. You didn't have to know *why*; you could predict with dead certainty and never know why. The equations worked; the curves were right.

"I was interested in astronomy too; it was the one science where individual figures worked out neatly, completely, and accurately, down to the last decimal point the instruments were good for. Compared with astronomy the other sciences were mere carpentry and kitchen chemistry.

"I found there were nooks and crannies in astronomy where individual numbers won't do, where you have to go over to statistics, and I became even more interested. I joined the Variable Star Association and I might have gone into astronomy professionally, instead of what I'm in now—business consultation—if I hadn't gotten interested in something else."

"'Business consultation'?" repeated Meade. "Income tax work?"

"Oh, no—that's too elementary. I'm the numbers boy for a firm of industrial engineers. I can tell a rancher exactly how many of his Hereford bull calves will be sterile. Or I tell a motion picture producer how much rain insurance to carry on location. Or maybe how big a company in a particular line must be to carry its own risk in industrial accidents. And I'm right. I'm always right."

"Wait a minute. Seems to me a big company would *have* to have insurance."

"Contrariwise. A really big corporation begins to resemble a statistical universe."

"Huh?"

"Never mind. I got interested in something else—cycles. Cycles are everything, Meade. And everywhere. The tides. The seasons. Wars. Love. Everybody knows that in the spring the young man's fancy lightly turns to what the girls never stopped thinking about, but did you know that it runs in an eighteen-year-plus cycle as well? And that a girl born at the wrong swing of the curve doesn't stand nearly as good a chance as her older or younger sister?"

"What? Is *that* why I'm a doddering old maid?"

"You're twenty-five?" He pondered. "Maybe—but your chances are picking up again; the curve is swinging up. Anyhow, remember you are just one statistic; the curve applies to the group. Some girls get married every year anyhow."

"Don't call me a statistic."

"Sorry. And marriages match up with acreage planted to wheat, with wheat cresting ahead. You could almost say that planting wheat makes people get married."

"Sounds silly."

"It *is* silly. The whole notion of cause-and-effect is probably super-stition. But the same cycle shows a peak in house building right after a peak in marriages, every time."

"Now that makes sense."

"Does it? How many newlyweds do you know who can afford to build a house? You might as well blame it on wheat acreage. We don't know *why*; it just *is*."

"Sun spots, maybe?"

"You can correlate sun spots with stock prices, or Columbia River salmon, or women's skirts. And you are just as much justified in blaming short skirts for sun spots as you are in blaming sun spots for salmon. We don't know. But the curves go on just the same."

"But there has to be some *reason* behind it."

"Does there? That's mere assumption. A fact has no 'why.' There it stands, self demonstrating. Why did you take your clothes off today?"

She frowned. "That's not fair."

"Maybe not. But I want to show you why I'm worried." He went into the bedroom, came out with a large roll of tracing paper. "We'll spread it on the floor. Here they are, all of them. The 54-year cycle— see the Civil War there? See how it matches in? The 18 & 1/3 year cycle, the 9-plus cycle, the 41-month shorty, the three rhythms of sun spots—everything, all combined in one grand chart. Mississippi River floods, fur catches in Canada, stock market prices, marriages, epidemics, freight-car loadings, bank clearings, locust plagues, divorces, tree growth, wars, rainfall, earth magnetism, building construction, patents applied for, murders—you name it; I've got it there."

She stared at the bewildering array of wavy lines. "But, Potty, what does it mean?"

"It means that these things all happen, in regular rhythm, whether we like it or not. It means that when skirts are due to go up, all the stylists in Paris can't make 'em go down. It means that when prices are going down, all the controls and supports and government planning can't make 'em go up." He pointed to a curve. "Take a look at the grocery ads. Then turn to the financial page and read how the Big Brains try to double-talk their way out of it. It means that when an epidemic is due, it happens, despite all the public health efforts. It means we're lemmings."

She pulled her lip. "I don't like it. 'I am the master of my fate,' and so forth. I've got free will, Potty. I know I have—I can feel it."

"I imagine every little neutron in an atom bomb feels the same way. He can go *sprung!* or he can sit still, just as he pleases. But statistical mechanics work out anyhow. And the bomb goes off—which is what I'm leading up to. See anything odd there, Meade?"

She studied the chart, trying not to let the curving lines confuse her. "They sort of bunch up over at the right end."

"You're dern tootin' they do! See that dotted vertical line? That's right now—and things are bad enough. But take a look at that solid vertical; that's about six months from now—and that's when we get it. Look at the cycles—the long ones, the short ones, all of them. Every single last one of them reaches either a trough or a crest exactly on— or almost on—that line."

"That's bad?"

"What do you think? Three of the big ones troughed in 1929 and the depression almost ruined us . . . even with the big 54-year cycle supporting things. Now we've got the big one troughing—and the few crests are not things that help. I mean to say, tent caterpillars and influenza don't do us any good. Meade, if statistics mean anything, this tired old planet hasn't seen a jackpot like this since Eve went into the apple business. I'm scared."

She searched his face. "Potty—you're not simply having fun with me? You know I can't check up on you."

"I wish to heaven I were. No, Meade, I can't fool about numbers; I wouldn't know how. This is it. The Year of the Jackpot."

▼

She was very silent as he drove her home. As they approached West Los Angeles, she said, "Potty?"

"Yes, Meade?"

"What do we *do* about it?"

"What do you do about a hurricane? You pull in your ears. What can you do about an atom bomb? You try to out-guess it, not be there when it goes off. What else can you do?"

"Oh." She was silent for a few moments, then added, "Potty? Will you tell me which way to jump?"

"Huh? Oh, sure! If I can figure it out."

He took her to her door, turned to go. She said, "Potty!"

He faced her. "Yes, Meade?"

She grabbed his head, shook it—then kissed him fiercely on the mouth. "There—is that just a statistic?"

"Uh, no."

"It had better not be," she said dangerously. "Potty, I think I'm going to have to change your curve."

II

"RUSSIANS REJECT UN NOTE"

"MISSOURI FLOOD DAMAGE EXCEEDS 1951 RECORD"

"MISSISSIPPI MESSIAH DEFIES COURT"

"NUDIST CONVENTION STORMS BAILEY'S BEACH"

"BRITISH-IRAN TALKS STILL DEAD-LOCKED"

"FASTER-THAN-LIGHT WEAPON PROMISED"

"TYPHOON DOUBLING BACK ON MANILA"

"MARRIAGE SOLEMNIZED ON FLOOR OF HUDSON—New York, 13 July, *In a specially-constructed diving suit built for two, Merydith Smithe, café society headline girl, and Prince Augie Schleswieg of New York and the*

Riviera were united today by Bishop Dalton in a service televised with the aid of the Navy's ultranew—"

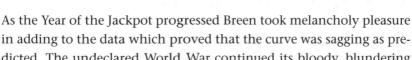

As the Year of the Jackpot progressed Breen took melancholy pleasure in adding to the data which proved that the curve was sagging as predicted. The undeclared World War continued its bloody, blundering way at half a dozen spots around a tortured globe. Breen did not chart it; the headlines were there for anyone to read. He concentrated on the odd facts in the other pages of the papers, facts which, taken singly, meant nothing, but taken together showed a disastrous trend.

He listed stock market prices, rainfall, wheat futures, but it was the "silly season" items which fascinated him. To be sure, some humans were always doing silly things—but at what point had prime damfoolishness become commonplace? When, for example, had the zombie-like professional models become accepted ideals of American womanhood? What were the gradations between National Cancer Week and National Athlete's Foot Week? On what day had the American people finally taken leave of horse sense?

Take transvestism—male-and-female dress customs were arbitrary, but they had seemed to be deeply rooted in culture. When did the breakdown start? With Marlene Dietrich's tailored suit? By the late forties there was no "male" article of clothing that a woman could not wear in public—but when had men started to slip over the line? Should he count psychological cripples who had made the word "drag" a byword in Greenwich Village and Hollywood long before this outbreak? Or were they "wild shots" not belonging on the curve? Did it start with some unknown normal man attending a masquerade and there discovering that skirts actually were more comfortable and practical than trousers? Or had it started with the resurgence of Scottish nationalism reflected in the wearing of kilts by many Scottish-Americans?

Ask a lemming to state his motives! The outcome was in front of him, a news story. Transvestism by draft-dodgers had at last resulted in a mass arrest in Chicago which was to have ended in a giant joint trial—only to have the deputy prosecutor show up in a pinafore and defy the judge to submit an examination to determine the judge's true sex. The judge suffered a stroke and died and the trial was post-poned—postponed forever in Breen's opinion; he doubted that this particular blue law would ever again be enforced.

Or the laws about indecent exposure, for that matter. The attempt to limit the Gypsy-Rose syndrome by ignoring it had taken the starch out of enforcement; now here was a report about the All Souls Com-munity Church of Springfield: the pastor had reinstituted ceremonial nudity. Probably the first time this thousand years, Breen thought, aside from some screwball cults in Los Angeles. The reverend gentle-man claimed that the ceremony was identical with the "dance of the high priestess" in the ancient temple of Karnak.

Could be—but Breen had private information that the "priestess" had been working the burlesque & nightclub circuit before her pre-sent engagement. In any case the holy leader was packing them in and had not been arrested.

Two weeks later a hundred and nine churches in thirty-three states offered equivalent attractions. Breen entered them on his curves.

This queasy oddity seemed to him to have no relation to the star-tling rise in the dissident evangelical cults throughout the country. These churches were sincere, earnest and poor—but growing, ever since the War. Now they were multiplying like yeast. It seemed a sta-tistical cinch that the United States was about to become godstruck again. He correlated it with Transcendentalism and the trek of the Lat-ter Day Saints—hmm . . . yes, it fitted. And the curve was pushing toward a crest.

Billions in war bonds were now falling due; wartime marriages were reflected in the swollen peak of the Los Angeles school popula-tion. The Colorado River was at a record low and the towers in Lake Mead stood high out of the water. But the Angelenos committed slow suicide by watering lawns as usual. The Metropolitan Water District commissioners tried to stop it—it fell between the stools of the police powers of fifty "sovereign" cities. The taps remained open, trickling away the life blood of the desert paradise.

The four regular party conventions—Dixiecrats, Regular Republicans, the other Regular Republicans, and the Democrats—attracted scant attention, as the Know-Nothings had not yet met. The fact that the "American Rally," as the Know-Nothings preferred to be called, claimed not to be a party but an educational society did not detract from their strength. But what was their strength? Their beginnings had been so obscure that Breen had had to go back and dig into the December 1951 files—but he had been approached twice this very week to join them, right inside his own office—once by his boss, once by the janitor.

He hadn't been able to chart the Know-Nothings. They gave him chills in his spine. He kept column-inches on them, found that their publicity was shrinking while their numbers were obviously zooming.

Krakatau blew up on July 18th. It provided the first important transPacific TV-cast; its effect on sunsets, on solar constant, on mean temperature, and on rainfall would not be felt until later in the year. The San Andreas fault, its stresses unrelieved since the Long Beach disaster of 1933, continued to build up imbalance—an unhealed wound running the full length of the West Coast. Pelée and Etna erupted; Mauna Loa was still quiet.

Flying saucers seemed to be landing daily in every state. No one had exhibited one on the ground—or had the Department of Defense sat on them? Breen was unsatisfied with the off-the-record reports he had been able to get; the alcoholic content of some of them had been high. But the sea serpent on Ventura Beach was real; he had seen it. The troglodyte in Tennessee he was not in a position to verify.

Thirty-one domestic air crashes the last week in July . . . was it sabotage? Or was it a sagging curve on a chart? And that neo-polio epidemic that skipped from Seattle to New York? Time for a big epidemic? Breen's chart said it was. But how about B.W.? Could a chart *know* that a Slav biochemist would perfect an efficient virus-and-vector at the right time? Nonsense!

But the curves, if they meant anything at all, included "free will;" they averaged in all the individual "wills" of a statistical universe— and came out as a smooth function. Every morning three million "free wills" flowed toward the center of the New York megapolis; every evening they flowed out again—all by "free will," and on a smooth and predictable curve.

Ask a lemming! Ask *all* the lemmings, dead and alive—let them take a vote on it! Breen tossed his notebook aside and called Meade. "Is this my favorite statistic?"

"Potty! I was thinking about you."

"Naturally. This is your night off."

"Yes, but for another reason, too. Potiphar, have you ever taken a look at the Great Pyramid?"

"I haven't even been to Niagara Falls. I'm looking for a rich woman, so I can travel."

"Yes, yes, I'll let you know when I get my first million, but—"

"That's the first time you've proposed to me this week."

"Shut up. Have you ever looked into the prophecies they found inside the pyramid?"

"Huh? Look, Meade, that's in the same class with astrology— strictly for squirrels. Grow up."

"Yes, of course. But Potty, I thought you were interested in anything odd. This is odd."

"Oh. Sorry. If it's 'silly season' stuff, let's see it."

"All right. Am I cooking for you tonight?"

"It's Wednesday, isn't it?"

"How soon?"

He glanced at his watch. "Pick you up in eleven minutes." He felt his whiskers. "No, twelve and a half."

"I'll be ready. Mrs. Megeath says that these regular dates mean that you are going to marry me."

"Pay no attention to her. She's just a statistic. And I'm a wild datum."

"Oh, well, I've got two hundred and forty-seven dollars toward that million. 'Bye!"

Meade's prize was the usual Rosicrucian come-on, elaborately printed, and including a photograph (retouched, he was sure) of the much disputed line on the corridor wall which was alleged to prophesy, by its various discontinuities, the entire future. This one had an unusual time scale but the major events were all marked on it—the fall of Rome, the Norman Invasion, the Discovery of America, Napoleon, the World Wars.

What made it interesting was that it suddenly stopped—now.

"What about it, Potty?"

"I guess the stonecutter got tired. Or got fired. Or they got a new head priest with new ideas." He tucked it into his desk. "Thanks. I'll think about how to list it." But he got it out again, applied dividers and a magnifying glass. "It says here," he announced, "that the end comes late in August—unless that's a fly speck."

"Morning or afternoon? I have to know how to dress."

"Shoes will be worn. All God's chilluns got shoes." He put it away.

She was quiet for a moment, then said, "Potty, isn't it about time to jump?"

"Huh? Girl, don't let *that* thing affect you! That's 'silly season' stuff."

"Yes. But take a look at *your* chart."

Nevertheless he took the next afternoon off, spent it in the reference room of the main library, confirmed his opinion of soothsayers. Nostradamus was pretentiously silly, Mother Shippey was worse. In any of them you could find what you looked for.

He did find one item in Nostradamus that he liked: "The Oriental shall come forth from his seat . . . he shall pass through the sky, through the waters and the snow, he shall strike each one with his weapon."

That sounded like what the Department of Defense expected the commies to try to do to the Western Allies.

But it was also a description of every invasion that had come out of the "heartland" in the memory of mankind. Nuts!

When he got home he found himself taking down his father's Bible and turning to Revelations. He could not find anything that he could understand but he got fascinated by the recurring use of precise numbers. Presently he thumbed through the Book at random; his eye lit on: "Boast not thyself of tomorrow; for thou knowest not what a day may bring forth." He put the Book away, feeling humbled but not cheered.

The rains started the next morning. The Master Plumbers elected Miss Star Morning "Miss Sanitary Engineering" on the same day that the morticians designated her as "The Body I would Like Best to Prepare," and her option was dropped by Fragrant Features. Congress voted $1.37 to compensate Thomas Jefferson Meeks for losses incurred while an emergency postman for the Christmas rush of 1936, approved the appointment of five lieutenant generals and one ambassador and adjourned in eight minutes. The fire extinguishers in a midwest orphanage turned out to be filled with air. The chancellor of the leading football institution sponsored a fund to send peace messages and vitamins to the Politburo. The stock market slumped nineteen points and the tickers ran two hours late. Wichita, Kansas, remained flooded while Phoenix, Arizona, cut off drinking water to areas outside city limits. And Potiphar Breen found that he had left his raincoat at Meade Barstow's rooming house.

He phoned her landlady, but Mrs. Megeath turned him over to Meade. "What are you doing home on a Friday?" he demanded.

"The theater manager laid me off. Now you'll have to marry me."

"You can't afford me. Meade—seriously, baby, what happened?"

"I was ready to leave the dump anyway. For the last six weeks the popcorn machine has been carrying the place. Today I sat through *I Was A Teen-Age Beatnik* twice. Nothing to do."

"I'll be along."

"Eleven minutes?"

"It's raining. Twenty—with luck."

It was more nearly sixty. Santa Monica Boulevard was a navigable stream; Sunset Boulevard was a subway jam. When he tried to ford the streams leading to Mrs. Megeath's house, he found that changing tires with the wheel wedged against a storm drain presented problems.

"Potty! You look like a drowned rat."

"I'll live." But presently he found himself wrapped in a blanket robe belonging to the late Mr. Megeath and sipping hot cocoa while Mrs. Megeath dried his clothing in the kitchen.

"Meade . . . I'm 'at liberty,' too."

"Huh? You quit your job?"

"Not exactly. Old Man Wiley and I have been having differences of opinion about my answers for months—too much 'Jackpot factor' in the figures I give him to turn over to clients. Not that I call it that, but he has felt that I was unduly pessimistic."

"But you were right!"

"Since when has being right endeared a man to his boss? But that wasn't why he fired me; that was just the excuse. He wants a man willing to back up the Know-Nothing program with scientific double-talk. And I wouldn't join." He went to the window. "It's raining harder."

"But they haven't got any program."

"I know that."

"Potty, you should have joined. It doesn't mean anything—I joined three months ago."

"The hell you did!"

She shrugged. "You pay your dollar and you turn up for two meetings and they leave you alone. It kept my job for another three months. What of it?"

"Uh, well—I'm sorry you did it; that's all. Forget it. Meade, the water is over the curbs out there."

"You had better stay here overnight."

"Mmm . . . I don't like to leave 'Entropy' parked out in this stuff all night. Meade?"

"Yes, Potty?"

"We're both out of jobs. How would you like to duck north into the Mojave and find a dry spot?"

"I'd love it. But look, Potty—is this a proposal, or just a proposition?"

"Don't pull that 'either-or' stuff on me. It's just a suggestion for a vacation. Do you want to take a chaperone?"

"No."

"Then pack a bag."

"Right away. But look, Potiphar—pack a bag *how?* Are you trying to tell me it's *time to jump?*"

He faced her, then looked back at the window. "I don't know," he said slowly, "but this rain might go on quite a while. Don't take anything you don't have to have—but don't leave anything behind you can't get along without."

He repossessed his clothing from Mrs. Megeath while Meade was upstairs. She came down dressed in slacks and carrying two large bags; under one arm was a battered and rakish Teddy bear. "This is Winnie."

"Winnie the Pooh?"

"No, Winnie Churchill. When I feel bad he promises me 'blood, toil, tears, and sweat;' then I feel better. You said to bring anything I couldn't do without?" She looked at him anxiously.

"Right." He took the bags. Mrs. Megeath had seemed satisfied with his explanation that they were going to visit his (mythical) aunt in Bakersfield before looking for jobs; nevertheless she embarrassed him by kissing him good-by and telling him to "take care of my little girl."

Santa Monica Boulevard was blocked off from use. While stalled in traffic in Beverly Hills he fiddled with the car radio, getting squawks and crackling noises, then finally one station nearby: "—in effect," a harsh, high, staccato voice was saying, "the Kremlin has given us till sundown to get out of town. This is your New York Reporter, who thinks that in days like these every American must personally keep his powder dry. And now for a word from—" Breen switched it off and glanced at her face. "Don't worry," he said. "They've been talking that way for years."

"You think they are bluffing?"

"I didn't say that. I said, 'don't worry.'"

But his own packing, with her help, was clearly on a "Survival Kit" basis—canned goods, all his warm clothing, a sporting rifle he had not fired in over two years, a first-aid kit and the contents of his medicine chest. He dumped the stuff from his desk into a carton, shoved it into the back seat along with cans and books and coats and covered the plunder with all the blankets in the house. They went back up the rickety stairs for a last check.

"Potty—where's your chart?"

"Rolled up on the back seat shelf. I guess that's all—hey, wait a minute!" He went to a shelf over his desk and began taking down small, sober-looking magazines. "I dern near left behind my file of *The Western Astronomer* and of the *Proceedings of the Variable Star Association.*"

"Why take them?"

"Huh? I must be nearly a year behind on both of them. Now maybe I'll have time to read."

"Hmm . . . Potty, watching you read professional journals is not my notion of a vacation."

"Quiet, woman! You took Winnie; I take these."

She shut up and helped him. He cast a longing eye at his electric calculator but decided it was too much like the White Knight's mouse trap. He could get by with his slide rule.

As the car splashed out into the street she said, "Potty, how are you fixed for cash?"

"Huh? Okay, I guess."

"I mean, leaving while the banks are closed, and everything." She held up her purse. "Here's my bank. It isn't much, but we can use it."

He smiled and patted her knee. "Stout fellow! I'm sitting on my bank; I started turning everything to cash about the first of the year."

"Oh. I closed my bank account right after we met."

"You did? You must have taken my maunderings seriously."

"I always take you seriously."

Mint Canyon was a five-mile-an-hour nightmare, with visibility limited to the tail lights of the truck ahead. When they stopped for coffee at Halfway, they confirmed what seemed evident: Cajon Pass was closed and long-haul traffic for Route 66 was being detoured through the secondary pass. At long, long last they reached the Victorville cut-off and lost some of the traffic— a good thing, as the windshield wiper on his side had quit working and they were driving by the committee system. Just short of Lancaster she said suddenly, "Potty, is this buggy equipped with a snorkel?"

"Nope."

"Then we had better stop. But I see a light off the road."

The light was an auto court. Meade settled the matter of economy versus convention by signing the book herself; they were placed in one cabin. He saw that it had twin beds and let the matter ride. Meade went to bed with her Teddy bear without even asking to be kissed goodnight. It was already gray, wet dawn.

They got up in the late afternoon and decided to stay over one more night, then push north toward Bakersfield. A high pressure area was alleged to be moving south, crowding the warm, wet mass that smothered Southern California. They wanted to get into it. Breen had the wiper repaired and bought two new tires to replace his ruined spare, added some camping items to his cargo, and bought for Meade a .32 automatic, a lady's social-purposes gun; he gave it to her somewhat sheepishly.

"What's this for?"

"Well, you're carrying quite a bit of cash."

"Oh. I thought maybe I was to use it to fight you off."

"Now, Meade—"

"Never mind. Thanks, Potty."

They had finished supper and were packing the car with their afternoon's purchases when the quake struck. Five inches of rain in twenty-four hours, more than three billion tons of mass suddenly loaded on a fault already overstrained, all cut loose in one subsonic, stomach-twisting rumble.

Meade sat down on the wet ground very suddenly; Breen stayed upright by dancing like a logroller. When the ground quieted down somewhat, thirty seconds later, he helped her up. "You all right?"

"My slacks are soaked." She added pettishly, "But, Potty, it never quakes in wet weather. *Never.*"

"It did this time."

"But—"

"Keep quiet, can't you?" He opened the car door and switched on the radio, waited impatiently for it to warm up. Shortly he was searching the entire dial. "Not a confounded Los Angeles station on the air!"

"Maybe the shock busted one of your tubes?"

"Pipe down." He passed a squeal and dialed back to it:

"—your Sunshine Station in Riverside, California. Keep tuned to this station for the latest developments. It is of now impossible to tell the size of the disaster. The Colorado River aqueduct is broken; nothing is known of the extent of the damage nor how long it will take to repair it. So far as we know the Owens River Valley aqueduct may be intact, but all persons in the Los Angeles area are advised to conserve water. My personal advice is to stick your washtubs out into this rain; it can't last forever. If we had time, we'd play *Cool Water*, just to give you the idea. I now read from the standard disaster instructions, quote: 'Boil all water. Remain quietly in your homes and do not panic. Stay off the highways. Cooperate with the police and render—' Joe! Joe! Catch that phone! '—render aid where necessary. Do not use the telephone except for—' Flash! An unconfirmed report from Long Beach states that the Wilmington and San Pedro waterfront is under five feet of water. I repeat, this is unconfirmed. Here's a message from the commanding general, March Field: 'official, all military personnel will report—'"

Breen switched it off. "Get in the car."

"Where are we going?"

"North."

"We've paid for the cabin. Should we—"

"Get in!"

He stopped in the town, managed to buy six five-gallon-tins and a jeep tank. He filled them with gasoline and packed them with blankets in the back seat, topping off the mess with a dozen cans of oil. Then they were rolling.

"What are we doing, Potiphar?"

"I want to get west on the valley highway."

"Any particular place west?"

"I think so. We'll see. You work the radio, but keep an eye on the road, too. That gas back there makes me nervous."

Through the town of Mojave and northwest on 466 into the Tehachapi Mountains—Reception was poor in the pass but what Meade could pick up confirmed the first impression—worse than the quake of '06, worse than San Francisco, Managua, and Long Beach taken together.

When they got down out of the mountains it was clearing locally; a few stars appeared. Breen swung left off the highway and ducked south of Bakersfield by the county road, reached the Route 99 superhighway just south of Greenfield. It was, as he had feared, already jammed with refugees; he was forced to go along with the flow for a couple of miles before he could cut west at Greenfield toward Taft. They stopped on the western outskirts of the town and ate at an all-night truckers' joint.

They were about to climb back into the car when there was suddenly "sunrise" due south. The rosy light swelled almost instantaneously, filled the sky, and died; where it had been a red-and-purple pillar of cloud was mounting, mounting—spreading to a mushroom top.

Breen stared at it, glanced at his watch, then said harshly, "Get in the car."

"Potty—that was . . . that was—"

"That was—that used to be—Los Angeles. Get in the car!"

He simply drove for several minutes. Meade seemed to be in a state of shock, unable to speak. When the sound reached them he again glanced at his watch. "Six minutes and nineteen seconds. That's about right."

"Potty—*we should have brought Mrs. Megeath.*"

"How was I to know?" he said angrily. "Anyhow, you can't transplant an old tree. If she got it, she never knew it."

"Oh, I hope so!"

"Forget it; straighten out and fly right. We're going to have all we can do to take care of ourselves. Take the flashlight and check the map. I want to turn north at Taft and over toward the coast."

"Yes, Potiphar."

"And try the radio."

She quieted down and did as she was told. The radio gave nothing, not even the Riverside station; the whole broadcast range was covered by a curious static, like rain on a window. He slowed down as they approached Taft, let her spot the turn north onto the state road, and turned into it. Almost at once a figure jumped out into the road in front of them, waved his arms violently. Breen tromped on the brake.

The man came up on the left side of the car, rapped on the window; Breen ran the glass down. Then he stared stupidly at the gun in the man's left hand. "Get out of the car," the stranger said sharply. "I've got to have it." He reached inside with his right hand, groped for the door lever.

Meade reached across Breen, stuck her little lady's gun in the man's face, pulled the trigger. Breen could feel the flash on his own face, never noticed the report. The man looked puzzled, with a neat, not-yet-bloody hole in his upper lip—then slowly sagged away from the car.

"Drive on!" Meade said in a high voice.

Breen caught his breath. "Good girl—"

"Drive on! *Get rolling!*"

They followed the state road through Los Padres National Forest, stopping once to fill the tank from their cans. They turned off onto a dirt road. Meade kept trying the radio, got San Francisco once but it was too jammed with static to read. Then she got Salt Lake City, faint but clear: "—since there are no reports of anything passing our radar screen the Kansas City bomb must be assumed to have been planted rather than delivered. This is a tentative theory but—" They passed into a deep cut and lost the rest.

When the squawk box again came to life it was a new voice: "Conelrad," said a crisp voice, "coming to you over the combined networks. The rumor that Los Angeles has been hit by an atom bomb is totally unfounded. It is true that the western metropolis has suffered a severe earthquake shock but that is all. Government officials and the Red Cross are on the spot to care for the victims, but—and I repeat—there has *been no atomic bombing.* So relax and stay in your homes. Such wild rumors can damage the United States quite as much as enemy's bombs. Stay off the highways and listen for—" Breen snapped it off.

"Somebody," he said bitterly, "has again decided that 'Mama knows best.' They won't tell us any bad news."

"Potiphar," Meade said sharply, "that *was* an atom bomb . . . wasn't it?"

"It was. And now we don't know whether it was just Los Angeles—and Kansas City—or all the big cities in the country. All we know is that they are lying to us."

"Maybe I can get another station?"

"The hell with it." He concentrated on driving. The road was very bad.

As it began to get light she said, "Potty—do you know where we're going? Are we just keeping out of cities?"

"I think I do. If I'm not lost." He stared around them. "Nope, it's all right. See that hill up forward with the triple gendarmes on its profile?"

"Gendarmes?"

"Big rock pillars. That's a sure landmark. I'm looking for a private road now. It leads to a hunting lodge belonging to two of my friends—an old ranch house actually, but as a ranch it didn't pay."

"Oh. They won't mind us using it?"

He shrugged. "If they show up, we'll ask them. If they show up. They lived in Los Angeles, Meade."

"Oh. Yes, I guess so."

The private road had once been a poor grade of wagon trail; now it was almost impassable. But they finally topped a hogback from which they could see almost to the Pacific, then dropped down into a sheltered bowl where the cabin was. "All out, girl. End of the line."

Meade sighed. "It looks heavenly."

"Think you can rustle breakfast while I unload? There's probably wood in the shed. Or can you manage a wood range?"

"Just try me."

Two hours later Breen was standing on the hogback, smoking a cigarette, and staring off down to the west. He wondered if that was a mushroom cloud up San Francisco way? Probably his imagination, he decided, in view of the distance. Certainly there was nothing to be seen to the south.

Meade came out of the cabin. "Potty!"

"Up here."

She joined him, took his hand, and smiled, then snitched his cigarette and took a deep drag. She expelled it and said, "I know it's sinful of me, but I feel more peaceful than I have in months and months."

"I know."

"Did you see the canned goods in that pantry? We could pull through a hard winter here."

"We might have to."

"I suppose. I wish we had a cow."

"What would you do with a cow?"

"I used to milk four cows before I caught the school bus, every morning. I can butcher a hog, too."

"I'll try to find one."

"You do and I'll manage to smoke it." She yawned. "I'm suddenly terribly sleepy."

"So am I. And small wonder."

"Let's go to bed."

"Uh, yes. Meade?"

"Yes, Potty?"

"We may be here quite a while. You know that, don't you?"

"Yes, Potty."

"In fact it might be smart to stay put until those curves all start turning up again. They will, you know."

"Yes. I had figured that out."

He hesitated, then went on, "Meade . . . will you marry me?"

"Yes." She moved up to him.

After a time he pushed her gently away and said, "My dear, my very dear, uh—we could drive down and find a minister in some little town?"

She looked at him steadily. "That wouldn't be very bright, would it? I mean, nobody knows we're here and that's the way we want it. And besides, your car might not make it back up that road."

"No, it wouldn't be very bright. But I want to do the right thing."

"It's all right, Potty. It's *all right*."

"Well, then . . . kneel down here with me. We'll say them together."

"Yes, Potiphar." She knelt and he took her hand. He closed his eyes and prayed wordlessly.

When he opened them he said, "What's the matter?"

"Uh, the gravel hurts my knees."

"We'll stand up, then."

"No. Look, Potty, why don't we just go in the house and say them there?"

"Huh? Hell's bells, woman, we might forget to say them entirely. Now repeat after me: I, Potiphar, take thee, Meade—"

"Yes, Potiphar. I, Meade, take thee, Potiphar—"

                                III

"OFFICIAL: STATIONS WITHIN RANGE RELAY TWICE. EXECUTIVE BUL-
LETIN NUMBER NINE—ROAD LAWS PREVIOUSLY PUBLISHED HAVE BEEN
IGNORED IN MANY INSTANCES. PATROLS ARE ORDERED TO SHOOT WITH-
OUT WARNING AND PROVOST MARSHALS ARE DIRECTED TO USE DEATH
PENALTY FOR UNAUTHORIZED POSSESSION OF GASOLINE. B.W. AND RADI-
ATION QUARANTINE REGULATIONS PREVIOUSLY ISSUED WILL BE RIGIDLY
ENFORCED. LONG LIVE THE UNITED STATES! HARLEY J. NEAL, LIEUTENANT
GENERAL, ACTING CHIEF OF GOVERNMENT. ALL STATIONS RELAY TWICE."

"THIS IS THE FREE RADIO AMERICA RELAY NETWORK, PASS THIS ALONG,
BOYS! GOVERNOR BRANDLEY WAS SWORN IN TODAY AS PRESIDENT BY ACT-
ING CHIEF JUSTICE ROBERTS UNDER THE RULE-OF-SUCCESSION. THE PRES-
IDENT NAMED THOMAS DEWEY AS SECRETARY OF STATE AND PAUL
DOUGLAS AS SECRETARY OF DEFENSE. HIS SECOND OFFICIAL ACT WAS TO
STRIP THE RENEGADE NEAL OF RANK AND TO DIRECT HIS ARREST BY ANY
CITIZEN OR OFFICIAL. MORE LATER, PASS THE WORD ALONG."

"HELLO, CQ, CQ, CQ. THIS IS W5KMR, FREEPORT. QRR, QRR! ANYBODY
READ ME? ANYBODY? WE'RE DYING LIKE FLIES DOWN HERE. WHAT'S HAP-
PENED? STARTS WITH FEVER AND A BURNING THIRST BUT YOU CAN'T
SWALLOW. WE NEED HELP. ANYBODY READ ME? HELLO, CQ 75 CQ 75 THIS
IS W5 KILO METRO ROMEO CALLING QRR AND CQ 75. BY FOR SOMEBODY.
. . . ANYBODY!!!"

"THIS IS THE LORD'S TIME, SPONSORED BY SWAN'S ELIXIR, THE TONIC THAT MAKES WAITING FOR THE KINGDOM OF GOD WORTHWHILE. YOU ARE ABOUT TO HEAR A MESSAGE OF CHEER FROM JUDGE BROOMFIELD, ANOINTED VICAR OF THE KINGDOM ON EARTH. BUT FIRST A BULLETIN: SEND YOUR CONTRIBUTIONS TO 'MESSIAH,' CLINT, TEXAS. DON'T TRY TO MAIL THEM: SEND THEM BY A KINGDOM MESSENGER OR BY SOME PILGRIM JOURNEYING THIS WAY. AND NOW THE TABERNACLE CHOIR FOLLOWED BY THE VOICE OF THE VICAR ON EARTH—"

"—THE FIRST SYMPTOM IS LITTLE RED SPOTS IN THE ARMPITS. THEY ITCH. PUT 'EM TO BED AT ONCE AND KEEP 'EM COVERED UP WARM. THEN GO SCRUB YOURSELF AND WEAR A MASK: WE DON'T KNOW YET HOW YOU CATCH IT. PASS IT ALONG, ED."

"—NO NEW LANDINGS REPORTED ANYWHERE ON THIS CONTINENT. THE PARATROOPERS WHO ESCAPED THE ORIGINAL SLAUGHTER ARE THOUGHT TO BE HIDING OUT IN THE POCONOS. SHOOT—BUT BE CAREFUL; IT MIGHT BE AUNT TESSIE. OFF AND CLEAR, UNTIL NOON TOMORROW—"

▼

The curves were turning up again. There was no longer doubt in Breen's mind about that. It might not even be necessary to stay up here in the Sierra Madres through the winter—though he rather thought they would. He had picked their spot to keep them west of the fallout; it would be silly to be mowed down by the tail of a dying epidemic, or be shot by a nervous vigilante, when a few months' wait would take care of everything.

Besides, he had chopped all that firewood. He looked at his calloused hands—he had done all that work and, by George, he was going to enjoy the benefits!

He was headed out to the hogback to wait for sunset and do an hour's reading; he glanced at his car as he passed it, thinking that he would like to try the radio. He suppressed the yen; two thirds of his reserve gasoline was gone already just from keeping the battery charged for the radio—and here it was only December. He really ought to cut down to twice a week. But it meant a lot to catch the noon bulletin of Free America and then twiddle the dial a few minutes to see what else he could pick up.

For the past three days Free America had not been on the air—solar static maybe, or perhaps just a power failure. But that rumor that President Brandley had been assassinated—while it hadn't come from the Free radio . . . and it hadn't been denied by them, either, which was a good sign. Still, it worried him.

And that other story that lost Atlantis had pushed up during the quake period and that the Azores were now a little continent—almost certainly a hang-over of the "silly season"—but it would be nice to hear a follow-up.

Rather sheepishly, he let his feet carry him to the car. It wasn't fair to listen when Meade wasn't around. He warmed it up, slowly spun the dial, once around and back. Not a peep at full gain, nothing but a terrible amount of static. Served him right.

He climbed the hogback, sat down on the bench he had dragged up there—their "memorial bench," sacred to the memory of the time Meade had hurt her knees on the gravel—sat down and sighed. His lean belly was stuffed with venison and corn fritters; he lacked only tobacco to make him completely happy. The evening cloud colors were spectacularly beautiful and the weather was extremely balmy for December; both, he thought, caused by volcanic dust, with perhaps an assist from atom bombs.

Surprising how fast things went to pieces when they started to skid! And surprising how quickly they were going back together, judging by the signs. A curve reaches trough and then starts right back up. World War III was the shortest big war on record—forty cities gone, counting Moscow and the other slave cities as well as the American ones—and then *whoosh!* neither side fit to fight. Of course, the fact that both sides had thrown their ICBMs over the pole through the most freakish arctic weather since Peary invented the place had a lot to do with it, he supposed. It was amazing that any of the Russians' paratroop transports had gotten through at all.

He sighed and pulled the November 1951 copy of the *Western Astronomer* out of his pocket. Where was he? Oh, yes, *Some Notes on the Stability of G-Type Stars with Especial Reference to Sol,* by A. G. M.

Dynkowski, Lenin Institute, translated by Heinrich Ley, F. R. A. S. Good boy, Ski—sound mathematician. Very clever application of harmonic series and tightly reasoned. He started to thumb for his place when he noticed a footnote that he had missed. Dynkowski's own name carried down to it: "This monograph was denounced by *Pravda* as romantic reactionariism shortly after it was published. Professor Dynkowski has been unreported since and must be presumed to be liquidated."

The poor geek! Well, he probably would have been atomized by now anyway, along with the goons who did him in. He wondered if they really had gotten all the Russki paratroopers? Well, he had killed his quota; if he hadn't gotten that doe within a quarter mile of the cabin and headed right back, Meade would have had a bad time. He had shot them in the back, the swine! and buried them beyond the woodpile—and then it had seemed a shame to skin and eat an innocent deer while those lice got decent burial.

Aside from mathematics, just two things worth doing—kill a man and love a woman. He had done both. He was rich.

He settled down to some solid pleasure. Dynkowski was a treat. Of course, it was old stuff that a G-type star, such as the sun, was potentially unstable; a G-O star could explode, slide right off the Russell diagram, and end up as a white dwarf. But no one before Dynkowski had defined the exact conditions for such a catastrophe, nor had anyone else devised mathematical means of diagnosing the instability and describing its progress.

He looked up to rest his eyes from the fine print and saw that the sun was obscured by a thin low cloud—one of those unusual conditions where the filtering effect is just right to permit a man to view the sun clearly with the naked eye. Probably volcanic dust in the air, he decided, acting almost like smoked glass.

He looked again. Either he had spots before his eyes or that was one fancy big sun spot. He had heard of being able to see them with the naked eye, but it had never happened to him. He longed for a telescope.

He blinked. Yep, it was still there, upper right. A *big* spot—no wonder the car radio sounded like a Hitler speech.

He turned back and continued on to the end of the article, being anxious to finish before the light failed. At first his mood was sheerest intellectual pleasure at the man's tight mathematical reasoning. A 3% imbalance in the solar constant—yes, that was standard stuff; the sun would *nova* with that much change. But Dynkowski went further; by means of a novel mathematical operator which he had dubbed "yokes" he bracketed the period in a star's history when this could happen and tied it down further with secondary, tertiary, and quaternary yokes, showing exactly the time of highest probability. Beautiful! Dynkowski even assigned dates to the extreme limit of his primary yoke, as a good statistician should.

But, as he went back and reviewed the equations, his mood changed from intellectual to personal. Dynkowski was not talking about just any G-O star; in the latter part he meant old Sol himself, Breen's personal sun, the big boy out there with the oversized freckle on his face.

That was one hell of a big freckle! It was a hole you could chuck Jupiter into and not make a splash. He could see it very clearly now.

Everybody talks about "when the stars grow old and the sun grows cold"—but it's an impersonal concept, like one's own death. Breen started thinking about it very personally. How long would it take, from the instant the imbalance was triggered until the expanding wave front engulfed earth? The mechanics couldn't be solved without a calculator even though they were implicit in the equations in front of him. Half an hour, for a horseback guess, from incitement until the earth went *phutt!*

It hit him with gentle melancholy. No more? Never again? Colorado on a cool morning . . . the Boston Post road with autumn wood smoke tanging the air . . . Bucks county bursting in the spring. The wet smells of the Fulton Fish Market—no, that was gone already. Coffee at the *Morning Call*. No more wild strawberries on a hillside in Jersey, hot and sweet as lips. Dawn in the South Pacific with the light airs cool velvet under your shirt and never a sound but the chuckling of the water against the sides of the old rust bucket—what was her name? That was a long time ago—the *S.S. Mary Brewster*.

No more moon if the earth was gone. Stars—but no one to look at them.

He looked back at the dates bracketing Dynkowski's probability yoke. "Thine Alabaster Cities gleam, undimmed by—"

He suddenly felt the need for Meade and stood up.

She was coming out to meet him. "Hello, Potty! Safe to come in now—I've finished the dishes."

"I should help."

"You do the man's work; I'll do the woman's work. That's fair." She shaded her eyes. "What a sunset! We ought to have volcanoes blowing their tops every year."

"Sit down and we'll watch it."

She sat beside him and he took her hand. "Notice the sun spot? You can see it with your naked eye."

She stared. "Is that a sun spot? It looks as if somebody had taken a bite out of it."

He squinted his eyes at it again. Damned if it didn't look bigger!

Meade shivered. "I'm chilly. Put your arm around me." He did so with his free arm, continuing to hold hands with the other. It *was* bigger—the thing was growing.

What good is the race of man? Monkeys, he thought, monkeys with a spot of poetry in them, cluttering and wasting a second-string planet near a third-string star. But sometimes they finish in style.

She snuggled to him. "Keep me warm."

"It will be warmer soon. I mean I'll keep you warm."

"Dear Potty."

She looked up. "Potty—something funny is happening to the sunset."

"No darling—to the sun."

"I'm frightened."

"I'm here, dear."

He glanced down at the journal, still open beside him. He did not need to add up the two figures and divide by two to reach the answer. Instead he clutched fiercely at her hand, knowing with an unexpected and overpowering burst of sorrow that this was

The End

Expendable

PHILIP K. DICK

Among all the unique and diverse writers whose work is considered science fiction, none is held in quite the same class as Philip K. Dick. During his life Dick wrote several dozen novels and more than a hundred short stories, but never made a lot of money.

Dick's work has continued to be published since his death; in fact, he is more popular now than he was during his lifetime. Some of this newfound fame may be attributed to the release of the film *Blade Runner*, based on his novel *Do Androids Dream of Electric Sheep?* Dick's work mirrors the chaos and deep unease that is reflected in today's music, film, television, and cyberculture. He uncannily felt the shifting currents of reality in the fifties and sixties.

Psychologists debate Dick's sanity; literary critics laud his vision. However he arrived at his strangely compelling narratives, one cannot deny their power, as this delightfully mordant piece from 1953 demonstrates.

The man came out on the front porch and examined the day. Bright and cold—with dew on the lawns. He buttoned his coat and put his hands in his pockets.

As the man started down the steps the two caterpillars waiting by the mailbox twitched with interest.

"There he goes," the first one said. "Send in your report."

As the other began to rotate his vanes the man stopped, turning quickly.

"I heard that," he said. He brought his foot down against the wall, scraping the caterpillars off, onto the concrete. He crushed them.

Then he hurried down the path to the sidewalk. As he walked he looked around him. In the cherry tree a bird was hopping, pecking bright-eyed at the cherries. The man studied him. All right? Or—The bird flew off. Birds all right. No harm from them.

He went on. At the corner he brushed against a spider web, crossed from the bushes to the telephone pole. His heart pounded. He tore away, batting the air. As he went on he glanced over his shoulder. The spider was coming slowly down the bush, feeling out the damage to his web.

Hard to tell about spiders. Difficult to figure out. More facts needed—No contact, yet.

He waited at the bus stop, stomping his feet to keep them warm.

The bus came and he boarded it, feeling a sudden pleasure as he took his seat with all the warm, silent people, staring indifferently ahead. A vague flow of security poured through him.

He grinned, and relaxed, the first time in days.

The bus went down the street.

Tirmus waved his antennae excitedly.

"Vote, then, if you want." He hurried past them, up onto the mound. "But let me say what I said yesterday, before you start."

"We already know it all," Lala said impatiently. "Let's get moving. We have the plans worked out. What's holding us up?"

"More reason for me to speak." Tirmus gazed around at the assembled gods. "The entire Hill is ready to march against the giant in question. Why? We know he can't communicate to his fellows— It's out of the question. The type of vibration, the language they use, makes it impossible to convey such ideas as he holds about us, about our—"

"Nonsense." Lala stepped up. "Giants communicate well enough."

"There is no record of a giant having made known information about us!"

The army moved restlessly.

"Go ahead," Tirmus said. "But it's a waste of effort. He's harmless—cut off. Why take all the time and—"

"Harmless?" Lala stared at him. "Don't you understand? He knows!"

Tirmus walked away from the mound. "I'm against unnecessary violence. We should save our strength. Someday we'll need it."

The vote was taken. As expected, the army was in favor of moving against the giant. Tirmus sighed and began stroking out the plans on the ground.

"This is the location that he takes. He can be expected to appear there at period-end. Now, as I see the situation—"

He went on, laying out the plans in the soft soil.

One of the gods leaned toward another, antennae touching. "This giant. He doesn't stand a chance. In a way, I feel sorry for him. How'd he happen to butt in?"

"Accident." The other grinned. "You know, the way they do, barging around."

"It's too bad for him, though."

It was nightfall. The street was dark and deserted. Along the sidewalk the man came, newspaper under his arm. He walked quickly, glancing around him. He skirted around the big tree growing by the curb and leaped agilely into the street. He crossed the street and gained the opposite side. As he turned the corner he entered the web, sewn from bush to telephone pole. Automatically he fought it, brushing it off him. As the strands broke a thin humming came to him, metallic and wiry.

". . . wait!"

He paused.

". . . careful . . . inside . . . wait . . ."

His jaw set. The last strands broke in his hands and he walked on. Behind him the spider moved in the fragment of his web, watching. The man looked back.

"Nuts to you," he said. "I'm not taking any chances, standing there all tied up."

He went on, along the sidewalk, to his path. He skipped up the path, avoiding he darkening bushes. On the porch he found his key, fitting it into the lock.

He paused. Inside? Better than outside, especially at night. Night a bad time. Too much movement under the bushes. Not good. He opened the door and stepped inside. The rug lay ahead of him, a pool of blackness. Across on the other side he made out the form of the lamp.

Four steps to the lamp. His foot came up. He stopped.

What did the spider say? Wait? He waited, listening. Silence.

He took his cigarette lighter and flicked it on.

The carpet of ants swelled toward him, rising up in a flood. He leaped aside, out onto the porch. The ants came rushing, hurrying, scratching across the floor in the half light.

The man jumped down to the ground and around the side of the house. When the first ants came flowing over the porch he was already spinning the faucet handle rapidly, gathering up the hose.

The burst of water lifted the ants up and scattered them, flinging them away. The man adjusted the nozzle, squinting through the mist. He advanced, turning the hard stream from side to side.

"God damn you," he said, his teeth locked. "Waiting inside—"

He was frightened. Inside—never before! In the night cold sweat came out on his face. Inside. They had never got inside before. Maybe a moth or two, and flies, of course. But they were harmless, fluttery, noisy—

A carpet of ants!

Savagely, he sprayed them until they broke rank and fled into the lawn, into the bushes, under the house.

He sat down on the walk, holding the hose, trembling from head to foot.

They really meant it. Not an anger raid, annoyed, spasmodic; but planned, an attack, worked out. They had waited for him. One more step.

Thank God for the spider.

Presently he shut the hose off and stood up. No sound; silence everywhere. The bushes rustled suddenly. Beetle? Something black scurried—he put his foot on it. A messenger, probably. Fast runner. He went gingerly inside the dark house, feeling his way by the cigarette lighter.

▼

Later, he sat at his desk, the spray gun beside him, heavy-duty steel and copper. He touched its damp surface with his fingers.

Seven o'clock. Behind him the radio played softly. He reached over and moved the desk lamp so that it shone on the floor beside the desk.

He lit a cigarette and took some writing paper and his fountain pen. He paused, thinking.

So they really wanted him, badly enough to plan it out. Bleak despair descended over him like a torrent. What could he do? Whom could he go to? Or tell. He clenched his fists, sitting bolt upright in the chair.

The spider slid down beside him onto the desk top. "Sorry. Hope you aren't frightened, as in the poem."

The man stared. "Are you the same one? The one at the corner? The one who warned me?"

"No. That's somebody else. A Spinner. I'm strictly a Cruncher. Look at my jaws." He opened and shut his mouth. "I bite them up."

The man smiled. "Good for you."

"Sure. Do you know how many there are of us in—say—an acre of land. Guess."

"A thousand."

"No. Two and a half million. Of all kinds. Crunchers, like me, or Spinners, or Stingers."

"Stingers?"

"The best. Let's see." The spider thought. "For instance, the black widow, as you call her. Very valuable." He paused. "Just one thing."

"What's that?"

"We have our problems. The gods—"

"Gods!"

"Ants, as you call them. The leaders. They're beyond us. Very unfortunate. They have an awful taste—makes one sick. We have to leave them for the birds."

The man stood up. "Birds? Are they—"

"Well, we have an arrangement. This has been going on for ages. I'll give you the story. We have some time left."

The man's heart contracted. "Time left? What do you mean?"

"Nothing. A little trouble later on, I understand. Let me give you the background. I don't think you know it."

"Go ahead. I'm listening." He stood up and began to walk back and forth.

"*They* were running the Earth pretty well, about a billion years ago. You see, men came from some other planet. Which one? I don't know. They landed and found the Earth quite well cultivated by them. There was a war."

"So we're the invaders," the man murmured.

"Sure. The war reduced both sides to barbarism, them and yourselves. You forgot how to attack, and they degenerated into closed social factions, ants, termites—"

"I see."

"The last group of you that knew the full story started us going. We were bred"—the spider chuckled in its own fashion—"bred some place for this worthwhile purpose. We keep them down very well. You know what they call us? The Eaters. Unpleasant, isn't it?"

Two more spiders came drifting down on their webstrands, alighting on the desk. The three spiders went into a huddle.

"More serious than I thought," the Cruncher said easily. "Didn't know the whole dope. The Stinger here—"

The black widow came to the edge of the desk. "Giant," she piped, metallically. "I'd like to talk with you."

"Go ahead," the man said.

"There's going to be some trouble here. They're moving, coming here, a lot of them. We thought we'd stay with you awhile. Get in on it."

"I see." The man nodded. He licked his lips, running his fingers shakily through his hair. "Do you think—that is, what are the chances—"

"Chances?" The Stinger undulated thoughtfully. "Well, we've been in this work for a long time. Almost a million years. I think that we have the edge over them, in spite of the drawbacks. Our arrangements with the birds, and of course, with the toads—"

"I think we can save you," the Cruncher put in cheerfully. "As a matter of fact, we look forward to events like this."

From under the floorboards came a distant scratching sound, the noise of a multitude of tiny claws and wings, vibrating faintly, remotely. The man heard. His body sagged all over.

"You're really certain? You think you can do it?" He wiped the perspiration from his lips and picked up the spray gun, still listening.

The sound was growing, swelling beneath them, under the floor, under their feet. Outside the house bushes rustled and a few moths flew up against the window. Louder and louder the sound grew, beyond and below, everywhere, a rising hum of anger and determination. The man looked from side to side.

"You're sure you can do it?" he murmured. "You can really save me?"

"Oh," the Stinger said, embarrassed. "I didn't mean *that*. I meant the species, the race . . . not you as an individual."

The man gaped at him and the three Eaters shifted uneasily. More moths burst against the window. Under them the floor stirred and heaved.

"I see," the man said. "I'm sorry I misunderstood you."

Finis

FRANK L. POLLACK

In the 1950s and 1960s there was a wave of disaster films in which the Earth was either attacked by aliens (*War of the Worlds*), collided with another planet (*When Worlds Collide*), or ended by nuclear holocaust (*On the Beach*). The common element among many of these were ordinary people trying to survive disaster with their humanity intact. "Finis," written in 1906, got the jump on all these, portraying a familiar catastrophe: Earth, in its journey with the sun around the Milky Way, comes too close to a star that is situated in the center of the universe. The result: Earth fries.

"They" tell us this is extremely unlikely to happen. Of course, "they" are the same people who keep changing their minds about how stars like our sun came to be, and how they actually might eventually die, and how the stars move in and around our own galaxy.

What's wonderful about "Finis" is the detail and realism Pollack manages to impart to something that seems so unlikely. It's almost as if he's been there. . . .

I'm getting tired," complained Davis, lounging in the window of the Physics Building, "and sleepy. It's after eleven o'clock. This makes the fourth night I've sat up to see your new star, and it'll be the last. Why, the thing was billed to appear three weeks ago."

"Are *you* tired, Miss Wardour?" asked Eastwood, and the girl glanced up with a quick flush and a negative murmur.

Eastwood made the reflection anew that she certainly was painfully shy. She was almost as plain as she was shy, though her hair had an unusual beauty of its own, fine as silk and coloured like palest flame.

Probably she had brains; Eastwood had seen her reading some extremely "deep" books, but she seemed to have no amusements, few interests. She worked daily at the Art Students' League, and boarded where he did, and he had thus come to ask her with the Davis's to watch for the new star from the laboratory windows on the Heights.

"Do you really think that it's worth while to wait any longer, professor?" enquired Mrs. Davis, concealing a yawn.

Eastwood was somewhat annoyed by the continued failure of the star to show itself and he hated to be called "professor," being only an assistant professor of physics.

"I don't know," he answered somewhat curtly. "This is the twelfth night that I have waited for it. Of course, it would have been a mathematical miracle if astronomers should have solved such a problem exactly, though they've been figuring on it for a quarter of a century."

The new Physics Building of Columbia University was about twelve storeys high. The physics laboratory occupied the ninth and tenth floors, with the astronomical rooms above it, an arrangement which would have been impossible before the invention of the oil vibration cushion, which practically isolated the instrument rooms from the earth.

Eastwood had arranged a small telescope at the window, and below them spread the illuminated map of Greater New York, sending up a faintly musical roar. All the streets were crowded, as they had been every night since the fifth of the month, when the great new star, or sun, was expected to come into view.

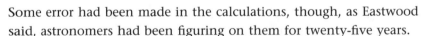

Some error had been made in the calculations, though, as Eastwood said, astronomers had been figuring on them for twenty-five years.

It was, in fact, nearly forty years since Professor Adolphe Bernier first announced his theory of a limited universe at the International Congress of Sciences in Paris, where it was counted as little more than a masterpiece of imagination.

Professor Bernier did not believe that the universe was infinite. Somewhere, he argued, the universe must have a centre, which is the pivot for its revolution.

The moon revolves around the earth, the planetary system revolves about the sun, the solar system revolves about one of the fixed stars, and this whole system in its turn undoubtedly revolves around some more distant point. But this sort of progression must definitely stop somewhere.

Somewhere there must be a central sun, a vast incandescent body which does not move at all. And as a sun is always larger and hotter than its satellites, therefore the body at the centre of the universe must be of an immensity and temperature beyond anything known or imagined.

It was objected that this hypothetical body should then be large enough to be visible from the earth, and Professor Bernier replied that some day it undoubtedly would be visible. Its light had simply not yet had time to reach the earth.

The passage of light from the nearest of the fixed stars is a matter of three years, and there must be many stars so distant that their rays have not yet reached us. The great central sun must be so inconceivably remote that perhaps hundreds, perhaps thousands of years would elapse before its light should burst upon the solar system.

All this was contemptuously classed as "newspaper science" till the extraordinary mathematical revival a little after the middle of the twentieth century afforded the means of verifying it.

Following the new theorems discovered by Professor Burnside, of Princeton, and elaborated by Dr. Taneka, of Tokyo, astronomers succeeded in calculating the arc of the sun's movements through space, its ratio to the orbit of its satellites. With this as a basis, it was possible to follow the widening circles, the consecutive systems of the heavenly bodies and their rotations.

The theory of Professor Bernier was justified. It was demonstrated that there really was a gigantic mass of incandescent matter, which, whether the central point of the universe or not, appeared to be without motion.

The weight and distance of this new sun were approximately calculated, and, the speed of light being known, it was an easy matter to reckon when its rays would reach the earth.

It was then estimated that the approaching rays would arrive at the earth in twenty-six years, and that was twenty-six years ago.

Three weeks had passed since the date when the new heavenly body was expected to become visible, and it had not yet appeared.

Popular interest had risen to a high pitch, stimulated by innumerable newspaper and magazine articles, and the streets were nightly thronged with excited crowds armed with opera-glasses and star maps, while at every corner a telescope man had planted his tripod instrument at a nickel a look.

Similar scenes were taking place in every civilized city on the globe.

It was generally supposed that the new luminary would appear in size about midway between Venus and the moon. Better informed persons expected something like the sun, and a syndicate of capitalists quietly leased large areas on the coast of Greenland in anticipation of a great rise in temperature and a northward movement in population.

Even the business situation was appreciably affected by the public uncertainty and excitement. There was a decline in stocks, and a minor religious sect boldly prophesied the end of the world.

"I've had enough of this," said Davis, looking at his watch again. "Are you ready to go, Grace? By the way, isn't it getting warmer?"

It had been a sharp February day, but the temperature was certainly rising. Water was dripping from the roofs, and from the icicles that fringed the window ledges, as if a warm wave had suddenly arrived.

"What's that light?" suddenly asked Alice Wardour, who was lingering by the open window.

"It must be moonrise," said Eastwood, though the illumination of the horizon was almost like daybreak.

Davis abandoned his intention of leaving, and they watched the east grow pale and flushed till at last a brilliant white disc heaved itself above the horizon.

It resembled the full moon, but as if trebled in lustre, and the streets grew almost as light as by day.

"Good heavens, that must be the new star, after all!" said Davis in an awed voice.

"No, it's only the moon. This is the hour and minute for her rising," answered Eastwood, who had grasped the cause of the phenomenon. "But the new sun must have appeared on the other side of the earth. Its light is what makes the moon so brilliant. It will rise here just as the sun does, no telling how soon. It must be brighter than was expected—and maybe hotter," he added with a vague uneasiness.

"Isn't it getting very warm in here?" said Mrs. Davis, loosening her jacket. "Couldn't you turn off some of the steam heat?"

Eastwood turned it off, for, in spite of the open window, the room was really growing uncomfortably close. But the warmth appeared to come from without; it was like a warm spring evening, and the icicles were breaking loose from the cornices.

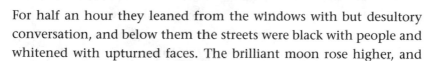

For half an hour they leaned from the windows with but desultory conversation, and below them the streets were black with people and whitened with upturned faces. The brilliant moon rose higher, and the mildness of the night sensibly increased.

It was after midnight when Eastwood first noticed the reddish flush tinging the clouds low in the east, and he pointed it out to his companions.

"That must be it at last," he exclaimed, with a thrill of vibrating excitement at what he was going to see, a cosmic event unprecedented in intensity.

The brightness waxed rapidly.

"By Jove, see it redden!" Davis ejaculated. "It's getting lighter than day—and hot! Whew!"

The whole eastern sky glowed with a deepening pink that extended half round the horizon. Sparrows chirped from the roofs, and it looked as if the disc of the unknown star might at any moment be expected to lift above the Atlantic, but it delayed long.

The heavens continued to burn with myriad hues, gathering at last to a fiery furnace glow on the skyline.

Mrs. Davis suddenly screamed. An American flag blowing freely from its staff on the roof of the tall building had all at once burst into flame.

Low in the east lay a long streak of intense fire which broadened as they squinted with watering eyes. It was as if the edge of the world had been heated to whiteness.

The brilliant moon faded to a feathery white film in the glare. There was a confused outcry from the observatory overhead, and a crash of something being broken, and as the strange new sunlight fell through the window the onlookers leaped back as if a blast furnace had been opened before them.

The glass cracked and fell inward. Something like the sun, but magnified fifty times in size and hotness, was rising out of the sea. An iron instrument-table by the window began to smoke with an acrid smell of varnish.

"What the devil is this, Eastwood?" shouted Davis accusingly.

From the streets rose a sudden, enormous wail of fright and pain, the outcry of a million throats at once, and the roar of a stampede followed. The pavements were choked with struggling, panic-stricken people in the fierce glare, and above the din arose the clanging rush of fire engines and trucks.

Smoke began to rise from several points below Central Park, and two or three church chimes pealed crazily.

The observers from overhead came running down the stairs with a thunderous trampling, for the elevator man had deserted his post.

"Here, we've got to get out of this," shouted Davis, seizing his wife by the arm and hustling her toward the door. "This place'll be on fire directly."

"Hold on. You can't go down into that crush on the street," Eastwood cried, trying to prevent him.

But Davis broke away and raced down the stairs, half carrying his terrified wife. Eastwood got his back against the door in time to prevent Alice from following them.

"There's nothing in this building that will burn, Miss Wardour," he said as calmly as he could. "We had better stay here for the present. It would be sure death to get involved in that stampede below. Just listen to it."

The crowds on the street seemed to sway to and fro in contending waves, and the cries, curses, and screams came up in a savage chorus.

The heat was already almost blistering to the skin, though they carefully avoided the direct rays, and instruments of glass in the laboratory cracked loudly one by one.

A vast cloud of dark smoke began to rise from the harbour, where the shipping must have caught fire, and something exploded with a terrific report. A few minutes later half a dozen fires broke out in the lower part of the city, rolling up volumes of smoke that faded to a thin mist in the dazzling light.

The great new sun was now fully above the horizon, and the whole east seemed ablaze. The stampede in the streets had quieted all at once, for the survivors had taken refuge in the nearest houses, and the pavements were black with motionless forms of men and women.

"I'll do whatever you say," said Alice, who was deadly pale, but remarkably collected. Even at that moment Eastwood was struck by the splendour of her ethereally brilliant hair that burned like pale flame above her pallid face. "But we can't stay here, can we?"

"No," replied Eastwood, trying to collect his faculties in the face of this catastrophic revolution of nature. "We'd better go to the basement, I think."

In the basement were deep vaults used for the storage of delicate instruments, and these would afford shelter for a time at least. It occurred to him as he spoke that perhaps temporary safety was the best that any living thing on earth could hope for.

But he led the way down the well staircase. They had gone down six or seven flights when a gloom seemed to grow upon the air, with a welcome relief.

It seemed almost cool, and the sky had clouded heavily, with the appearance of polished and heated silver.

A deep but distant roaring arose and grew from the south-east, and they stopped on the second landing to look from the window.

▼

A vast black mass seemed to fill the space between sea and sky, and it was sweeping towards the city, probably from the harbour, Eastwood thought, at a speed that made it visibly grow as they watched it.

"A cyclone—and a waterspout!" muttered Eastwood, appalled.

He might have foreseen it from the sudden, excessive evaporation and the heating of the air. The gigantic black pillar drove towards them swaying and reeling, and a gale came with it, and a wall of impenetrable mist behind.

As Eastwood watched its progress he saw its cloudy bulk illumined momentarily by a dozen lightning-like flashes, and a moment later, above its roar, came the tremendous detonations of heavy cannon.

The forts and the warships were firing shells to break the waterspout, but the shots seemed to produce no effect. It was the city's last and useless attempt at resistance. A moment later forts and ships alike must have been engulfed.

"Hurry! This building will collapse!" Eastwood shouted.

They rushed down another flight, and heard the crash with which the monster broke over the city. A deluge of water, like the emptying of a reservoir, thundered upon the street, and the water was steaming hot as it fell.

There was a rending crash of falling walls, and in another instant the Physics Building seemed to be twisted around by a powerful hand. The walls blew out, and the whole structure sank in a chaotic mass.

But the tough steel frame was practically unwreckable, and in fact, the upper portion was simply bent down upon the lower storeys, peeling off most of the shell of masonry and stucco.

Eastwood was stunned as he was hurled to the floor, but when he came to himself he was still upon the landing, which was tilted at an alarming angle. A tangled mass of steel rods and beams hung a yard over his head, and a huge steel girder had plunged down perpendicularly from above, smashing everything in its way.

Wreckage choked the well of the staircase, a mass of plaster, bricks, and shattered furniture surrounded him, and he could look out in almost every direction through the rent iron skeleton.

A yard away Alice was sitting up, mechanically wiping the mud and water from her face, and apparently uninjured. Tepid water was pouring through the interstices of the wreck in torrents, though it did not appear to be raining.

A steady, powerful gale had followed the whirlwind, and it brought a little coolness with it. Eastwood enquired perfunctorily of Alice if she were hurt, without being able to feel any degree of interest in the matter. His faculty of sympathy seemed paralyzed.

"I don't know. I thought—I thought that we were all dead!" the girl murmured in a sort of daze. "What was it? Is it all over?"

"I think it's only beginning," Eastwood answered dully.

The gale had brought up more clouds and the skies were thickly overcast, but shining white-hot. Presently the rain came down in almost scalding floods and as it fell upon the hissing streets it steamed again into the air.

In three minutes all the world was choked with hot vapour, and from the roar and splash the streets seemed to be running rivers.

The downpour seemed too violent to endure, and after an hour it did cease, while the city reeked with mist. Through the whirling fog Eastwood caught glimpses of ruined buildings, vast heaps of debris, all the wreckage of the greatest city of the twentieth century.

Then the torrents fell again, like a cataract, as if the waters of the earth were shuttlecocking between sea and heaven. With a jarring tremor of the ground a landslide went down into the Hudson.

The atmosphere was like a vapour bath, choking and sickening. The physical agony of respiration aroused Alice from a sort of stupor, and she cried out pitifully that she would die.

The strong wind drove the hot spray and steam through the shattered building till it seemed impossible that human lungs could extract life from the semi-liquid that had replaced the air, but the two lived.

After hours of this parboiling the rain slackened, and, as the clouds parted, Eastwood caught a glimpse of a familiar form halfway up the heavens. It was the sun, the old sun, looking small and watery.

But the intense heat and brightness told that the enormous body still blazed behind the clouds. The rain seemed to have ceased definitely, and the hard, shining whiteness of the sky grew rapidly hotter.

The heat of the air increased to an oven-like degree; the mists were dissipated, the clouds licked up, and the earth seemed to dry itself almost immediately. The heat from the two suns beat down simultaneously till it became a monstrous terror, unendurable.

An odour of smoke began to permeate the air; there was a dazzling shimmer over the streets, and great clouds of mist arose from the bay, but these appeared to evaporate before they could darken the sky.

The piled wreck of the building sheltered the two refugees from the direct rays of the new sun, now almost overhead, but not from the penetrating heat of the air. But the body will endure almost anything, short of tearing asunder, for a time at least; it is the finer mechanism of the nerves that suffers most.

Alice lay face down among the bricks, gasping and moaning. The blood hammered in Eastwood's brain, and the strangest mirages flickered before his eyes.

Alternately he lapsed into heavy stupors, and awoke to the agony of the day. In his lucid moments he reflected that this could not last long, and tried to remember what degree of heat would cause death.

Within an hour after the drenching rains he was feverishly thirsty, and the skin felt as if peeling from his whole body.

This fever and horror lasted until he forgot that he had ever known another state; but at last the west reddened, and the flaming sun went down. It left the familiar planet high in the heavens, and there was no darkness until the usual hour, though there was a slight lowering of the temperature.

But when night did come it brought life-giving coolness, and though the heat was still intense it seemed temperate by comparison. More than all, the kindly darkness seemed to set a limit to the cataclysmic disorders of the day.

"Ouf! This is heavenly!" said Eastwood, drawing long breaths and feeling mind and body revived in the gloom.

"It won't last long," replied Alice, and her voice sounded extraordinarily calm through the darkness. "The heat will come again when the new sun rises in a few hours."

"We might find some better place in the meanwhile—a deep cellar; or we might get into the subway," Eastwood suggested.

"It would be no use. Don't you understand? I have been thinking it all out. After this, the new sun will always shine, and we could not endure it even another day. The wave of heat is passing around the world as it revolves, and in a few hours the whole earth will be a burnt-up ball. Very likely we are the only people left alive in New York, or perhaps in America."

She seemed to have taken the intellectual initiative, and spoke with an assumption of authority that amazed him.

"But there must be others," said Eastwood, after thinking for a moment. "Other people have found sheltered places, or miners, or men underground."

"They would have been drowned by the rain. At any rate, there will be none left alive by tomorrow night.

"Think of it," she went on dreamily, "for a thousand years this wave of fire has been rushing towards us, while life has been going on so happily in the world, so unconscious that the world was doomed all the time. And now this is the end of life."

"I don't know," Eastwood said slowly. "It may be the end of human life, but there must be some forms that will survive—some micro-organisms perhaps capable of resisting high temperatures, if nothing higher. The seed of life will be left at any rate, and that is everything. Evolution will begin over again, producing new types to suit the changed conditions. I only wish I could see what creatures will be here in a few thousand years.

"But I can't realize it at all—this thing!" he cried passionately, after a pause. "Is it real? Or have we all gone mad? It seems too much like a bad dream."

The rain crashed down again as he spoke, and the earth steamed, though not with the dense reek of the day. For hours the waters roared and splashed against the earth in hot billows till the streets were foaming yellow rivers, dammed by the wreck of fallen buildings.

There was a continual rumble as earth and rock slid into the East River, and at last the Brooklyn Bridge collapsed with a thunderous crash and splash that made all Manhattan vibrate. A gigantic billow like a tidal wave swept up the river from its fall.

The downpour slackened and ceased soon after the moon began to shed an obscured but brilliant light through the clouds.

Presently the east commenced to grow luminous, and this time there could be no doubt as to what was coming.

Alice crept closer to the man as the grey light rose upon the watery air.

"Kiss me!" she whispered suddenly, throwing her arms around his neck. He could feel her trembling. "Say you love me; hold me in your arms. There is only an hour."

"Don't be afraid. Try to face it bravely," stammered Eastwood.

"I don't fear it—not death. But I have never lived. I have always been timid and wretched and afraid—afraid to speak—and I've almost wished for suffering and misery or anything rather than to be stupid and dumb and dead, the way I've always been.

"I've never dared to tell anyone what I was, what I wanted. I've been afraid all my life, but I'm not afraid now. I have never lived; I have never been happy; and now we must die together!"

It seemed to Eastwood the cry of the perishing world. He held her in his arms and kissed her wet, tremulous face that was strained to his.

------------▼------------

The twilight was gone before they knew it. The sky was blue already, with crimson flakes mounting to the zenith, and the heat was growing once more intense.

"This is the end, Alice," said Eastwood, and his voice trembled.

She looked at him, her eyes shining with an unearthly softness and brilliancy, and turned her face to the east.

There, in crimson and orange, flamed the last dawn that human eyes would ever see.

A Guide to
Virtual Death

J. G. BALLARD

Best known for his extraordinary memoir, *Empire of the Sun*, Ballard has been one of the most literate and entertaining critics of the foibles of Western society. He has used the tools and tropes of SF in many of his stories and novels to poke dark fun at our social institutions, our fears, and our ridiculous behavior in the face of change.

"A Guide to Virtual Death," first published in 1992, is a droll speculation on the end of the world as we know it. Characteristically, Ballard portrays the terrible truth about ourselves that most of us either ignore or deny. He has accurately pinpointed the invention that possesses the greatest potential for destruction of anything yet devised by mankind: television. Sad, but true.

For reasons amply documented elsewhere, intelligent life on earth became extinct in the closing hours of the 20th Century. Among the clues left to us, the following schedule of a day's television programmes transmitted to an unnamed city in the northern hemisphere on December 23, 1999, offers its own intriguing insight into the origins of the disaster.

6.00 A.M.   Porno-Disco. Wake yourself up with his-and-her hard-core sex images played to a disco beat.

7.00   Weather Report. Today's expected microclimates in the city's hotel atriums, shopping malls and office complexes. Hilton International promises an afternoon snowshower as a Christmas appetizer.

7.15   News Round-up. What our newsmakers have planned for
              you. Maybe a small war, a synthetic earthquake or a
              famine-zone/charity tie-in.

7.45   Breakfast Time. Gourmet meals to watch as you eat your
              diet cellulose.

8.30   Commuter Special. The rush-hour game-show. How
              many bottoms can you pinch, how many faces can you
              slap?

9.30   The Travel Show. Visit the world's greatest airports and
              underground car-parks.

10.30   Home-makers of Yesterday. Nostalgic scenes of old-fash-
              ioned house-work. No. 7—The Vacuum Cleaner.

11.00   Office War. Long-running serial of office gang-wars.

12.00   Newsflash. The networks promise either a new serial
              killer or a deadly food toxin.

1.00 P.M.   Live from Parliament. No. 12—The Alcoholic M.P.

1.30   The Nose-Pickers. Hygiene programme for the kiddies.

2.00   Caress Me. Soft-porn for the siesta hour.

2.30   Your Favourite Commercials. Popular demand re-runs of
              golden-oldie TV ads.

3.00   Housewives' Choice. Rape, and how to psychologically
              prepare yourself.

4.00   Count-down. Game show in which contestants count
              backwards from one million.

5.00   Newsflash. Either an airliner crash or a bank collapse.
              Viewers express preference.

6.00   *Today's Special.* Virtual Reality TV presents "The Kennedy
              Assassination." The Virtual Reality head-set takes you to
              Dallas, Texas on November 22, 1963. First you fire the
              assassin's rifle from the Book Depository window, and
              then you sit between Jackie and JFK in the Presidential
              limo as the bullet strikes. For premium subscribers
              only—feel the Presidential brain tissue spatter your face
              OR wipe Jackie's tears onto your handkerchief.

8.00   Dinner Time. More gourmet dishes to view with your
              evening diet-cellulose.

9.00	Science Now. Is there life after death? Micro-electrodes pick up ultra-faint impulses from long-dead brains. Relatives question the departed.
10.00	Crime-Watch. Will it be your home that is broken into tonight by the TV Crime Gang?
11.00	*Today's Special.* Tele-Orgasm. Virtual Reality TV takes you to an orgy. Have sex with the world's greatest movie-stars. Tonight: Marilyn Monroe and Madonna *OR* Warren Beatty and Tom Cruise. For premium subscribers only— experience transexualism, paedophilia, terminal syphilis, gang-rape, and bestiality (choice: German Shepherd or Golden Retriever).
1.00 A.M.	Newsflash. Tonight's surprise air-crash.
2.00	The Religious Hour. Imagine being dead. Priests and neuro-scientists construct a life-like mock-up of your death.
3.00	Night-Hunter. Will the TV Rapist come through your bedroom window?
4.15	Sex for Insomniacs. Soft porn to rock you to sleep.
5.00	The Charity Hour. Game show in which Third-World contestants beg for money.

Emissary from a Green and Yellow World

ROBERT SHECKLEY

In the mid-1960s, Robert Sheckley may have been the single most brilliant SF short-story writer in America. Combining the storytelling skill of Ray Bradbury and the off-the-wall imagination of Philip K. Dick, Sheckley turned out dozens of outrageously creative and original short stories.

In "Emissary from a Green and Yellow World," published in early 1999 in *The Magazine of Fantasy & Science Fiction,* Sheckley poses a simple question that raises complicated issues: If someone else knew our world was going to be destroyed and offered us refuge elsewhere, what would we do? Sheckley's Everyman in the story happens to be the President of the United States; a very human, down-to-earth kind of guy. I'd like to think that if a similar scenario ever happened, whoever was president would do the same.

O ne thing about President Rice. He was able to make up his mind. When Ong came to Earth with his contention, Rice believed him. Not that it made any difference in the end.

It began when the Marine guard came into the Oval Office, his face ashen.

"What is it?" said President Rice, looking up from his papers.

"Someone wants to see you," the guard said.

"So? A lot of people want to see the President of the United States. Is his name on the morning list?"

"You don't understand, sir. This guy—he just—materialized! One moment he wasn't there and the next moment, there he was, standing in front of me in the corridor. And he isn't a man, sir. He stands on two legs but he isn't a man. He's—he's—I don't know what he is!"

And the guard burst into tears.

Rice had seen other men cave in from the pressures of government. But what did a Marine guard have to do with pressures?

"Listen, son," Rice said.

The guard hastily rubbed tears out of his eyes. "Yes, sir." His voice was shaky, but it wasn't hysterical.

"What I want you to do," Rice said, "is take the rest of the day off. Go home. Get some rest. Come back here tomorrow refreshed. If your supervisor asks about it, tell him I ordered it. Will you do that for me?"

"Yes, sir."

"And on your way, send in that fellow you met in the corridor. The one you say doesn't look human. Don't talk to him. Just tell him I'm waiting to see him."

▼

The fellow was not long in coming. He was about six feet tall. He wore a silver one-piece jump suit that shimmered when you looked at it. His features were difficult to describe. All you could say for sure was, he didn't look human.

"I know what you're thinking," the fellow said. "You are thinking that I don't look human."

"That's right," Rice said.

"You're correct. I'm not human. Intelligent, yes. Human, no. You can call me Ong. I'm from Omair, a planet in the constellation you call Sagittarius. Omair is a yellow and green world. Do you believe me?"

"Yes, I believe you," Rice said.

"May I ask why?"

"It's just a hunch," Rice said. "I think that if you stayed around here and submitted to an examination by a team of our scientists, they'd conclude that you were an alien. So let's get right to it. You're an alien. I accept that you're from a green and yellow world named Omair. Now what?"

"You're asking, I suppose, why I've come here, at this time?"

"That's right."

"Well, sir, I've come to warn you that your sun is going to go nova in about one hundred and fifty of your years."

"You're sure?"

"Quite sure."

"Why'd you wait so long to get around to telling us?"

"We just found out ourselves. As soon as it was confirmed, my people sent me as emissary to give your planet the information and offer what assistance we could."

"Why did they pick you?"

"I was chosen at random for off-planet service. It could have been any of us."

"If you say so."

"Now I have delivered the message. How can we help?"

Rice was feeling very peculiar. He didn't understand it, but he really did believe the emissary. But he also knew his belief was futile in terms of saving Earth's people. Ong's contention would have to be submitted to scientific proof. Before any conclusions could be reached, the Earth would vaporize in the expanding sun. Rice knew that if he wanted to do anything about it, it would have to begin now.

Rice said, "Some of our scientists have made similar conjectures as to our eventual doom."

"They're right. Within approximately one hundred and fifty years this planet will no longer be habitable. May I be blunt? You're going to have to get off. All of you. And you must begin immediately."

"Great," President Rice said. "Oh, that's just great."

"Is something wrong?"

"I'm just having a little trouble assimilating this." Rice put a hand to his forehead. "This is a nightmare situation. But I have to deal with it as if it's real. Because it probably is." He wiped his forehead again. "Let's say I believe you. How could we do anything about it?"

"We of Omair are ready to help. We will give you detailed plans explaining what you must do to make starships for all Earth's people. There will be further instructions for getting all the people together and into the ships in an orderly manner. Please understand, we're just trying to help, not impose ourselves on you."

"I believe you," Rice said, and he did.

"There's a lot to be done," the emissary said. "It's a big task, but you humans are just as smart as we Omairians—we checked on that, no use wasting our time on dummies. With your present level of technology, and with our assistance, you can do this and be away within the next hundred years."

"It's a tremendously exciting prospect," Rice said.

"We thought you'd feel that way. You aren't the only planetary civilization we've been able to rescue."

"That is very much to your credit."

"Nothing to praise. This is how we Omairians are."

"I'm going to have to ask something that may sound a little strange," Rice said. "But this is Earth so I have to ask it. Who's going to pay for all this?"

"If it's necessary," Ong said, "we of Omair are willing to defray the costs."

"Thank you. That's very good of you."

"We know."

"So what will be necessary?"

"To begin with, you'll need to clear out the center of one of your continents for the launching pads. But that's not too difficult, because you can distribute the people in the other continents. That will disrupt commerce and farming, of course. But we will supply whatever food is needed."

Rice could imagine it now—the slow convening of experts from all over the globe, the quarreling, the demands for more and more proofs. And even if a consensus of scientists came to agreement after many years, what about the population at large? Before any sizeable portion of the Earth's people could be convinced, the Earth would long since have vaporized in the expanding sun.

"Simultaneous to the building of the starships," the emissary went on, "you'll have to get your populations indoctrinated, inoculated—we'll supply the medicines—and in general prepared for a long journey by starship. During the transition period you'll require temporary housing for millions. We can help there."

"Is the indoctrination really necessary? Earth people hate that sort of thing."

"Absolutely essential. Your people will not be prepared for a lifetime of shipboard life. Hypnotherapy may be needed in many cases. We can supply the machines. I know your people won't like it, being uprooted this way. But it's either that or perish in about a hundred years."

"I'm convinced," Rice said. "The question is, can I sell it?"

"I beg your pardon?"

"Well, it's not just a case of convincing me, you know. There are tens of millions of people out there who won't believe you."

"But surely if you order them to take the necessary measures for their own good . . ."

"I'm just the ruler of one country, not the whole planet. And I can't even order my own countrymen to do what you're suggesting."

"You don't have to order it. Just suggest it and show the proofs. Humans are intelligent. They'll accept your view."

Rice shook his head. "Believe me, they won't believe me. Most of them will think this is a diabolical plot on the part of government, or some church, or the Islamic Conspiracy, or some other. Some will think little gray aliens are trying to trick us into captivity. Others will believe it's the work of a long-vanished Elder Race, here to do us in. Whatever the reason, everyone will be sure it's a plot of some kind."

"A plot to do what?" Ong asked.

"To enslave us."

"We of Omair don't do that sort of thing. We have a perfect record in that regard. I can offer proofs."

"You keep on talking about proofs," Rice said. "But most humans are proof-proof."

"Is that really true?"

"Sad to say, it's true."

"It goes against accepted theory. We have always believed that intelligence invariably produces rationality."

"Not in these parts. Not with us."

"I'm sorry to hear that. We Omairians thought this was just a matter of one colleague calling on another and warning him of danger, then advising him on what steps to take. I had no idea humans might resist believing. It's not rational, you know. Are you quite sure of this?"

"That's how humans are. And above all, they're conditioned from earliest age against taking orders from aliens."

"I wouldn't be giving any orders."

"You'd be advising the government. In people's minds, that would be the equivalent of giving orders."

"I don't know what to tell you," the emissary said. "Is there really no way you could convince people otherwise?"

"I can tell you here and now, it'll never work."

Ong gave a slight inclination of his head. "Well, it has been nice meeting you. Have a nice day."

The emissary turned to go.

"Just one moment," Rice said.

The alien paused, turned. "Yes?"

"What about just taking those of us who do believe, who want to go?"

"It's unprecedented," the emissary said. "In all our experience, races either can change their thinking and get away from their doomed worlds by their own efforts, or they cannot."

"We're different," Rice said.

"All right," the emissary said. "I'll do it. Gather your people. I'll be back in ten years to take those who want to go. We can't wait any longer than that."

"We'll be ready."

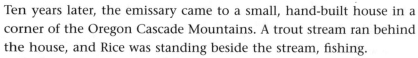

Ten years later, the emissary came to a small, hand-built house in a corner of the Oregon Cascade Mountains. A trout stream ran behind the house, and Rice was standing beside the stream, fishing.

Rice said, "How did you find me here?"

"Once we Omairians have met you, we can always find you again. But I think you are not president any longer."

"No," Rice said. "My term ended and I didn't get reelected. I tried to convince people of the destruction that lay ahead. Nearly everyone thought I was a crackpot. Those who did believe me were worse than those who didn't. A crazy man tried to shoot me and killed my wife instead. My children hold me responsible. They changed their names and moved away."

"I am sorry to hear that," the emissary said. "But I think you'll have to admit that those other people, the ones who despise and disbelieve you, do not have your grasp, your intelligence, your intuition. You're probably the most unusual man of your century, Mr. Rice. You believed in us from the start. You didn't think we were sent by God or the devil. You accepted what we said. Evidently you were the only one."

"Evidently."

"Perhaps it's for the best," the emissary said. "Your people, in their present state, could never have made it out there. But you could."

"Me?"

"Your true place is with us, Mr. Rice, out in the galaxy. There is still time. You are not an old man. We have rejuvenation treatments. We can add many years to your life. We have women of our species who would be honored to mate with you. We have a civilization that would welcome you. I beg of you, leave this doomed Earth behind and come away with me."

"No, I think not," Rice said. "I can still look forward to living another thirty or so years on Earth before things get too bad, can't I?"

"Yes, but no longer."

"It's enough. I'll stay."

"You choose to die here with your people? But they will perish because of their own ignorance."

"Yes. But they are Earth's children, as I am. My place is here with them."

"I find it difficult to believe you're saying this."

"I did a lot of thinking about it. It occurred to me that I was really no different from the other humans. Not fundamentally. And certainly no better."

"I can't accept that. Anyhow, what is your inference?"

"It seemed to me that if my species was incapable of believing in its own doom, it was not for me to believe in it, either. So I've decided that all that stuff you talked about is not going to happen. In fact, I'm pretty sure I've dreamed all this up."

"It is not intelligence," said the emissary, "to take refuge in solipsism."

"My mind's made up. I'll stay here with my trout stream. You've never done any fly fishing, have you, emissary?"

"Where I come from," the emissary said, "we don't fish. We respect all life."

"Does that mean you don't eat flesh of any kind?"

"That is correct."

"What about vegetables? They're living things."

"We don't eat vegetables, either. We convert our energy from inert chemicals, or, if necessary, we transform it directly from solar radiation. We can re-engineer you so you can do that, too."

"I'll just bet you can," Rice said.

"I beg your pardon?"

"You heard me. Or rather, you heard my implication. The sort of life you offer wouldn't be human. It would be hellish. It wouldn't be worth living for a fellow like me, to say nothing of my friends. I refer to the rest of the human race."

"You mentioned hell. There is no hell."

"Yes there is. Hell is me talking to you. Now do me a favor and get out of my face."

---▼---

The emissary left, and, outside, paused for a moment, looking back at the house. Would Rice change his mind? No indication of it. Ong shrugged and returned to his vehicle. With a gesture he brought it up to full visibility and got aboard.

Soon he was high in the air, with the green and blue planet receding below him. Soon he would put in the faster than light drive.

But just before he did, he turned back and took a last look. A good-looking planet, and intelligent people. A pity to see it all lost.

He brooded for a moment, but only a moment. Then he consoled himself with the knowledge that this represented no real loss to the Cosmos. After all, intelligent life had evolved again and again on planets all over the universe.

But what had evolved was intelligent life much like that of Ong and his people. That was the standard, the norm. But intelligent life like Earth's? Intelligent irrational life? It had to be a fluke, a one-of-a-kind thing, this mating of intelligence and irrationality. The emissary didn't think the universe had seen Earth's like before. It probably would not again.

He looked down once more at the Earth. It looked like a nice place. But of course, there were more where that came from. Sort of. In any event, it was time to get back to his own green and yellow world.

The Portable Phonograph

WALTER VAN TILBURG CLARK

In the 1960s, before science fiction was as widely accepted in academic circles as it is today, very few SF stories found their way into the high school curriculum. "The Portable Phonograph" was a notable exception. Clark, with a solid literary reputation for his novel *The Oxbow Incident*, really wasn't considered a SF writer, so his work was acceptable to school boards.

Of course, this quietly powerful tale is science fiction in the finest tradition of post-holocaust stories. He paints an elegant image of the phonograph and those who cling to its magic when all other traces of civilization are gone. Originally published in 1950, the technology may have dated, but not the power of the story's indelible impact.

The red sunset, with narrow, black cloud strips like threats across it, lay on the curved horizon of the prairie. The air was still and cold, and in it settled the mute darkness and greater cold of night. High in the air there was wind, for through the veil of the dusk clouds could be seen gliding rapidly south and changing shapes. A sensation of torment, of two-sided, unpredictable nature, arose from the stillness of the earth air beneath the violence of the upper air. Out of the sunset, through the dead, matted grass and isolated weed stalks of the prairie, crept the narrow and deeply rutted remains of a road. In the road, in places, there were crusts of shallow, brittle ice. There was little islands of an old oiled pavement in the road too, but most of it was mud, now frozen rigid. The frozen mud still bore the toothed impress of great tanks, and a wanderer on the neighboring undulations might have stumbled, in this light, into large, partially filled-in and weed-grown cavities, their banks channeled and beginning to spread into badlands. These pits were such as might have been made by falling meteors, but they were not. They were the scars of gigantic bombs, their rawness already made a little natural by rain, seed and time. Along the road there were rakish remnants of fence. There were also, just visible, one portion of tangled and multiple barbed wire still erect, behind which was a shelving ditch with small caves, now very quiet and empty, at intervals in its back wall. Otherwise there was no structure or remnant of a structure visible over the dome of the darkling earth, but only, in sheltered hollows, the darker shadows of young trees trying again.

Under the wuthering arch of the high wind a V of wild geese fled south. The rush of their pinions sounded briefly, and the faint, plaintive notes of their expeditionary talk. Then they left a still greater vacancy. There was the smell and expectation of snow, as there is likely to be when the wild geese fly south. From the remote distance, toward the red sky, came faintly the protracted howl and quick yap-yap of a prairie wolf.

North of the road, perhaps a hundred yards, lay the parallel and deeply entrenched course of a small creek, lined with leafless alders and willow. The creek was already silent under ice. Into the bank above it was dug a sort of cell, with a single opening, like the mouth of a mine tunnel. Within the cell there was a little red of fire, which showed dully through the opening, like a reflection or a deception of the imagination. The light came from the chary burning of four blocks of poorly aged peat, which gave off a petty warmth and much acrid smoke. But the precious remnants of wood, old fence posts and timbers from the long-deserted dugouts, had to be saved for the real cold, for the time when a man's breath blew white, the moisture in his nostrils stiffened at once when he stepped out, and the expansive blizzards paraded for days over the vast open, swirling and settling and thickening, till the dawn of the cleared day when the sky was a thin blue-green and the terrible cold, in which a man could not live for three hours unwarmed, lay over the uniformly drifted swell of the plain.

Around the smoldering peat four men were seated cross-legged. Behind them, traversed by their shadows, was the earth bench, with two old and dirty army blankets, where the owner of the cell slept. In a niche in the opposite wall were a few tin utensils which caught the glint of the coals. The host was rewrapping in a piece of daubed burlap, four fine, leather-bound books. He worked slowly and very carefully, and at last tied the bundle securely with a piece of grass-woven cord. The other three looked intently upon the process, as if a great significance lay in it. As the host tied the cord, he spoke. He was an old man, his long, matted beard and hair gray to nearly white. The shadows made his brows and cheekbones appear gnarled, his eyes and cheeks deeply sunken. His big hands, rough with frost and swollen by rheumatism, were awkward but gentle at their task. He was like a prehistoric priest performing a fateful ceremonial rite. Also his voice had in it a suitable quality of deep, reverent despair, yet perhaps, at the moment, a sharpness of selfish satisfaction.

"When I perceived what was happening," he said, "I told myself, 'It is the end. I cannot take much; I will take these.'

"Perhaps I was impractical," he continued. "But for myself, I do not regret, and what do we know of those who will come after us? We are the doddering remnant of a race of mechanical fools. I have saved what I love; the soul of what was good in us here; perhaps the new ones will make a strong enough beginning not to fall behind when they become clever."

He rose with slow pain and placed the wrapped volumes in the niche with his utensils. The others watched him with the same ritualistic gaze.

"Shakespeare, the Bible, *Moby Dick*, *The Divine Comedy*," one of them said softly. "You might have done worse; much worse."

"You will have a little soul left until you die," said another harshly. "That is more than is true of us. My brain becomes thick, like my hands." He held the big, battered hands, with their black nails, in the glow to be seen.

"I want paper to write on," he said. "And there is none."

The fourth man said nothing. He sat in the shadow farthest from the fire, and sometimes his body jerked in its rags from the cold.

Although he was still young, he was sick, and coughed often. Writing implied a greater future than he now felt able to consider.

The old man seated himself laboriously, and reached out, groaning at the movement, to put another block of peat on the fire. With bowed heads and averted eyes, his three guests acknowledged his magnanimity.

"We thank you, Doctor Jenkins, for the reading," said the man who had named the books.

They seemed then to be waiting for something. Doctor Jenkins understood, but was loath to comply. In an ordinary moment he would have said nothing. But the words of *The Tempest*, which he had been reading, and the religious attention of the three, made this an unusual occasion.

"You wish to hear the phonograph," he said grudgingly.

The two middle-aged men stared into the fire, unable to formulate and expose the enormity of their desire.

The young man, however, said anxiously, between suppressed coughs, "Oh, please," like an excited child.

The old man rose again in his difficult way, and went to the back of the cell. He returned and placed tenderly upon the packed floor, where the firelight might fall upon it, an old, portable phonograph in a black case. He smoothed the top with his hand, and then opened it. The lovely green-felt-covered disk became visible.

"I have been using thorns as needles," he said. "But tonight, because we have a musician among us"—he bent his head to the young man, almost invisible in the shadow—"I will use a steel needle. There are only three left."

The two middle-aged men stared at him in speechless adoration. The one with the big hands, who wanted to write, moved his lips, but the whisper was not audible.

"Oh, don't," cried the young man, as if he were hurt. "The thorns will do beautifully."

"No," the old man said. "I have become accustomed to the thorns, but they are not really good. For you, my young friend, we will have good music tonight.

"After all," he added generously, and beginning to wind the phonograph, which creaked, "they can't last forever."

"No, nor we," the man who needed to write said harshly. "The needle, by all means."

"Oh, thanks," said the young man. "Thanks," he said again, in a low, excited voice, and then stifled his coughing with a bowed head.

"The records, though," said the old man when he had finished winding, "are a different matter. Already they are very worn. I do not play them more than once a week. One, once a week, that is what I allow myself.

"More than a week I cannot stand it; not to hear them," he apologized.

"No, how could you?" cried the young man. "And with them here like this."

"A man can stand anything," said the man who wanted to write, in his harsh, antagonistic voice.

"Please, the music," said the young man.

"Only the one," said the old man. "In the long run we will remember more that way."

He had a dozen records with luxuriant gold and red seals. Even in that light the others could see that the threads of the records were becoming worn. Slowly he read out the titles, and the tremendous, dead names of the composers and the artists and the orchestras. The three worked upon the names in their minds, carefully. It was difficult to select from such a wealth what they would at once most like to remember. Finally the man who wanted to write named Gershwin's "New York."

"Oh, no," cried the sick young man, and then could say nothing more because he had to cough. The others understood him, and the harsh man withdrew his selection and waited for the musician to choose.

The musician begged Doctor Jenkins to read the titles again, very slowly, so that he could remember the sounds. While they were read, he lay back against the wall, his eyes closed, his thin, horny hand pulling at his light beard, and listened to the voices and the orchestras and the single instruments in his mind.

When the reading was done he spoke despairingly. "I have forgotten," he complained. "I cannot hear them clearly.

"There are things missing," he explained.

"I know," said Doctor Jenkins. "I thought that I knew all of Shelley by heart. I should have brought Shelley."

"That's more soul than we can use," said the harsh man. "*Moby Dick* is better.

"By God, we can understand that," he emphasized.

The doctor nodded.

"Still," said the man who had admired the books, "we need the absolute if we are to keep a grasp on anything.

"Anything but these sticks and peat clods and rabbit snares." he said bitterly.

"Shelley desired an ultimate absolute," said the harsh man. "It's too much," he said. "It's no good; no earthly good."

The musician selected a Debussy nocturne. The others considered and approved. They rose to their knees to watch the doctor prepare for the playing, so that they appeared to be actually in an attitude of worship. The peat glow showed the thinness of their bearded faces, and the deep lines in them, and revealed the condition of their garments. The other two continued to kneel as the old man carefully lowered the needle onto the spinning disk, but the musician suddenly drew back against the wall again, with his knees up, and buried his face in his hands.

At the first notes of the piano the listeners were startled. They stared at each other. Even the musician lifted his head in amazement, but then quickly bowed it again, strainingly, as if he were suffering from a pain he might not be able to endure. They were all listening deeply, without movement. The wet, blue-green notes tinkled forth from the old machine, and were individual, delectable presences in the cell. The individual, delectable presences swept into a sudden tide of unbearably beautiful dissonance, and then continued fully the swelling and ebbing of that tide, the dissonant in-pourings, and the resolutions, and the diminishments, and the little, quiet wavelets of interlude lapping between. Every sound was piercing and singularly sweet. In all the men except the musician, there occurred rapid sequences of tragically heightened recollection. He heard nothing but what was there. At the final, whispering disappearance, but moving quietly, so that the others would not hear him and look at him, he let his head fall back in agony, as if it were drawn there by the hair, and clenched the fingers of one hand over his teeth. He sat that way while the others were silent, and until they began to breathe again normally. His drawn-up legs were trembling violently.

Quickly Doctor Jenkins lifted the needle off, to save it, and not to spoil the recollection with scraping. When he had stopped the whirling of the sacred disk, he courteously left the phonograph open and by the fire, in sight.

The others, however, understood. The musician rose last, but then abruptly, and went quickly out at the door without saying anything. The others stopped at the door and gave their thanks in low voices. The doctor nodded magnificently.

"Come again," he invited, "in a week. We will have the 'New York.'"

When the two had gone together, out toward the rimed road, he stood in the entrance, peering and listening. At first there was only the resonant boom of the wind overhead, and then, far over the dome of the dead, dark plain, the wolf cry lamenting. In the rifts of clouds the doctor saw four stars flying. It impressed the doctor that one of them had just been obscured by the beginning of a flying cloud at the very moment he heard what he had been listening for, a sound of suppressed coughing. It was not near by, however. He believed that down against the pale alders he could see the moving shadow.

With nervous hands he lowered the piece of canvas which served as his door, and pegged it at the bottom. Then quickly and quietly, looking at the piece of canvas frequently, he slipped the records into the case, snapped the lid shut, and carried the phonograph to his couch. There, pausing often to stare at the canvas and listen, he dug earth from the wall and disclosed a piece of board. Behind this there was a deep hole in the wall, into which he put the phonograph. After a moment's consideration, he went over and reached down to his bundle of books and inserted it also. Then, guardedly, he once more sealed up the hole with the board and the earth. He also changed his blankets, and the grass-stuffed sack which served as a pillow, so that he could lie facing the entrance. After carefully placing two more blocks of peat on the fire, he stood for a long time watching the stretched canvas, but it seemed to billow naturally with the first gusts of a lowering wind. At last he prayed, and got in under his blankets, and closed his smoke-smarting eyes. On the inside of the bed, next to the wall, he could feel with his hand, the comfortable piece of lead pipe.

Fermi and Frost

FREDERIK POHL

Winner of multiple Hugo and Nebula awards, editor of award-winning magazines, innovator of the original-stories anthology, editor of a line of SF books, solo author, collaborator, agent, critic, president in turn of both World SF and the Science Fiction Writers of America—Frederik Pohl has done it all, and extraordinarily well.

"Fermi and Frost," first published in *Isaac Asimov's Science Fiction Magazine* in 1985, shows how Pohl's style, with roots in the 1940s, has changed and matured over the years. What is especially notable about this Hugo Award–winning story is that it follows its protagonist through a post-nuclear ordeal that shows some light at the end of the tunnel.

For a writer who has witnessed the coming of the nuclear age and the nuclear gamesmanship of the second half of the twentieth century, Pohl's optimism is reason to keep hope for our future.

O n Timothy Clary's ninth birthday he got no cake. He spent all of it in a bay of the TWA terminal at John F. Kennedy Airport in New York, sleeping fitfully, crying now and then from exhaustion or fear. All he had to eat was stale Danish pastries from the buffet wagon and not many of them, and he was fearfully embarrassed because he had wet his pants. Three times. Getting to the toilets over the packed refugee bodies was just about impossible. There were twenty-eight hundred people in a space designed for a fraction that many, and all of them with the same idea. Get away! Climb the highest mountain! Drop yourself splat, spang, right in the middle of the widest desert! Run! Hide!—

And pray. Pray as hard as you can, because even the occasional planeload of refugees that managed to fight their way aboard and even take off had no sure hope of refuge when they got wherever the plane was going. Families parted. Mothers pushed their screaming children aboard a jet and melted back into the crowd before screaming, more quietly, themselves.

Because there had been no launch order yet, or none that the public had heard about anyway, there might still be time for escape. A little time. Time enough for the TWA terminal, and every other airport terminal everywhere, to jam up with terrified lemmings. There was no doubt that the missiles were poised to fly. The attempted Cuban coup had escalated wildly, and one nuclear sub had attacked another with a nuclear charge. That, everyone agreed, was the signal. The next event would be the final one.

Timothy knew little of this, but there would have been nothing he could have done about it—except perhaps cry, or have nightmares, or wet himself, and young Timothy was doing all of those anyway. He did not know where his father was. He didn't know where his mother was, either, except that she had gone somewhere to try to call his father; but then there had been a surge that could not be resisted when three 747s at once had announced boarding, and Timothy had been carried far from where he had been left. Worse than that. Wet as he was, with a cold already, he was beginning to be very sick. The young woman who had brought him the Danish pastries put a worried hand to his forehead and drew it away helplessly. The boy needed a doctor. But so did a hundred others, elderly heart patients and hungry babies and at least two women close to childbirth.

If the terror had passed and the frantic negotiations had succeeded, Timothy might have found his parents again in time to grow up and marry and give them grandchildren. If one side or the other had been able to preempt, and destroy the other, and save itself, Timothy forty years later might have been a graying, cynical colonel in the American military government of Leningrad. (Or body servant to a Russian one in Detroit.) Or if his mother had pushed just a little harder earlier on, he might have wound up in the plane of refugees that reached Pittsburgh just in time to become plasma. Or if the girl who was watching him had become just a little more scared, and a little more brave, and somehow managed to get him through the throng to the improvised clinics in the main terminal, he might have been given medicine, and found somebody to protect him, and take him to a refuge, and live. . . .

But that is in fact what did happen!

Because Harry Malibert was on his way to a British Interplanetary Society seminar in Portsmouth, he was already sipping Beefeater Martinis in the terminal's Ambassador Club when the unnoticed TV at the bar suddenly made everybody notice it.

Those silly nuclear-attack communications systems that the radio stations tested out every now and then, and nobody paid any attention to any more—why, this time it was real! They were serious! Because it was winter and snowing heavily Malibert's flight had been delayed anyway. Before its rescheduled departure time came, all flights had been embargoed. Nothing would leave Kennedy until some official somewhere decided to let them go.

Almost at once the terminal began to fill with would-be refugees. The Ambassador Club did not fill at once. For three hours the ground-crew stew at the desk resolutely turned away everyone who rang the bell who could not produce the little red card of admission; but when the food and drink in the main terminals began to run out the Chief of Operations summarily opened the club to everyone. It didn't help relieve the congestion outside, it only added to what was within. Almost at once a volunteer doctors' committee seized most of the club to treat the ill and injured from the thickening crowds, and people like Harry Malibert found themselves pushed into the bar area. It was one of the Operations staff, commandeering a gin and tonic at the bar for the sake of the calories more than the booze, who recognized him. "You're Harry Malibert. I heard you lecture once, at Northwestern."

Malibert nodded. Usually when someone said that to him he answered politely, "I hope you enjoyed it," but this time it did not seem appropriate to be normally polite. Or normal at all.

"You showed slides of Arecibo," the man said dreamily. "You said that radio telescope could send a message as far as the Great Nebula in Andromeda, two million light-years away—if only there was another radio telescope as good as that one there to receive it."

"You remember very well," said Malibert, surprised.

"You made a big impression, Dr. Malibert." The man glanced at his watch, debated, took another sip of his drink. "It really sounded wonderful, using the big telescopes to listen for messages from alien civilizations somewhere in space—maybe hearing some, maybe making contact, maybe not being alone in the universe any more. You made me wonder why we hadn't seen some of these people already, or anyway heard from them—but maybe," he finished, glancing bitterly at the ranked and guarded aircraft outside, "maybe now we know why."

Malibert watched him go, and his heart was leaden. The thing he had given his professional career to—SETI, the Search for Extra-Terrestrial Intelligence—no longer seemed to matter. If the bombs went off, as everyone said they must, then that was ended for a good long time, at least—

Gabble of voices at the end of the bar; Malibert turned, leaned over the mahogany, peered. The *Please Stand By* slide had vanished, and a young black woman with pomaded hair, voice trembling, was delivering a news bulletin:

"—the president has confirmed that a nuclear attack has begun against the United States. Missiles have been detected over the Arctic, and they are incoming. Everyone is ordered to seek shelter and remain there pending instructions—"

Yes. It was ended, thought Malibert, at least for a good long time.

▼

The surprising thing was that the news that it had begun changed nothing. There were no screams, no hysteria. The order to seek shelter meant nothing at John F. Kennedy Airport, where there was no shelter any better than the building they were in. And that, no doubt, was not too good. Malibert remembered clearly the strange aerodynamic shape of the terminal's roof. Any blast anywhere nearby would tear that off and send it sailing over the bay to the Rockaways, and probably a lot of the people inside with it.

But there was nowhere else to go.

There were still camera crews at work, heaven knew why. The television set was showing crowds in Times Square and Newark, a clot of automobiles stagnating on the George Washington Bridge, their drivers abandoning them and running for the Jersey shore. A hundred people were peering around each other's heads to catch glimpses of the screen, but all that anyone said was to call out when he recognized a building or a street.

Orders rang out: "You people will have to move back! We need the room! Look, some of you, give us a hand with these patients." Well, that seemed useful, at least. Malibert volunteered at once and was given the care of a young boy, teeth chattering, hot with fever. "He's had tetracycline," said the doctor who turned the boy over to him. "Clean him up if you can, will you? He ought to be all right if—"

If any of them were, thought Malibert, not requiring her to finish the sentence. How did you clean a young boy up? The question answered itself when Malibert found the boy's trousers soggy and the smell told him what the moisture was. Carefully he laid the child on a leather love seat and removed the pants and sopping undershorts. Naturally the boy had not come with a change of clothes. Malibert solved that with a pair of his own jockey shorts out of his briefcase—far too big for the child, of course, but since they were meant to fit tightly and elastically they stayed in place when Malibert pulled them up to the waist. Then he found paper towels and pressed the blue jeans as dry as he could. It was not very dry. He grimaced, laid them over a bar stool and sat on them for a while, drying them with body heat. They were only faintly wet ten minutes later when he put them back on the child—

San Francisco, the television said, had ceased to transmit.

Malibert saw the Operations man working his way toward him and shook his head. "It's begun," Malibert said, and the man looked around. He put his face close to Malibert's.

"I can get you out of here," he whispered. "There's an Icelandic DC-8 loading right now. No announcement. They'd be rushed if they did. There's room for you, Dr. Malibert."

It was like an electric shock. Malibert trembled. Without knowing why he did it, he said, "Can I put the boy on instead?"

The Operations man looked annoyed. "Take him with you, of course," he said. "I didn't know you had a son."

"I don't," said Malibert. But not out loud. And when they were in the jet he held the boy in his lap as tenderly as though he were his own.

If there was no panic in the Ambassador Club at Kennedy there was plenty of it everywhere else in the world. What everyone in the superpower cities knew was that their lives were at stake. Whatever they did might be in vain, and yet they had to do something. Anything! Run, hide, dig, brace, stow . . . pray. The city people tried to desert the metropolises for the open safety of the country, and the farmers and the exurbanites sought the stronger, safer buildings of the cities.

And the missiles fell.

The bombs that had seared Hiroshima and Nagasaki were struck matches compared to the hydrogen-fusion flares that ended eighty million lives in those first hours. Firestorms fountained above a hundred cities. Winds of three hundred kilometers an hour pulled in cars and debris and people, and they all became ash that rose to the sky. Splatters of melted rock and dust sprayed into the air.

They sky darkened.

Then it grew darker still.

When the Icelandic jet landed at Keflavik Airport Malibert carried the boy down the passage to the little stand marked *Immigration*. The line was long, for most of the passengers had no passports at all, and the immigration woman was very tired of making out temporary entrance permits by the time Malibert reached her. "He's my son," Malibert lied. "My wife has his passport, but I don't know where my wife is."

She nodded wearily. She pursed her lips, looked toward the door beyond which her superior sat sweating and initialing reports, then shrugged and let them through. Malibert took the boy to a door marked *Snirting*, which seemed to be the Icelandic word for toilets, and was relieved to see that at least Timothy was able to stand by himself while he urinated, although his eyes stayed half closed. His head was very hot. Malibert prayed for a doctor in Reykjavik.

In the bus the English-speaking tour guide in charge of them— she had nothing else to do, for her tour would never arrive—sat on the arm of a first-row seat with a microphone in her hand and chattered vivaciously to the refugees. "Chicago? Ya, is gone, Chicago. And Detroit and Pittisburrug—is bad. New York? Certainly New York too!" she said severely, and the big tears rolling down her cheek made Timothy cry too.

Malibert hugged him. "Don't worry, Timmy," he said. "No one would bother bombing Reykjavik." And no one would have. But when the bus was ten miles farther along there was a sudden glow in the clouds ahead of them that made them squint. Someone in the USSR had decided that it was time for neatening up loose threads. That someone, whoever remained in whatever remained of their central missile control, had realized that no one had taken out that supremely, insultingly dangerous bastion of imperialist American interests in the North Atlantic, the United States airbase at Keflavik.

Unfortunately, by then EMP and attrition had compromised the accuracy of their aim. Malibert had been right. No one would have bothered bombing Reykjavik—on purpose—but a forty-mile miss did the job anyway, and Reykjavik ceased to exist.

They had to make a wide detour inland to avoid the fires and the radiation. And as the sun rose on their first day in Iceland, Malibert, drowsing over the boy's bed after the Icelandic nurse had shot him full of antibiotics, saw the daybreak in awful, sky-drenching red.

It was worth seeing, for in the days to come there was no daybreak at all.

▼

The worst was the darkness, but at first that did not seem urgent. What was urgent was rain. A trillion trillion dust particles nucleated water vapor. Drops formed. Rain fell torrents of rain; sheets and cascades of rain. The rivers swelled. The Mississippi overflowed, and the Ganges, and the Yellow. The High Dam at Aswan spilled water over its lip, then crumbled. The rains came where rains came never. The Sahara knew flash floods. The Flaming Mountains at the edge of the Gobi flamed no more; a ten-year supply of rain came down in a week and rinsed the dusty slopes bare.

And the darkness stayed.

The human race lives always eighty days from starvation. That is the sum of stored food, globe wide. It met the nuclear winter with no more and no less.

The missiles went off on the 11th of June. If the world's larders had been equally distributed, on the 30th of August the last mouthful would have been eaten. The starvation deaths would have begun and ended in the next six weeks; exit the human race.

The larders were not equally distributed. The Northern Hemisphere was caught on one foot, fields sown, crops not yet grown. Nothing did grow there. The seedlings poked up through the dark earth for sunlight, found none, died. Sunlight was shaded out by the dense clouds of dust exploded out of the ground by H-bombs. It was the Cretaceous repeated; extinction was in the air.

There were mountains of stored food in the rich countries of North America and Europe, of course, but they melted swiftly. The rich countries had much stored wealth in the form of their livestock. Every steer was a million calories of protein and fat. When it was slaughtered, it saved thousands of other calories of grain and roughage for every day loped off its life in feed. The cattle and pigs and sheep—even the goats and horses; even the pet bunnies and the chicks; even the very kittens and hamsters—they all died quickly and were eaten, to eke out the stores of canned foods and root vegetables and grain. There was no rationing of the slaughtered meat. It had to be eaten before it spoiled.

Of course, even in the rich countries the supplies were not equally distributed. The herds and the grain elevators were not located on Times Square or in the Loop. It took troops to convey corn from Iowa to Boston and Dallas and Philadelphia. Before long, it took killing. Then it could not be done at all.

So the cities starved first. As the convoys of soldiers made the changeover from seizing food for the cities to seizing food for themselves, the riots began, and the next wave of mass death. These casualties didn't usually die of hunger. They died of someone else's.

It didn't take long. By the end of "summer" the frozen remnants of the cities were all the same. A few thousand skinny, freezing desperadoes survived in each, sitting guard over their troves of canned and dried and frozen foodstuffs.

Every river in the world was running sludgy with mud to its mouth, as the last of the trees and grasses died and relaxed their grip on the soil. Every rain washed dirt away. As the winter dark deepened the rains turned to snow. The Flaming Mountains were sheeted in ice now, ghostly, glassy fingers uplifted to the gloom. Men could walk across the Thames at London now, the few men who were left. And across the Hudson, across the Whangpoo, across the Missouri between the two Kansas Cities. Avalanches rumbled down on what was left of Denver. In the stands of dead timber grubs flourished. The starved predators scratched them out and devoured them. Some of the predators were human. The last of the Hawaiians were finally grateful for their termites.

A Western human being—comfortably pudgy on a diet of 2800 calories a day, resolutely jogging to keep the flab away or mournfully conscience-stricken at the thickening thighs and the waistbands that won't quite close—can survive for forty-five days without food. By then the fat is gone. Protein reabsorptions of the muscles is well along. The plump housewife or businessman is a starving scarecrow. Still, even then care and nursing can still restore health.

Then it gets worse.

Dissolution attacks the nervous system. Blindness begins. The flesh of the gums recedes, and the teeth fall out. Apathy becomes pain, then agony, then coma.

Then death. Death for almost every person on Earth. . . .

▼

For forty days and forty nights the rain fell, and so did the temperature. Iceland froze over.

To Harry Malibert's astonishment and dawning relief, Iceland was well equipped to do that. It was one of the few places on Earth that could be submerged in snow and ice and still survive.

There is a ridge of volcanoes that goes almost around the Earth. The part that lies between America and Europe is called the Mid-Atlantic Ridge, and most of it is under water. Here and there, like boils erupting along a forearm, volcanic islands poke up above the surface. Iceland is one of them. It was because Iceland was volcanic that it could survive when most places died of freezing, but it was also because it had been cold in the first place.

The survival authorities put Malibert to work as soon as they found out who he was. There was no job opening for a radio astronomer interested in contacting far-off (and very likely non-existent) alien races. There was, however, plenty of work for persons with scientific training, especially if they had the engineering skills of a man who had run Arecibo for two years. When Malibert was not nursing Timothy Clary through the slow and silent convalescence from his pneumonia, he was calculating heat losses and pumping rates for the piped geothermal water.

Iceland filled itself with enclosed space. It heated the spaces with water from the boiling underground springs.

Of heat it had plenty. Getting the heat from the geyser fields to the enclosed spaces was harder. The hot water was as hot as ever, since it did not depend at all on sunlight for its calories, but it took a lot more of it to keep out a −30°C chill than a +5°C one. It wasn't just to keep the surviving people warm that they needed energy. It was to grow food.

Iceland had always had a lot of geothermal greenhouses. The flowering ornamentals were ripped out and food plants put in their place. There was no sunlight to make the vegetables and grains grow, so the geothermal power-generating plants were put on max output. Solar-spectrum incandescents flooded the trays with photons. Not just in the old greenhouses. Gymnasia, churches, schools—they all began to grow food under the glaring lights. There was other food, too, metric tons of protein baaing and starving in the hills. The herds of sheep were captured and slaughtered and dressed—and put outside again, to freeze until needed. The animals that froze to death on the slopes were bulldozed into heaps of a hundred, and left where they were. Geodetic maps were carefully marked to show the locations of each heap.

It was, after all, a blessing that Reykjavik had been nuked. That meant half a million fewer people for the island's resources to feed.

When Malibert was not calculating load factors, he was out in the desperate cold, urging on the workers. Sweating navvies tried to muscle shrunken fittings together in icy foxholes that their body heat kept filling with icewater. They listened patiently as Malibert tried to give orders—his few words of Icelandic was almost useless, but even the navvies sometimes spoke tourist-English. They checked their radiation monitors, looked up at the storms overhead, returned to their work and prayed. Even Malibert almost prayed when one day, trying to locate the course of the buried coastal road, he looked out on the sea ice and saw a gray-white ice hummock that was not an ice hummock. It was just at the limits of visibility, dim on the fringe of the road crew's work lights, and it moved. "A polar bear!" he whispered to the head of the work crew, and everyone stopped while the beast shambled out of sight.

From then on they carried rifles.

▼

When Malibert was not (incompetent) technical advisor to the task of keeping Iceland warm or (almost incompetent, but learning) substitute father to Timothy Clary, he was trying desperately to calculate survival chances. Not just for them; for the entire human race. With all the desperate flurry of survival work, the Icelanders spared time to think of the future. A study team was created, physicists from the University of Reykjavik, the surviving Supply officer from the Keflavik airbase, a meteorologist on work-study from the University of Leyden to learn about North Atlantic air masses. They met in the gasthuis where Malibert lived with the boy, and usually Timmy sat silent next to Malibert while they talked. What they wanted was to know how long the dust cloud would persist. Some day the particles would finish dropping from the sky, and then the world could be reborn—if enough survived to parent a new race, anyway. But when? They could not tell. They did not know how long, how cold, how killing the nuclear winter would be. "We don't know the megatonnage," said Malibert, "we don't know what atmospheric changes have taken place, we don't know the rate of isolation. We only know it will be bad."

"It is already bad," grumbled Thorsid Magnesson, Director of Public Safety. (Once that office had had something to do with catching criminals, when the major threat to safety was crime.)

"It will get worse," said Malibert, and it did. The cold deepened. The reports from the rest of the world dwindled. They plotted maps to show what they knew to show. One set of missile maps, to show where the strikes had been—within a week that no longer mattered, because the deaths from cold already began to outweigh those from blast. They plotted isotherm maps, based on the scattered weather reports that came in—maps that had to be changed every day, as the freezing line marched toward the Equator. Finally the maps were irrelevant. The whole world was cold then. They plotted fatality maps—the percentages of deaths in each area, as they could infer them from the reports they received, but those maps soon became too frightening to plot.

The British Isles died first, not because they were nuked, but because they were not. There were too many people alive there. Britain never owned more than a four-day supply of food. When the ships stopped coming they starved. So did Japan. A little later, so did Bermuda and Hawaii and Canada's off-shore provinces; and then it was continents' turn.

And Timmy Clary listened to every word.

The boy didn't talk much. He never asked after his parents, not after the first few days. He did not hope for good news, and did not want bad. The boy's infection was cured, but the boy himself was not. He ate half of what a hungry child should devour. He ate that only when Malibert coaxed him.

The only thing that made Timothy look alive was the rare times when Malibert could talk to him about space. There were many in Iceland who knew about Harry Malibert and SETI, and a few who cared about it almost as much as Malibert himself. When time permitted they would get together, Malibert and his groupies. There was Lars the postman (now pick-and-shovel ice excavator, since there was no mail), Ingar the waitress from the Loftleider Hotel (now stitching heavy drapes to help insulate dwelling walls), Elda the English teacher (now practical nurse, frostbite cases a specialty). There were others, but those three were always there when they could get away. They were Harry Malibert fans who had read his books and dreamed with him of radio messages from weird aliens from Aldebaran, or worldships that could carry million-person populations across the galaxy, on voyages of a hundred thousand years. Timmy listened, and drew sketches of the worldships. Malibert supplied him with dimensions. "I talked to Gerry Webb," he said, "and he'd worked it out in detail. It is a matter of rotation rates and strength of materials. To provide the proper simulated gravity for the people in the ships, the shape has to be a cylinder and it has to spin—sixteen kilometers is what the diameter must be. Then the cylinder must be long enough to provide space, but not so long that the dynamics of spin cause it to wobble or bend—perhaps sixty kilometers long. One part to live in. One part to store fuel. And at the end, a reaction chamber where hydrogen fusion thrusts the ship across the Galaxy."

"Hydrogen bombs," said the boy. "Harry? Why don't the bombs wreck the worldship?"

"It's engineering," said Malibert honestly, "and I don't know the details. Gerry was going to give his paper at the Portsmouth meeting; it was one reason I was going." But, of course, there would never be a British Interplanetary Society meeting in Portsmouth now, ever again.

Elda said uneasily, "It is time for lunch soon. Timmy? Will you eat some soup if I make it?" And did make it, whether the boy promised or not. Elda's husband had worked at Keflavik in the PX, an accountant; unfortunately he had been putting in overtime there when the follow-up missile did what the miss had failed to do, and so Elda had no husband left, not enough even to bury.

Even with the earth's hot water pumped full velocity through the straining pipes it was not warm in the gasthuis. She wrapped the boy in blankets and sat near him while he dutifully spooned up the soup. Lars and Ingar sat holding hands and watching the boy eat. "To hear a voice from another star," Lars said suddenly, "that would have been fine."

"There are no voices," said Ingar bitterly. "Not even ours now. We have the answer to the Fermi paradox."

And when the boy paused in his eating to ask what that was, Harry Malibert explained it as carefully as he could:

"It is named after Enrico Fermi, a scientist. He said, 'We know that there are many billions of stars like our sun. Our sun has planets, therefore it is reasonable to assume that some of the other stars do also. One of our planets has living things on it. Us, for instance, as well as trees and germs and horses. Since there are so many stars, it seems almost certain that some of them, at least, have also living things. People. People as smart as we are—or smarter. People who can build spaceships, or send radio messages to other stars, as we can.' Do you understand so far, Timmy?" The boy nodded, frowning, but—Malibert was delighted to see—kept on eating his soup. "Then, the question Fermi asked was, 'Why haven't some of them come to see us?'"

"Like in the movies," the boy nodded. "The flying saucers."

"All those movies are made-up stories, Timmy. Like Jack and the Beanstalk, or Oz. Perhaps some creatures from space have come to see us sometime, but there is no good evidence that this is so. I feel sure there would be evidence if it had happened. There would have to be. If there were many such visits, ever, then at least one would have dropped the Martian equivalent of a McDonald's Big Mac box, or a used Sirian flash cube, and it would have been found and shown to be from somewhere other than the Earth. None ever has. So there are only three possible answers to Dr. Fermi's question. One, there is no other life. Two, there is, but they want to leave us alone. They don't want to contact us, perhaps because we frighten them with our violence, or for some reason we can't even guess at. And the third reason—" Elda made a quick gesture, but Malibert shook his head—"is that perhaps as soon as any people get smart enough to do all those things that get them into space—when they have all the technology we do—they also have such terrible bombs and weapons that they can't control them any more. So a war breaks out. And they kill themselves off before they are fully grown up."

"Like now," Timothy said, nodding seriously to show he understood. He had finished his soup, but instead of taking the plate away Elda hugged him in her arms and tried not to weep.

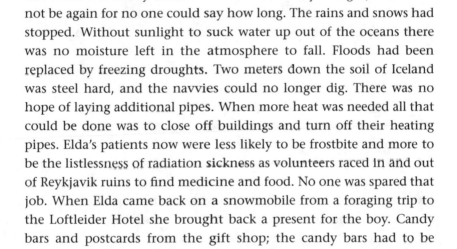

The world was totally dark now. There was no day or night, and would not be again for no one could say how long. The rains and snows had stopped. Without sunlight to suck water up out of the oceans there was no moisture left in the atmosphere to fall. Floods had been replaced by freezing droughts. Two meters down the soil of Iceland was steel hard, and the navvies could no longer dig. There was no hope of laying additional pipes. When more heat was needed all that could be done was to close off buildings and turn off their heating pipes. Elda's patients now were less likely to be frostbite and more to be the listlessness of radiation sickness as volunteers raced in and out of Reykjavik ruins to find medicine and food. No one was spared that job. When Elda came back on a snowmobile from a foraging trip to the Loftleider Hotel she brought back a present for the boy. Candy bars and postcards from the gift shop; the candy bars had to be shared, but the postcards were all for him. "Do you know what these are?" she asked. The cards showed huge, squat, ugly men and women in the costumes of a thousand years ago. "They're trolls. We have myths in Iceland that the trolls lived here. They're still here, Timmy, or so they say; the mountains are trolls that just got too old and tired to move any more."

"They're made-up stories, right?" the boy asked seriously, and did not grin until she assured him they were. Then he made a joke. "I guess the trolls won," he said.

"Ach, Timmy!" Elda was shocked. But at least the boy was capable of joking, she told herself, and even graveyard humor was better than none. Life had become a little easier for her with the new patients—easier because for the radiation-sick there was very little that could be done—and she bestirred herself to think of ways to entertain the boy.

And found a wonderful one.

Since fuel was precious there were no excursions to see the sights of Iceland-under-the-ice. There was no way to see them anyway in the eternal dark. But when a hospital chopper was called up to travel empty to Stokksnes on the eastern shore to bring back a child with a broken back, she begged space for Malibert and Timmy. Elda's own ride was automatic, as duty nurse for the wounded child. "An avalanche crushed his house," she explained. "It is right under the mountains, Stokksnes, and landing there will be a little tricky, I think. But we can come in from the sea and make it safe. At least in the landing lights of the helicopter something can be seen."

They were luckier than that. There was more light. Nothing came through the clouds, where the billions of particles that had once been Elda's husband added to the trillions of trillions that had been Detroit and Marseilles and Shanghai to shut out the sky. But in the clouds and under them were snakes and sheets of dim color, sprays full of dull red, fans of pale green. The aurora borealis did not give much light. But there was no other light at all except for the faint glow from the pilot's instrument panel. As their eyes widened they could see the dark shapes of the Vatnajökull slipping by below them. "*Big* trolls," cried the boy happily, and Elda smiled too as she hugged him.

The pilot did as Elda had predicted, down the slopes of the eastern range, out over the sea, and cautiously back into the little fishing village. As they landed, red-tipped flashlights guiding them, the copter's landing lights picked out a white lump, vaguely saucer-shaped. "Radar dish," said Malibert to the boy, pointing.

Timmy pressed his nose to the freezing window. "Is it one of them, Daddy Harry? The things that could talk to the stars?"

The pilot answered: "Ach, no, Timmy—military, it is." And Malibert said:

"They wouldn't put one of those here, Timothy. It's too far north. You wanted a place for a big radio telescope that could search the whole sky, not just the little piece of it you can see from Iceland."

And while they helped slide the stretcher with the broken child into the helicopter, gently, kindly as they could be, Malibert was thinking about those places, Arecibo and Woomara and Socorro and all the others. Every one of them was now dead and certainly broken with a weight of ice and shredded by the mean winds. Crushed, rusted, washed away, all those eyes on space were blinded now; and the thought saddened Harry Malibert, but not for long. More gladdening than anything sad was the fact that, for the first time, Timothy had called him "Daddy."

▼

In one ending to the story, when at last the sun came back it was too late. Iceland had been the last place where human beings survived, and Iceland had finally starved. There was nothing alive anywhere on Earth that spoke, or invented machines, or read books. Fermi's terrible third answer was the right one after all.

But there exists another ending. In this one the sun came back in time. Perhaps it was just barely in time, but the food had not yet run out when daylight brought the first touches of green in some parts of the world, and plants began to grow again from frozen or hoarded seed. In this ending Timothy lived to grow up. When he was old enough, and after Malibert and Elda got around to marrying, he married one of their daughters. And of their descendants—two generations or a dozen generations later—one was alive on the day when Fermi's paradox became a quaintly amusing old worry, as irrelevant and comical as a fifteenth-century mariner's fear of falling off the edge of the flat Earth. On that day the skies spoke, and those who lived in them came to call.

Perhaps that is the true ending of the story, and in it the human race chose not to squabble and struggle with itself, and so extinguish itself finally into the dark. In this ending human beings survived, and saved all the science and beauty of life, and greeted their star-born visitors with joy. . . .

But that is in fact what did happen!

At least, one would like to think so.

Ultimate Construction

C. C. SHACKLETON

There's a long tradition in speculative fiction of stories that seem to be about one thing when they're really about another. Here C. C. Shackleton, writing in mid-century, offers a decidedly unusual and rather *different* take on what might happen.

The shifting sands moved over the face of the Earth and would soon engulf it.

For millennia now the oceans had been dry and the last tide had washed against the unending shore. The Earth was old. Its heart was cold, its skin dry and wrinkled with encroaching dust. Like a living thing, the sands multiplied, wombed in the deserts where navies once sailed.

The death of moisture meant the death of man. A human being is not watertight; his vital juices evaporate like water from an unglazed pitcher. One by one, and then tribe by tribe and nation by nation, man disappeared as magically as he had come. His bones were powdered by the moving grit, his mineral salts dissolved into the sand.

Yet for a long time he managed to postpone his final extinction. With every technological device at his command, he fought off the deserts in a losing battle that was not lost for centuries.

Now the battle was almost over. The old pastures, the woodlands, the hills, even the regions of ice at either pole—all were covered by the sand. All the works of man, his cities, roads and bridges, were engulfed by the dunes. Every insect, bird and animal lay sleeping under that treacherous yellow blanket. Only in one last valley, in one last house, did one last spark of life survive.

The Last Man on Earth came out of his door and stood regarding the scene. His valley was small and shallow, and completely ringed round the top with glass walls. This morning there was something new to see: the sand had arrived.

The sand pressed and surged against the glass like a living thing, tawnier and more terrible than lions. It rose and spread round the invisible obstacle. It could be heard whispering against the glass, trying to get in.

The glass cracked. Breaking under the pressure behind it, a whole section of it fell inward. At once a great arm of yellow sand reached into the valley and spread its fingers around the house. More followed, and more behind that, until a great wedge sliding in from the rear buried the back of the house up to its eaves.

Without revealing any great emotion, the Last Man on Earth watched this invasion from the front garden. Over the lawn at his feet spread the tide, looking golden and soft and almost inviting. It seemed harmless; it was irresistible.

So little time now remained. There was one last thing the Last Man could do. Turning, he ran through the sand that lay ankle-deep over the porch and hurried into the house to find a bucket and a spade.

A moment later he emerged triumphant. The Last Man on Earth was only six years old. He started to build a sandcastle.

The Manhattan Phone Book (Abridged)

JOHN VARLEY

At the end of the 1960s and in the early 1970s science fiction went through a period of depression. Some of the most famous writers—Heinlein, Clarke, Asimov—weren't writing anything, and what was being written tended to be extremely downbeat.

You couldn't blame writers for seeing the dark side of things. The turbulence of the '60s was extremely unsettling to the entire nation, and many SF writers felt the need to respond to the serious issues of the day with piercing tales that explored such problems as pollution, overpopulation, and war.

Then this dark mood began to lift, and by 1975 writers were once again writing upbeat stories. John Varley was especially prolific, turning out about twenty stories within just a couple of years, each seemingly more imaginative than the previous one.

The following story is one of Varley's rather less optimistic stories. First published in 1984, "The Manhattan Phone Book (Abridged)" puts a human face on mass destruction. Perhaps all soldiers should have to read this story before they go to war.

This is the best story and the worst story anybody ever wrote. There's lots of ways to judge the merit of a story, right? One of them is, are there a lot of people in it, and are they real. Well, this story has more people in it than any story in the history of the world. The Bible? Forget it. Ten thousand people, tops. (I didn't count, but I suspect it's less than that, even with all the begats.)

And real? Each and every character is a certified living human being. You can fault me on the depth of characterization, no question about it. If I'd had the time and space, I could have told you a lot more about each of these people . . . but a writer has dramatic constraints to consider. If only I had more room. Wow! What stories you'd hear!

Admittedly, the plot is skimpy. You can't have everything. The strength of this story is its people. I'm in it. So are you.

It goes like this:

Jerry L. Aab moved to New York six years ago from his home in Valdosta, Georgia. He still speaks with a southern accent, but he's gradually losing it. He's married to a woman named Elaine, and things haven't been going too well for the Aab family. Their second child died, and Elaine is pregnant again. She thinks Jerry is seeing another woman. He isn't, but she's talking divorce.

Roger Aab isn't related to Jerry. He's a native New Yorker. He lives in a third-floor walk-up at 1 Maiden Lane. It's his first place; Roger is just nineteen, a recent high school graduate, thinking about attending City College. Right now, while he makes up his mind, he works in a deli and tries to date Linda Cooper, who lives two blocks away. He hasn't really decided what to do with his life yet, but is confident a decision will come.

Kurt Aach is on parole. He served two years in Attica, up-state, for armed robbery. It wasn't his first stretch. He had vague ideas of going straight when he got out. If he could join the merchant marine he figures he just might make it, but the lousy jobs he's been offered so far aren't worth the trouble. He just bought a .38 Smith and Wesson from a guy on the docks. He cleans and oils it a lot.

Robert Aach is Kurt's older brother. He never visited Kurt in prison because he hates the worthless bum. When he thinks of his brother, he hopes the state will bring back the electric chair real soon. He has a wife and three kids. They like to go to Florida when he gets a vacation.

Adrienne Aaen has worked at the Woolworth's on East 14th Street since she was twenty-one. She's pushing sixty now, and will be retired soon, involuntarily. She never married. She has a sour disposition, mostly because of her feet, which have hurt for forty years. She has a cat and a parakeet. The cat is too lazy to chase the bird. Adrienne has managed to save a little money. Every night she thanks God for all her blessings, and the City of New York for rent control.

Molly Aagard is thirty, and works for the New York Transit Police. She rides the subway every day. She's charged with stopping the serious crimes that infest the underground city, and she works very hard at it. She *hates* the wall-to-wall graffiti that blooms in every car like a malign fungus.

Irving Aagard is no relation. He's fifty-five, and owns an Oldsmobile dealership in New Jersey. People ask him why he lives in Manhattan, and he is always puzzled by that question. Would they rather he lived in Jersey, for chrissake? To Irving, Manhattan is the only place to live. He has enough money to send his three kids Gerald, Morton, and Barbara—to good schools. He frets about crime, but no more than anyone else.

Shiela Aagre is a seventeen-year-old streetwalker from St. Paul. Her life isn't so great, but it's better than Minnesota. She uses heroin, but knows she can stop whenever she wants to.

Theodore Aaker and his wife, Beatrice, live in a fine apartment a block away from the Dakota, where John Lennon was killed. They went out that night and stood in the candlelight vigil, remembering Woodstock, remembering the summer of love in the Haight-Ashbury. Theodore sometimes wonders how and why he got into stocks and bonds. Beatrice is pregnant with their first child. She is deciding how much time she should take off from her law practice. It's a hard question.

(162,000 characters omitted)

Clemanzo Cruz lives on East 120th Street. He's unemployed, and has been since he arrived from Puerto Rico. He hangs out in a bar at the corner of Lexington and 122nd. He didn't used to drink much back in San Juan, but now that's about all he does. It's been fifteen years. You might say he is discouraged. His wife, Ilona, goes to work at five P.M. at the Empire State Building, where she scrubs floors and toilets. She's been mugged a dozen times on the way home on the number 6 Lexington local.

Zelad Cruz shares an apartment with two other secretaries. Even with roommates it's hard to make ends meet with New York rents the way they are. She always has a date Saturday night—she's quite a beauty—and she swings very hard, but Sunday morning always finds her at early mass at St. Patrick's. There's this guy who she thinks may ask her to get married. She's decided she'll say yes. She's tired of sharing an apartment. She hopes he won't beat her up.

Richard Cruzado drives a cab. He's a good-natured guy. He's been known to take fares into darkest Brooklyn. His wife's name is Sabina. She's always after him to buy a house in Queens. He thinks one of these days he will. They have six children, and life is tough for them in Manhattan. Those houses out in Queens have back yards, pools, you name it.

(1,250,000 characters omitted)

Ralph Zzyzzmjac changed his name two years ago. His real name is Ralph Zyzzmjac. A friend persuaded him to add a Z to be the last guy in the phone book. He's a bachelor, a librarian working for the City of New York. For a good time he goes to the movies, alone. He's sixty-one.

Edward Zzzzyniewski is crazy. He's been in and out of Bellevue. He spends most of his time thinking about that bastard Zzyzzmjac, who two years ago knocked him out of last place, his only claim to fame. He broods about him—a man he's never met—fantasizing that Zzyzzmjac is out to get him. Last year he added two Z's to his name. Now he's thinking about stealing a march on that bastard Zzyzzmjac. He's sure Zzyzzmjac is adding two more Z's this year, so he's going to add *seven*. Ed Zzzzzzzzzzzzyniewski. That'd be nice, he decides.

Then one day seventeen thermonuclear bombs exploded in the air over Manhattan, The Bronx, and Staten Island, too. They had a yield of between five and twenty megatons each. This was more than enough to kill everyone in this story. Most of them died instantly. A few lingered for minutes or hours, but they *all* died, just like that. I died. So did you.

I was lucky. In less time than it takes for one neuron to nudge another I was turned into radioactive atoms, and so was the building I was in, and the ground beneath me to a depth of three hundred meters. In a millisecond it was all as sterile as Edward Teller's soul.

You had a tougher time of it. You were in a store, standing near a window. The huge pressure wave turned the glass into ten thousand slivers of pain, one thousand of which tore the flesh from your body. One sliver went into your left eye. You were hurled to the back of the store, breaking a lot of bones and suffering internal injuries, but you still lived. There was a big piece of plate glass driven through your body. The bloody point emerged from your back. You touched it carefully, trying to pull it out, but it hurt too much.

On the piece of glass was a rectangular decal and the message "Mastercard Gladly Accepted."

The store caught fire around you, and you started to cook slowly. You had time to think "Is this what I pay my taxes for?" and then you died.

This story is brought to you courtesy of The Phone Company. Copies of the story can be found near every telephone in Manhattan, and thousands of stories just like it have been compiled for every community in the United States. They make interesting reading. I urge you to read a few pages every night. Don't forget that many wives are listed only under their husband's name. And there are the children to consider: very few have their own phone. Many people—such as single women—pay extra for an unlisted number. And there are the very poor, the transients, the street people, and folks who were unable to pay the last bill. Don't forget any of them as you read the story. Read as much or as little as you can stand, and ask yourself if this is what you want to pay your taxes for. Maybe you'll stop.

Aw, c'mon, I hear you protest. *Some*body will survive.

Perhaps. Possibly. Probably.

But that's not the point. We all love after-the-bomb stories. If we didn't, why would there be so many of them? There's something attractive about all those people being gone, about wandering in a depopulated world, scrounging cans of Campbell's pork and beans, defending one's family from marauders. Sure, it's horrible, sure we weep for all those dead people. But some secret part of us thinks it would be good to survive, to start over.

Secretly, we know we'll survive. All those *other* folks will die. That's what after-the-bomb stories are all about.

All those after-the-bomb stories were lies. Lies, lies, lies.

This is the only true after-the-bomb story you will ever read.

Everybody dies. Your father and mother are decapitated and crushed by a falling building. Rats eat their severed heads. Your husband is disemboweled. Your wife is blinded, flashburned, and gropes along a street of cinders until fear-crazed dogs eat her alive. Your brother and sister are incinerated in their homes, their bodies turned into fine powdery ash by firestorms. Your children . . . ah, I'm sorry. I hate to tell you this, but your children live a *long* time. Three eternal days. They spend those days puking their guts out, watching the flesh fall from their bodies, smelling the gangrene in their lacerated feet, and asking you why it happened. But you aren't there to tell them. I already told you how you died.

It's what you pay your taxes for.

The Man Who
Walked Home

JAMES TIPTREE, JR.

The 1970s was, in addition to its other designations, the decade that ushered in the feminist movement, and women began to participate in many fields formerly dominated by men. Science fiction was no exception.

In the early days of the field there were very few women, and most of them used names that could have belonged to someone of either gender: C. L. (Catherine) Moore, Leigh Brackett, Andre Norton. What does all this have to do with James Tiptree, Jr.?

Tip, as his friends called him, was the biggest ball of fire to hit SF in the early '70s. He wrote stories that shook things up, and they were as feminist as any written by women, despIte having what Robert Silverberg described as "an ineffable maleness" to his prose.

Tiptree was famously reclusive. When he was finally unmasked, it turned out he was actually Alice Sheldon, an ex–CIA agent and a woman. Her writing was so powerful that an award was created in her name to honor the best gender-bending fiction. "The Man Who Walked Home" is a heartbreaking story about a guy just doing a job, with a disastrously bad result.

T ransgression! Terror! And *he thrust and lost there—punched into impossibility, abandoned never to be known how, the wrong man in the most wrong of all wrong places in that unimaginable collapse of never-to-be-reimagined mechanism—he stranded, undone, his lifeline severed, he in that nanosecond knowing his only tether parting, going away, the longest line to life withdrawing, winking out, disappearing forever beyond his grasp—telescoping away from him into the closing vortex beyond which lay his home, his life, his only possibility of being; seeing it sucked back into the deepest maw, melting, leaving him orphaned on what never-to-be-known shore of total wrongness—of beauty beyond joy, perhaps? Of horror? Of nothingness? Of profound otherness only, certainly—whatever it was, that place into which he transgressed, it could not support his life there, his violent and violating aberrance; and he, fierce, brave, crazy—clenched into total protest, one body-fist of utter repudiation of himself there in that place, forsaken there—what did he do? Rejected, exiled, hungering home-ward more desperate than any lost beast driving for its unreachable home, his home, his HOME—and no way, no transport, no vehicle, means, machin-ery, no force but his intolerable resolve aimed homeward along that van-ishing vector, that last and only lifeline—he did, what?*

He walked.

Home.

▼

Precisely what hashed up in the work of the major industrial lessee of the Bonneville Particle Acceleration Facility in Idaho was never known. Or rather, all those who might have been able to diagnose the original malfunction were themselves obliterated almost at once in the greater catastrophe which followed.

The nature of this second cataclysm was not at first understood either. All that was ever certain was that at 1153.6 of May 2, 1989 Old Style, the Bonneville laboratories and all their personnel were transformed into an intimately disrupted form of matter resembling a high-energy plasma, which became rapidly airborne to the accom-paniment of radiating seismic and atmospheric events.

The disturbed area unfortunately included an operational MIRV Watchdog womb.

In the confusion of the next hours the Earth's population was sub-stantially reduced, the biosphere was altered, and the Earth itself was marked with numbers of more conventional craters. For some years thereafter, the survivors were existentially preoccupied and the pecu-liar dust bowl at Bonneville was left to weather by itself in the chang-ing climatic cycles.

It was not a large crater; just over a kilometer in width and lack-ing the usual displacement lip. Its surface was covered with a finely divided substance which dried into dust. Before the rains began it was almost perfectly flat. Only in certain lights, had anyone been there to inspect it, a small surface-marking or abraded place could be detected almost exactly at the center.

Two decades after the disaster a party of short brown people appeared from the south, together with a flock of somewhat atypical sheep. The crater at this time appeared as a wide shallow basin in which the grass did not grow well, doubtless from the almost complete lack of soil microorganisms. Neither this nor the surrounding vigorous grass was found to harm the sheep. A few crude hogans went up at the southern edge and a faint path began to be traced across the crater itself, passing by the central bare spot.

One spring morning two children who had been driving sheep across the crater came screaming back to camp. A monster had burst out of the ground before them, a huge flat animal making a dreadful roar. It vanished in a flash and a shaking of the earth, leaving an evil smell. The sheep had run away.

Since this last was visibly true, some elders investigated. Finding no sign of the monster and no place in which it could hide, they settled for beating the children, who settled for making a detour around the monster-spot, and nothing more occurred for a while.

The following spring the episode was repeated. This time an older girl was present, but she could add only that the monster seemed to be rushing flat out along the ground without moving at all. And there was a scraped place in the dirt. Again nothing was found; an evil-ward in a cleft stick was placed at the spot.

When the same thing happened for the third time a year later, the detour was extended and other charm-wands were added. But since no harm seemed to come of it and the brown people had seen far worse, sheep-tending resumed as before. A few more instantaneous apparitions of the monster were noted, each time in the spring.

At the end of the third decade of the new era a tall old man limped down the hills from the south, pushing his pack upon a bicycle wheel. He camped on the far side of the crater, and soon found the monster-site. He attempted to question people about it, but no one understood him, so he traded a knife for some meat. Although he was obviously feeble, something about him dissuaded them from killing him, and this proved wise because he later assisted the women in treating several sick children.

He spent much time around the place of the apparition and was nearby when it made its next appearance. This excited him very much and he did several inexplicable but apparently harmless things, including moving his camp into the crater by the trail. He stayed on for a full year watching the site and was close by for its next manifestation. After this he spent a few days making a charm-stone for the spot and left northward, hobbling as he had come.

More decades passed. The crater eroded, and a rain-gully became an intermittent streamlet across the edge of the basin. The brown people and their sheep were attacked by a band of grizzled men, after which the survivors went away eastward. The winters of what had been Idaho were now frost-free; aspen and eucalyptus sprouted in the moist plain. Still the crater remained treeless, visible as a flat bowl of grass; and the bare place at the center remained. The skies cleared somewhat.

After another three decades a larger band of black people with ox-drawn carts appeared and stayed for a time, but left again when they too saw the thunderclap-monster. A few other vagrants straggled by.

Five decades later a small permanent settlement had grown up on the nearest range of hills, from which men riding on small ponies with dark stripes down their spines herded humped cattle near the crater. A herdsman's hut was built by the streamlet, which in time became the habitation of an olive-skinned, red-haired family. In due course one of this clan again observed the monster-flash, but these people did not depart. The stone the tall man had placed was noted and left undisturbed.

The homestead at the crater's edge grew into a group of three and was joined by others, and the trail across it became a cart road with a log bridge over the stream. At the center of the still faintly discernible crater the cart road made a bend, leaving a grassy place which bore on its center about a square meter of curiously impacted bare earth and a deeply etched sandstone rock.

The apparition of the monster was now known to occur regularly each spring on a certain morning in this place, and the children of the community dared each other to approach the spot. It was referred to in a phrase that could be translated as "the Old Dragon." The Old Dragon's appearance was always the same: a brief violent thunder-burst which began and cut off abruptly, in the midst of which a drag-onlike creature was seen apparently in furious motion on the earth, although it never actually moved. Afterward there was a bad smell and the earth smoked. People who saw it from close by spoke of a shivering sensation.

Early in the second century two young men rode into town from the north. Their ponies were shaggier than the local breed, and the equip-ment they carried included two boxlike objects which the young men set up at the monster-site. They stayed in the area a full year, observing two materializations of the Old Dragon, and they provided much news and maps of roads and trading towns in the cooler regions to the north. They built a windmill which was accepted by the com-munity and offered to build a lighting machine, which was refused. Then they departed with their boxes after unsuccessfully attempting to persuade a local boy to learn to operate one.

In the course of the next decades other travelers stopped by and marveled at the monster, and there was sporadic fighting over the mountains to the south. One of the armed bands made a cattle raid into the crater hamlet. It was repulsed, but the raiders left a spotted sickness which killed many. For all this time the bare place at the crater's center remained, and the monster made his regular appear-ances, observed or not.

The hill-town grew and changed, and the crater hamlet grew to be a town. Roads widened and linked into networks. There were gray-green conifers in the hills now, spreading down into the plain, and chirruping lizards lived in their branches.

At century's end a shabby band of skin-clad squatters with stunted milk-beasts erupted out of the west and were eventually killed or driven away, but not before the local herds had contracted a vicious parasite. Veterinaries were fetched from the market city up north, but little could be done. The families near the crater left, and for some decades the area was empty. Finally cattle of a new strain reappeared in the plain and the crater hamlet was reoccupied. Still the bare center continued annually to manifest the monster, and he became an accepted phenomenon of the area. On several occasions parties came from the distant Northwest Authority to observe it.

The crater hamlet flourished and grew into the fields where cattle had grazed, and part of the old crater became the town park. A small seasonal tourist industry based on the monster-site developed. The townspeople rented rooms for the appearances, and many more-or-less authentic monster-relics were on display in the local taverns.

Several cults now grew up around the monster. One persistent belief held that it was a devil or damned soul forced to appear on Earth in torment to expiate the catastrophe of three centuries back. Others believed that it, or he, was some kind of messenger whose roar portended either doom or hope according to the believer. One very vocal sect taught that the apparition registered the moral conduct of the townspeople over the past year, and scrutinized the annual apparition for changes which could be interpreted for good or ill. It was considered lucky, or dangerous, to be touched by some of the dust raised by the monster. In every generation at least one small boy would try to hit the monster with a stick, usually acquiring a broken arm and a lifelong tavern tale. Pelting the monster with stones or other objects was a popular sport, and for some years people systematically flung prayers and flowers at it. Once a party tried to net it and were left with strings and vapor. The area itself had long since been fenced off at the center of the park.

Through all this the monster made his violently enigmatic annual appearance, sprawled furiously motionless, unreachably roaring.

Only as the fourth century of the new era went by was it apparent that the monster had been changing slightly. He was now no longer on the earth but had an arm and a leg thrust upward in a kicking or flailing gesture. As the years passed he began to change more quickly until at the end of the century he had risen to a contorted crouching pose, arms outflung as if frozen in gyration. His roar, too, seemed somewhat differently pitched, and the earth after him smoked more and more.

It was then widely felt that the man-monster was about to do something, to make some definitive manifestation, and a series of natural disasters and marvels gave support to a vigorous cult teaching this doctrine. Several religious leaders journeyed to the town to observe the apparitions.

However, the decades passed and the man-monster did nothing more than turn slowly in place, so that he now appeared to be in the act of sliding or staggering while pushing himself backward like a creature blown before a gale. No wind, of course, could be felt, and presently the general climate quieted and nothing came of it all.

Early in the fifth century New Calendar three survey parties from the North Central Authority came through the area and stopped to observe the monster. A permanent recording device was set up at the site, after assurances to the townsfolk that no hardscience was involved. A local boy was trained to operate it; he quit when his girl left him but another volunteered. At this time nearly everyone believed that the apparition was a man, or the ghost of one. The record-machine boy and a few others including the school mechanics teacher referred to him as The Man John. In the next decades the roads were greatly improved; all forms of travel increased, and there was talk of building a canal to what had been the Snake River.

▼

One May morning at the end of Century Five a young couple in a smart green mule-trap came jogging up the highroad from the Sandreas Rift Range to the southwest. The girl was golden-skinned and chatted with her young husband in a language unlike that ever heard by The Man John either at the end or the beginning of his life. What she said to him has, however, been heard in every age and tongue.

"Oh, Serli, I'm so glad we're taking this trip now! Next summer I'll be busy with the baby!"

To which Serli replied as young husbands often have, and so they trotted up to the town's inn. Here they left trap and bags and went in search of her uncle, who was expecting them there. The morrow was the day of The Man John's annual appearance, and her Uncle

Laban had come from the MacKenzie History Museum to observe it and to make certain arrangements.

They found him with the town school instructor of mechanics, who was also the recorder at the monster-site. Presently Uncle Laban took them all with him to the town mayor's office to meet with various religious personages. The mayor was not unaware of tourist values, but he took Uncle Laban's part in securing the cultists' grudging assent to the MacKenzie authorities' secular interpretation of the monster, which was made easier by the fact that the cults disagreed among themselves. Then, seeing how pretty the niece was, the mayor took them all home to dinner.

When they returned to the inn for the night it was abrawl with holidaymakers.

"Whew," said Uncle Laban. "I've talked myself dry, sister's daughter. What a weight of holy nonsense is that Moksha female! Serli, my lad, I know you have questions. Let me hand you this to read, it's the guidebook we're giving them to sell. Tomorrow I'll answer for it all." And he disappeared into the crowded tavern.

So Serli and his bride took the pamphlet upstairs to bed with them, but it was not until the next morning at breakfast that they found time to read it.

"'All that is known of John Delgano,'" read Serli with his mouth full, "'comes from two documents left by his brother Carl Delgano in the archives of the MacKenzie Group in the early years after the holocaust.' Put some honey on this cake, Mira my dove. Verbatim transcript follows, this is Carl Delgano speaking:

"'I'm not an engineer or an astronaut like John, I ran an electronics repair shop in Salt Lake City. John was only trained as a spaceman, he never got to space; the slump wiped all that out. So he tied up with this commercial group who were leasing part of Bonneville. They wanted a man for some kind of hard vacuum tests, that's all I knew about it. John and his wife moved to Bonneville, but we all got together several times a year, our wives were like sisters. John had two kids, Clara and Paul.

"'The tests were supposed to be secret, but John told me confidentially they were trying for an antigravity chamber. I don't know if it ever worked. That was the year before.

"'Then that winter they came down for Christmas and John said they had something far out. He was excited. A temporal displacement, he called it; some kind of time effect. He said their chief honcho was like a real mad scientist. Big ideas. He kept adding more angles every time some other project would quit and leave equipment he could lease. No, I don't know who the top company was—maybe an insurance conglomerate, they had all the cash, didn't they? I guess they'd pay to catch a look at the future, that figures. Anyway, John was go, go, go. Katharine was scared, that's natural. She pictured him like, you know, H. G. Wells—walking around in some future world. John told her it wasn't like that at all. All they'd get would be this flicker, like a second or two. All kinds of complications.'—Yes, yes, my greedy piglet, some brew for me too. This is thirsty work!

"So. 'I remember I asked him, what about Earth moving? I mean, you could come back in a different place, right? He said they had that all figured. A spatial trajectory. Katharine was so scared we dropped it. John told her, don't worry. I'll come home. But he didn't. Not that it makes any difference, of course, everything was wiped out. Salt Lake too. The only reason I'm here is that I went up by Calgary to see Mom, April twenty-ninth. May second it all blew. I didn't find you folks at MacKenzie until July. I guess I may as well stay. That's all I know about John, except that he was a solid guy. If that accident started all this it wasn't his fault.

"'The second document'—in the name of love, little mother, do I have to read all this? Oh, very well, but you will kiss me first, madam. Must you look so delicious? 'The second document. Dated in the year eighteen, New Style, written by Carl'—see the old handwriting, my plump plump pigeon? Oh, very well, *very* well.

"'Written at Bonneville Crater: I have seen my brother John Delgano. When I knew I had the rad sickness I came down here to look around. Salt Lake's still hot. So I hiked up here by Bonneville. You can see the crater where the labs were, it's grassed over. It's different, not radioactive; my film's okay. There's a bare place in the middle. Some Indios here told me a monster shows up here every year in the spring. I saw it myself a couple of days after I got here, but I was too far away to see much, except I was sure it's a man. In a vacuum suit. There was a lot of noise and dust, took me by surprise. It was all over in a second. I figured it's pretty close to the day, I mean, May second, old.

"'So I hung around a year and he showed up again yesterday. I was on the face side, and I could see his face through the visor. It's John, all right. He's hurt. I saw blood on his mouth and his suit is frayed some. He's lying on the ground. He didn't move while I could see him but the dust boiled up, like a man sliding onto base without moving. His eyes are open like he was looking. I don't understand it anyway, but I know it's John, not a ghost. He was in exactly the same position each time and there's a loud crack like thunder and another sound like a siren, very fast. And an ozone smell, and smoke. I felt a kind of shudder.

"'I know it's John there and I think he's alive. I have to leave here now to take this back while I can still walk. I think somebody should come here and see. Maybe you can help John. Signed, Carl Delgano.'

"'These records were kept by the MacKenzie Group, but it was not for several years'—etcetera, first light-print, etcetera, archives, analysts, etcetera—very good! Now it is time to meet your uncle, my edible one, after we go upstairs for just a moment."

"No, Serli, I will wait for you downstairs," said Mira prudently.

------▼------

When they came into the town park Uncle Laban was directing the installation of a large durite slab in front of the enclosure around The Man John's appearance-spot. The slab was wrapped in a curtain to await the official unveiling. Townspeople and tourists and children thronged the walks, and a Ride-for-God choir was singing in the band shell. The morning was warming up fast. Vendors hawked ices and straw toys of the monster and flowers and good-luck confetti to throw at him. Another religious group stood by in dark robes; they belonged to the Repentance church beyond the park. Their pastor was directing somber glares at the crowd in general and Mira's uncle in particular.

Three official-looking strangers who had been at the inn came up and introduced themselves to Uncle Laban as observers from Alberta

Central. They went on into the tent which had been erected over the closure, carrying with them several pieces of equipment which the townsfolk eyed suspiciously.

The mechanics teacher finished organizing a squad of students to protect the slab's curtain, and Mira and Serli and Laban went on into the tent. It was much hotter inside. Benches were set in rings around a railed enclosure about twenty feet in diameter. Inside the railing the earth was bare and scuffed. Several bunches of flowers and blooming poinciana branches leaned against the rail. The only thing inside the rail was a rough sandstone rock with markings etched on it.

Just as they came in, a small girl raced across the open center and was yelled at by everybody. The officials from Alberta were busy at one side of the rail, where the light-print box was mounted.

"Oh, no," muttered Mira's uncle, as one of the officials leaned over to set up a tripod stand inside the rails. He adjusted it, and a huge horsetail of fine feathery filaments blossomed out and eddied through the center of the space.

"Oh, *no*," Laban said again. "Why can't they let it be?"

"They're trying to pick up dust from his suit, is that right?" Serli asked.

"Yes, insane. Did you get time to read?"

"Oh, yes," said Serli.

"Sort of," added Mira.

"Then you know. He's falling. Trying to check his—well, call it velocity. Trying to slow down. He must have slipped or stumbled. We're getting pretty close to when he lost his footing and started to fall. What did it? Did somebody trip him?" Laban looked from Mira to Serli, dead serious now. "How would you like to be the one who made John Delgano fall?"

"Ooh," said Mira in quick sympathy. Then she said, "Oh."

"You mean," asked Serli, "whoever made him fall caused all the, caused—"

"Possible," said Laban.

"Wait a minute." Serli frowned. "He did fall. So somebody had to do it—I mean, he has to trip or whatever. If he doesn't fall the past would all be changed, wouldn't it? No war, no—"

"Possible," Laban repeated. "God knows. All *I* know is that John Delgano and the space around him is the most unstable, improbable, highly charged area ever known on Earth, and I'm damned if I think anybody should go poking sticks in it."

"Oh, come now, Laban!" One of the Alberta men joined them, smiling. "Our dust mop couldn't trip a gnat. It's just vitreous monofilaments."

"Dust from the future," grumbled Laban. "What's it going to tell you? That the future has dust in it?"

"If we could only get a trace from that thing in his hand."

"In his hand?" asked Mira. Serli started leafing hurriedly through the pamphlet.

"We've had a recording analyzer aimed at it," the Albertan lowered his voice, glancing around. "A spectroscope. We know there's something there, or was. Can't get a decent reading. It's severely deteriorated."

"People poking at him, grabbing at him," Laban muttered. "You—"

"TEN MINUTES!" shouted a man with a megaphone. "Take your places, friends and strangers."

The Repentance people were filing in at one side, intoning an ancient incantation, "Mi-seri-cordia, Ora pro nobis!"

The atmosphere suddenly became tense. It was now very close and hot in the big tent. A boy from the mayor's office wiggled through the crowd, beckoning Laban's party to come and sit in the guest chairs on the second level on the "face" side. In front of them at the rail one of the Repentance ministers was arguing with an Albertan official over his right to occupy space taken by a recorder, it being his special duty to look into The Man John's eyes.

"Can he really see us?" Mira asked her uncle.

"Blink your eyes," Laban told her. "A new scene every blink, that's what he sees. Phantasmagoria. Blink-blink-blink—for god knows how long."

"Mi-sere-re, pec-cavi," chanted the penitentials. A soprano neighed. "May the red of sin pa-aa-ass from us!"

"They believe his oxygen tab went red because of the state of their souls," Laban chuckled. "Their souls are going to have to stay damned awhile; John Delgano has been on oxygen reserve for five centuries—or rather, he *will be* low for five centuries more. At a half-second per year his time, that's fifteen minutes. We know from the audio trace he's still breathing more or less normally, and the reserve was good for twenty minutes. So they should have their salvation about the year seven hundred, if they last that long."

"FIVE MINUTES! Take your seats, folks. Please sit down so everyone can see. Sit down, folks."

"It says we'll hear his voice through his suit speaker," Serli whispered. "Do you know what he's saying?"

"You get mostly a twenty-cycle howl," Laban whispered back. "The recorders have spliced up something like *ayt*, part of an old word. Take centuries to get enough to translate."

"Is it a message?"

"Who knows? Could be his word for 'date' or 'hate.' 'Too late,' maybe. Anything."

The tent was quieting. A fat child by the railing started to cry and was pulled back onto a lap. There was a subdued mumble of praying. The Holy Joy faction on the far side rustled their flowers.

"Why don't we set our clocks by him?"

"It's changing. He's on sidereal time."

"ONE MINUTE."

In the hush the praying voices rose slightly. From outside a chicken cackled. The bare center space looked absolutely ordinary. Over it the recorder's silvery filaments eddied gently in the breath from a hundred lungs. Another recorder could be heard ticking faintly.

For long seconds nothing happened.

The air developed a tiny hum. At the same moment Mira caught a movement at the railing on her left.

The hum developed a beat and vanished into a peculiar silence and suddenly everything happened at once.

Sound burst on them, raced shockingly up the audible scale. The air cracked as something rolled and tumbled in the space. There was a grinding, wailing roar and—

He was there.

Solid, huge—a huge man in a monster-suit, his head was a dull bronze transparent globe, holding a human face, a dark smear of open mouth. His position was impossible, legs strained forward thrusting himself back, his arms frozen in a whirlwind swing. Although he seemed to be in frantic forward motion nothing moved, only one of his legs buckled or sagged slightly—

—And then he was gone, utterly and completely gone in a thunderclap, leaving only the incredible afterimage in a hundred pairs of staring eyes. Air boomed, shuddering; dust rolled out mixed with smoke.

"Oh! Oh, my god," gasped Mira, unheard, clinging to Serli. Voices were crying out, choking. "He saw me, he saw me!" a woman shrieked. A few people dazedly threw their confetti into the empty dust-cloud, most had failed to throw at all. Children began to howl. "He *saw* me!" the woman screamed hysterically. "Red, oh, Lord have mercy!" a deep male voice intoned.

Mira heard Laban swearing furiously and looked again into the space. As the dust settled she could see that the recorder's tripod had tipped over into the center. There was a dusty mound lying against it—flowers. Most of the end of the stand seemed to have disappeared or been melted. Of the filaments nothing could be seen.

"Some damn fool pitched flowers into it. Come on, let's get out."

"Was it under, did it trip him?" asked Mira, squeezed in the crowd.

"It was still red, his oxygen thing," Serli said over her head. "No mercy this trip, eh, Laban?"

"Shsh!" Mira caught the Repentance pastor's dark glance. They jostled through the enclosure gate and were out in the sunlit park, voices exclaiming, chattering loudly in excitement and relief.

"It was terrible," Mira cried softly. "Oh, I never thought it was a real live man. There he is, he's *there.* Why can't we help him? Did we trip him?"

"I don't know, I don't think so," her uncle grunted. They sat down near the new monument, fanning themselves. The curtain was still in place.

"Did we change the past?" Serli laughed, looked lovingly at his little wife. For a moment he wondered why she was wearing such odd earrings; then he remembered he had given them to her at that Indian pueblo they'd passed.

"But it wasn't just those Alberta people," said Mira. She seemed obsessed with the idea. "It was the flowers really." She wiped at her forehead.

"Mechanics or superstition," chuckled Serli. "Which is the culprit, love or science?"

"Shsh." Mira looked about nervously. "The flowers were love, I guess. . . . I feel so strange. It's hot. Oh, thank you." Uncle Laban had succeeded in attracting the attention of the iced-drink vendor.

People were chatting normally now, and the choir struck into a cheerful song. At one side of the park a line of people were waiting to sign their names in the visitors' book. The mayor appeared at the park gate, leading a party up the bougainvillea alley for the unveiling of the monument.

"What did it say on that stone by his foot?" Mira asked. Serli showed her the guidebook picture of Carl's rock with the inscription translated below: WELCOME HOME JOHN.

"I wonder if he can see it."

The mayor was about to begin his speech.

Much later when the crowd had gone away the monument stood alone in the dark, displaying to the moon the inscription in the language of that time and place:

ON THIS SPOT THERE APPEARS ANNUALLY THE FORM OF MAJOR JOHN DELGANO, THE FIRST AND ONLY MAN TO TRAVEL IN TIME.

MAJOR DELGANO WAS SENT INTO THE FUTURE SOME HOURS BEFORE THE HOLOCAUST OF DAY ZERO. ALL KNOWLEDGE OF THE MEANS BY WHICH HE WAS SENT IS LOST, PERHAPS FOREVER. IT IS BELIEVED THAT AN ACCIDENT OCCURRED WHICH SENT HIM MUCH FARTHER THAN WAS

INTENDED. SOME ANALYSTS SPECULATE THAT HE MAY HAVE GONE AS FAR AS FIFTY THOUSAND YEARS AHEAD. HAVING REACHED THIS UNKNOWN POINT MAJOR DELGANO APPARENTLY WAS RECALLED, OR ATTEMPTED TO RETURN, ALONG THE COURSE IN SPACE AND TIME THROUGH WHICH HE WAS SENT. HIS TRAJECTORY IS THOUGHT TO START AT THE POINT WHICH OUR SOLAR SYSTEM WILL OCCUPY AT A FUTURE TIME AND IS TANGENT TO THE COMPLEX HELIX WHICH OUR EARTH DESCRIBES AROUND THE SUN.

HE APPEARS ON THIS SPOT IN THE ANNUAL INSTANTS IN WHICH HIS COURSE INTERSECTS OUR PLANET'S ORBIT, AND HE IS APPARENTLY ABLE TO TOUCH THE GROUND IN THOSE INSTANTS. SINCE NO TRACE OF HIS PASSAGE INTO THE FUTURE HAS BEEN MANIFESTED, IT IS BELIEVED THAT HE IS RETURNING BY A DIFFERENT MEANS THAN HE WENT FORWARD. HE IS ALIVE IN OUR PRESENT. OUR PAST IS HIS FUTURE AND OUR FUTURE IS HIS PAST. THE TIME OF HIS APPEARANCES IS SHIFTING GRADUALLY IN SOLAR TIME TO CONVERGE ON THE MOMENT OF 1153.6, ON MAY 2, 1989 OLD STYLE, OR DAY ZERO.

THE EXPLOSION WHICH ACCOMPANIED HIS RETURN TO HIS OWN TIME AND PLACE MAY HAVE OCCURRED WHEN SOME ELEMENTS OF THE PAST INSTANTS OF HIS COURSE WERE CARRIED WITH HIM INTO THEIR OWN PRIOR EXISTENCE. IT IS CERTAIN THAT THIS EXPLOSION PRECIPITATED THE WORLDWIDE HOLOCAUST WHICH ENDED FOREVER THE AGE OF HARD-SCIENCE.

—He was falling, losing control, failing in his fight against the terrible momentum he had gained, fighting with his human legs shaking in the inhuman stiffness of his armor, his soles charred, not gripping well now, not enough traction to break, battling, thrusting as the flashes came, the punishing alternation of light, dark, light, dark, which he had borne so long, the claps of air thickening and thinning against his armor as he skidded through space which was time, desperately braking as the flicker of Earth hammered against his feet—only his feet mattered now, only to slow and stay on course—and the pull, the beacon was getting slacker; as he came near home it was fanning out, hard to stay centered; he was becoming, he supposed, more probably; the wound he had punched in time was healing itself. In the beginning it had been so tight—a single ray of light in a closing tunnel—he had hurled himself after it like an electron flying to the

anode, aimed surely along that exquisitely complex single vector of possibility of life, shot and been shot like a squeezed pip into the last chink in that rejecting and rejected nowhere through which he, John Delgano, could conceivably continue to exist, the hole leading to home—had pounded down it across time, across space, pumping with desperate legs as the real Earth of that unreal time came under him, his course as certain as the twisting dash of an animal down its burrow, he a cosmic mouse on an interstellar, intertemporal race for his nest with the wrongness of everything closing round the rightness of that one course, the atoms of his heart, his blood, his every cell crying Home—HOME!—as he drove himself after that fading breath-hole, each step faster, surer, stronger, until he raced with invincible momentum upon the rolling flickers of Earth as a man might race a rolling log in a torrent. Only the stars stayed constant around him from flash to flash, he looking down past his feet at a million strobes of Crux, of Triangulum; once at the height of his stride he had risked a century's glance upward and seen the Bears weirdly strung out from Polaris—but a Polaris not the Pole Star now, he realized, jerking his eyes back to his racing feet, thinking, I am walking home to Polaris, home! to the strobing beat. He had ceased to remember where he had been, the beings, people or aliens or things, he had glimpsed in the impossible moment of being where he could not be; had ceased to see the flashes of worlds around him, each flash different, the jumble of bodies, shapes, walls, colors, landscapes—some lasting a breath, some changing pell-mell—the faces, limbs, things poking at him; the nights he had pounded through, dark or lit by strange lamps, roofed or unroofed; the days flashing sunlight, gales, dust, snow, interiors innumerable, strobe after strobe into night again; he was in daylight now, a hall of some kind; I am getting closer at last, he thought, the feel is changing— but he had to slow down, to check; and that stone near his feet, it had stayed there some time now, he wanted to risk a look but he did not dare, he was so tired, and he was sliding, was going out of control, fighting to kill the merciless velocity that would not let him slow down; he was hurt, too, something had hit him back there, they had done something, he didn't know what, back somewhere in the kaleidoscope of faces, arms, hooks, beams, centuries of creatures grabbing at him—and his oxygen was going, never mind, it would last—it had to last, he was going home, home! And he had forgotten now the message he had tried to shout, hoping it could be picked up somehow, the important thing he had repeated; and the thing he had carried, it was gone now, his camera was gone, too, something had torn it away—but he was coming home! Home! If only he could kill this momentum, could stay on the failing course, could slip, scramble, slide, somehow ride this avalanche down to home, to home—and his throat said Home!—called Kate, Kate! And his heart shouted, his lungs almost gone now, as his legs fought, fought and failed, as his feet gripped and skidded and held and slid, as he pitched, flailed, pushed, strove in the gale of time-rush across space, across time, at the end of the longest path ever: the path of John Delgano, coming home.

Interview with a Lemming

JAMES THURBER

James Thurber was one of the greatest humorists of the twentieth century. In his fiction, poetry, and cartoons he ruthlessly lambasted the human race for its failings, but was always funny as he applied his sharp wit to overinflated egos, concepts, or institutions. Perhaps his most famous work is the oft-reprinted short story "The Secret Life of Walter Mitty."

His work appeared often in *The New Yorker* magazine, and he was a great part of the magazine's reputation. He was even a part of their offices, and when they moved from one location to another, they literally brought with them walls on which he had scribbled cartoons.

Lemmings have long suffered from a bad reputation, but I wouldn't say that Thurber was out to right this wrong when he wrote "Interview with a Lemming" in 1942. I think it more likely that he thought humans were not so different from the poor little mouselike creatures. The result, I'm sure you'll agree, is a delight.

The weary scientist, trampling through the mountains of northern Europe in the winter weather, dropped his knapsack and prepared to sit on a rock.

"Careful, brother," said a voice.

"Sorry," murmured the scientist, noting with some surprise that a lemming which he had been about to sit on had addressed him. "It is a source of considerable astonishment to me," said the scientist, sitting down beside the lemming, "that you are capable of speech."

"You human beings are always astonished," said the lemming, "when any other animal can do anything you can. Yet there are many things animals can do that you cannot, such as stridulate, or chirr, to name just one. To stridulate, or chirr, one of the minor achievements of the cricket, your species is dependent on the intestines of the sheep and the hair of the horse."

"We are a dependent animal," admitted the scientist.

"You are an amazing animal," said the lemming.

"We have always considered you rather amazing, too," said the scientist. "You are perhaps the most mysterious of creatures."

"If we are going to indulge in adjectives beginning with 'm,'" said the lemming, sharply, "let me apply a few to your species— murderous, maladjusted, maleficent, malicious and muffle-headed."

"You find our behavior as difficult to understand as we do yours?"

"You, as you would say, said it," said the lemming. "You kill, you mangle, you torture, you imprison, you starve each other. You cover the nurturing earth with cement, you cut down elm trees to put up institutions for people driven insane by the cutting down of elm trees, you—"

"You could go on all night like that," said the scientist, "listing our sins and our shames."

"I could go on all night and up to four o'clock tomorrow after-noon," said the lemming. "It just happens that I have made a life-long study of the self-styled higher animal. Except for one thing, I know all there is to know about you, and a singularly dreary, dolor-ous and distasteful store of information it is, too, to use only adjec-tives beginning with 'd.'"

"You say you have made a lifelong study of my species—" began the scientist.

"Indeed I have," broke in the lemming. "I know that you are cruel, cunning and carnivorous, sly, sensual and selfish, greedy, gullible and guileful—"

"Pray don't wear yourself out," said the scientist, quietly. "It may interest you to know that I have made a lifelong study of lem-mings, just as you have made a lifelong study of people. Like you, I have found but one thing about my subject which I am not able to understand."

"And what is that?" asked the lemming.

"I don't understand," said the scientist, "why you lemmings all rush down to the sea and drown yourselves."

"How curious," said the lemming. "The one thing I don't understand is why you human beings don't."

The Last Question

ISAAC ASIMOV

It's only fitting that the last story in this book should be one by Isaac Asimov. There was a period in Asimov's career when he tackled a lot of major questions, and he especially delighted in speculating about computers and how they would develop in the future. It was almost inevitable that he would write a story with this title. That doesn't mean that I'm going to give away the ending. You'll have to read for yourself to find out the answer.

Though he wrote far more non-fiction (mostly about science), Asimov always considered himself first and foremost a science fiction writer. SF was what inspired him to become a writer, and he was in love with the wondrous future he held in his imagination. He wrote many short stories and more than a dozen novels, including *The Caves of Steel* (a mystery set in a marvelously imagined future New York) and his most famous work, *The Foundation Trilogy*, a long series of stories that became world renowned, even winning a Hugo for "Best All-Time SF Series." "The Last Question" was first published in 1956. The science may seem a bit dated because of certain elements of scale, but the story remains no less full of wonder. It is reprinted from a collection of Asimov's stories, *Nine Tomorrows*, which I recommend as a marvelous introduction to Asimov's SF and the field in general.

The last question was asked for the first time, half in jest, on May 21, 2061, at a time when humanity first stepped into the light. The question came about as a result of a five-dollar bet over highballs, and it happened this way:

Alexander Adell and Bertram Lupov were two of the faithful attendants of Multivac. As well as any human beings could, they knew what lay behind the cold, clicking, flashing face—miles and miles of face—of that giant computer. They had at least a vague notion of the general plan of relays and circuits that had long since grown past the point where any single human could possibly have a firm grasp of the whole.

Multivac was self-adjusting and self-correcting. It had to be, for nothing human could adjust and correct it quickly enough or even adequately enough. —So Adell and Lupov attended the monstrous giant only lightly and superficially, yet as well as any men could. They fed it data, adjusted questions to its needs and translated the answers that were issued. Certainly they, and all others like them, were fully entitled to share in the glory that was Multivac's.

For decades, Multivac had helped design the ships and plot the trajectories that enabled men to reach the Moon, Mars, and Venus, but past that, Earth's poor resources could not support the ships. Too much energy was needed for the long trips. Earth exploited its coal and uranium with increasing efficiency, but there was only so much of both.

But slowly Multivac learned enough to answer deeper questions more fundamentally, and on May 14, 2061, what had been theory, became fact.

The energy of the sun was stored, converted, and utilized directly on a planet-wide scale. All Earth turned off its burning coal, its fissioning uranium, and flipped the switch that connected all of it to a small station, one mile in diameter, circling the Earth at half the distance of the Moon. All Earth ran by invisible beams of sunpower.

Seven days had not sufficed to dim the glory of it and Adell and Lupov finally managed to escape from the public function, and to meet in quiet where no one would think of looking for them, in the deserted underground chambers, where portions of the mighty buried body of Multivac showed. Unattended, idling, sorting data with contented lazy clickings, Multivac, too, had earned its vacation and the boys appreciated that. They had no intention, originally, of disturbing it.

They had brought a bottle with them, and their only concern at the moment was to relax in the company of each other and the bottle.

"It's amazing when you think of it," said Adell. His broad face had lines of weariness in it, and he stirred his drink slowly with a glass rod, watching the cubes of ice slur clumsily about. "All the energy we can possibly ever use for free. Enough energy, if we wanted to draw on it, to melt all Earth into a big drop of impure liquid iron, and still never miss the energy so used. All the energy we could ever use, forever and forever and forever."

Lupov cocked his head sideways. He had a trick of doing that when he wanted to be contrary, and he wanted to be contrary now, partly because he had had to carry the ice and glassware. "Not forever," he said.

"Oh, hell, just about forever. Till the sun runs down, Bert."

"That's not forever."

"All right, then. Billions and billions of years. Twenty billion, maybe. Are you satisfied?"

Lupov put his fingers through his thinning hair as though to reassure himself that some was still left and sipped gently at his own drink. "Twenty billion years isn't forever."

"Well, it will last our time, won't it?"

"So would the coal and uranium."

"All right, but now we can hook up each individual spaceship to the Solar Station, and it can go to Pluto and back a million times without ever worrying about fuel. You can't do *that* on coal and uranium. Ask Multivac, if you don't believe me."

"I don't have to ask Multivac. I know that."

"Then stop running down what Multivac's done for us," said Adell, blazing up. "It did all right."

"Who says it didn't? What I say is that a sun won't last forever. That's all I'm saying. We're safe for twenty billion years, but then what?" Lupov pointed a slightly shaky finger at the other. "And don't say we'll switch to another sun."

There was silence for a while. Adell put his glass to his lips only occasionally, and Lupov's eyes slowly closed. They rested.

Then Lupov's eyes snapped open. "You're thinking we'll switch to another sun when ours is done, aren't you?"

"I'm not thinking."

"Sure you are. You're weak on logic, that's the trouble with you. You're like the guy in the story who was caught in a sudden shower and who ran to a grove of trees and got under one. He wasn't worried, you see, because he figured when one tree got wet through, he would just get under another one."

"I get it," said Adell. "Don't shout. When the sun is done, the other stars will be gone, too."

"Darn right they will," muttered Lupov. "It all had a beginning in the original cosmic explosion, whatever that was, and it'll all have an end when all the stars run down. Some run down faster than others. Hell, the giants won't last a hundred million years. The sun will last twenty billion years and maybe the dwarfs will last a hundred billion for all the good they are. But just give us a trillion years and everything will be dark. Entropy has to increase to maximum, that's all."

"I know all about entropy," said Adell, standing on his dignity.

"The hell you do."

"I know as much as you do."

"Then you know everything's got to run down someday."

"All right. Who says they won't?"

"You did, you poor sap. You said we had all the energy we needed, forever. You said 'forever.'"

It was Adell's turn to be contrary. "Maybe we can build things up again someday," he said.

"Never."

"Why not? Someday."

"Never."

"Ask Multivac."

"*You* ask Multivac. I dare you. Five dollars says it can't be done."

Adell was just drunk enough to try, just sober enough to be able to phrase the necessary symbols and operations into a question which, in words, might have corresponded to this: Will mankind one day without the net expenditure of energy be able to restore the sun to its full youthfulness even after it had died of old age?

Or maybe it could be put more simply like this: How can the net amount of entropy of the universe be massively decreased?

Multivac fell dead and silent. The slow flashing of lights ceased, the distant sounds of clicking relays ended.

Then, just as the frightened technicians felt they could hold their breath no longer, there was a sudden springing to life of the teletype attached to that portion of Multivac. Five words were printed: INSUF-FICIENT DATA FOR MEANINGFUL ANSWER.

"No bet," whispered Lupov. They left hurriedly.

By next morning, the two, plagued with throbbing head and cottony mouth, had forgotten the incident.

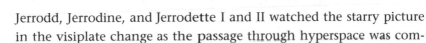

Jerrodd, Jerrodine, and Jerrodette I and II watched the starry picture in the visiplate change as the passage through hyperspace was completed in its non-time lapse. At once, the even powdering of stars gave way to the predominance of a single bright marble-disk, centered.

"That's X-23," said Jerrodd confidently. His thin hands clamped tightly behind his back and the knuckles whitened.

The little Jerrodettes, both girls, had experienced the hyperspace passage for the first time in their lives and were self-conscious over the momentary sensation of inside-outness. They buried their giggles and chased one another wildly about their mother, screaming, "We've reached X-23—we've reached X-23—we've—"

"Quiet, children," said Jerrodine sharply. "Are you sure, Jerrodd?"

"What is there to be but sure?" asked Jerrodd, glancing at the bulge of featureless metal just under the ceiling. It ran the length of the room, disappearing through the wall at either end. It was as long as the ship.

Jerrodd scarcely knew a thing about the thick rod of metal except that it was called a Microvac, that one asked it questions if one wished; that if one did not it still had its task of guiding the ship to a preordered destination; of feeding on energies from the various

Sub-galactic Power Stations; of computing the equations for the hyper-spatial jumps.

Jerrodd and his family had only to wait and live in the comfort-able residence quarters of the ship.

Someone had once told Jerrodd that the "ac" at the end of "Microvac" stood for "analog computer" in ancient English, but he was on the edge of forgetting even that.

Jerrodine's eyes were moist as she watched the visiplate. "I can't help it. I feel funny about leaving Earth."

"Why, for Pete's sake?" demanded Jerrodd. "We had nothing there. We'll have everything on X-23. You won't be alone. You won't be a pioneer. There are over a million people on the planet already. Good Lord, our great-grandchildren will be looking for new worlds because X-23 will be overcrowded." Then, after a reflective pause, "I tell you, it's a lucky thing the computers worked out interstellar travel the way the race is growing."

"I know, I know," said Jerrodine miserably.

Jerrodette I said promptly, "Our Microvac is the best Microvac in the world."

"I think so, too," said Jerrodd, tousling her hair.

It *was* a nice feeling to have a Microvac of your own and Jerrodd was glad he was part of his generation and no other. In his father's youth, the only computers had been tremendous machines taking up a hundred square miles of land. There was only one to a planet. Plan-etary ACS they were called. They had been growing in size steadily for a thousand years and then, all at once, came refinement. In place of transistors had come molecular valves so that even the largest Plane-tary AC could be put into a space only half the volume of a spaceship.

Jerrodd felt uplifted, as he always did when he thought that his own personal Microvac was many times more complicated than the ancient and primitive Multivac that had first tamed the Sun, and almost complicated as Earth's Planetary AC (the largest) that had first solved the problem of hyperspatial travel and had made trips to the stars possible.

"So many stars, so many planets," sighed Jerrodine, busy with her own thoughts. "I suppose families will be going out to new planets forever, the way we are now."

"Not forever," said Jerrodd, with a smile. "It will all stop someday, but not for billions of years. Many billions. Even the stars run down, you know. Entropy must increase."

"What's entropy, daddy?" shrilled Jerrodette II.

"Entropy, little sweet, is just a word which means the amount of running-down of the universe. Everything runs down, you know, like your little walkie-talkie robot, remember?"

"Can't you just put in a new power-unit, like with my robot?"

"The stars *are* the power-units, dear. Once they're gone, there are no more power-units."

Jerrodette I at once set up a howl. "Don't let them, daddy. Don't let the stars run down."

"Now look what you've done," whispered Jerrodine, exasperated.

"How was I to know it would frighten them?" Jerrodd whispered back.

"Ask the Microvac," wailed Jerrodette I. "Ask him how to turn the stars on again."

"Go ahead," said Jerrodine. "It will quiet them down." (Jerrodette II was beginning to cry, also.)

Jerrodd shrugged. "Now, now, honeys. I'll ask Microvac. Don't worry, he'll tell us."

He asked Microvac, adding quickly, "Print the answer."

Jerrodd cupped the strip of thin cellufilm and said cheerfully, "See now, the Microvac says it will take care of everything when the time comes so don't worry."

Jerrodine said, "And now, children, it's time for bed. We'll be in our new home soon."

Jerrodd read the words on the cellufilm again before destroying it: INSUFFICIENT DATA FOR A MEANINGFUL ANSWER.

He shrugged and looked at the visiplate. X-23 was just ahead.

▼

VJ-23X of Lameth stared into the black depths of the three-dimensional, small-scale map of the Galaxy and said, "Are we ridiculous, I wonder, in being so concerned about the matter?"

MQ-17J of Nicron shook his head. "I think not. You know the Galaxy will be filled in five years at the present rate of expansion."

Both seemed in their early twenties, both were tall and perfectly formed.

"Still," said VJ-23X, "I hesitate to submit a pessimistic report to the Galactic Council."

"I wouldn't consider any other kind of report. Stir them up a bit. We've got to stir them up."

VJ-23X sighed. "Space is infinite. A hundred billion Galaxies are there for the taking. More."

"A hundred billion is *not* infinite and it's getting less infinite all the time. Consider! Twenty thousand years ago, mankind first solved the problem of utilizing stellar energy, and a few centuries later, interstellar travel became possible. It took mankind a million years to fill one small world and then only fifteen thousand years to fill the rest of the Galaxy. Now the population doubles every ten years—"

VJ-23X interrupted. "We can thank immortality for that."

"Very well. Immortality exists and we have to take it into account. I admit it has its seamy side, this immortality. The Galactic AC has solved many problems for us, but in solving the problem of preventing old age and death, it has undone all its other solutions."

"Yet you wouldn't want to abandon life, I suppose."

"Not at all," snapped MQ-17J, softening it at once to, "Not yet. I'm by no means old enough. How old are you?"

"Two hundred twenty-three. And you?"

"I'm still under two hundred. —But to get back to my point. Population doubles every ten years. Once this Galaxy is filled, we'll have filled another in ten years. Another ten years and we'll have filled two more. Another decade, four more. In a hundred years, we'll have filled a thousand Galaxies. In a thousand years, a million Galaxies. In ten thousand years, the entire known Universe. Then what?"

VJ-23X said, "As a side issue, there's a problem of transportation. I wonder how many sunpower units it will take to move Galaxies of individuals from one Galaxy to the next."

"A very good point. Already, mankind consumes two sunpower units per year."

"Most of it's wasted. After all, our own Galaxy alone pours out a thousand sunpower units a year and we only use two of those."

"Granted, but even with a hundred percent efficiency, we only stave off the end. Our energy requirements are going up in a geometric progression even faster than our population. We'll run out of energy even sooner than we run out of Galaxies. A good point. A very good point."

"We'll just have to build new stars out of interstellar gas."

"Or out of dissipated heat?" asked MQ-17J, sarcastically.

"There may be some way to reverse entropy. We ought to ask the Galactic AC."

VJ-23X was not really serious, but MQ-17J pulled out his AC-contact from his pocket and placed it on the table before him.

"I've half a mind to," he said. "It's something the human race will have to face someday."

He stared somberly at his small AC-contact. It was only two inches cubed and nothing in itself, but it was connected through hyperspace with the great Galactic AC that served all mankind. Hyperspace considered, it was an integral part of the Galactic AC.

MQ-17J paused to wonder if someday in his immortal life he would get to see the Galactic AC. It was on a little world of its own, a spider webbing of force-beams holding the matter within which surges of sub-mesons took the place of the old clumsy molecular valves. Yet despite its sub-etheric workings, the Galactic AC was known to be a full thousand feet across.

MQ-17J asked suddenly of his AC-contact, "Can entropy ever be reversed?"

VJ-23X looked startled and said at once, "Oh, say, I didn't really mean to have you ask that."

"Why not?"

"We both know entropy can't be reversed. You can't turn smoke and ash back into a tree."

"Do you have trees on your world?" asked MQ-17J.

The sound of the Galactic AC startled them into silence. Its voice came thin and beautiful out of the small AC-contact on the desk. It said: THERE IS INSUFFICIENT DATA FOR A MEANINGFUL ANSWER.

VJ-23X said, "See!"

The two men thereupon returned to the question of the report they were to make to the Galactic Council.

Zee Prime's mind spanned the new Galaxy with a faint interest in the countless twists of stars that powdered it. He had never seen this one before. Would he ever see them all? So many of them, each with its load of humanity. —But a load that was almost a dead weight. More and more, the real essence of men was to be found out here, in space.

Minds, not bodies! The immortal bodies remained back on the planets, in suspension over the eons. Sometimes they roused for material activity but that was growing rarer. Few new individuals were coming into existence to join the incredibly mighty throng, but what matter? There was little room in the Universe for new individuals.

Zee Prime was roused out of his reverie upon coming across the wispy tendrils of another mind.

"I am Zee Prime," said Zee Prime. "And you?"

"I am Dee Sub Wun. Your Galaxy?"

"We call it only the Galaxy. And you?"

"We call ours the same. All men call their Galaxy their Galaxy and nothing more. Why not?"

"True. Since all Galaxies are the same."

"Not all Galaxies. On one particular Galaxy the race of man must have originated. That makes it different."

Zee Prime said, "On which one?"

"I cannot say. The Universal AC would know."

"Shall we ask him? I am suddenly curious."

Zee Prime's perceptions broadened until the Galaxies themselves shrank and became a new, more diffuse powdering on a much larger background. So many hundreds of billions of them, all with their immortal beings, all carrying their load of intelligences with minds that drifted freely through space. And yet one of them was unique among them all in being the original Galaxy. One of them had, in its vague and distant past, a period when it was the only Galaxy populated by man.

Zee Prime was consumed with curiosity to see this Galaxy and he called out: "Universal AC! On which Galaxy did mankind originate?"

The Universal AC heard, for on every world and throughout space, it had its receptors ready, and each receptor led through hyperspace to some unknown point where the Universal AC kept itself aloof.

Zee Prime knew of only one man whose thoughts had penetrated within sensing distance of Universal AC, and he reported only a shining globe, two feet across, difficult to see.

"But how can that be all of Universal AC?" Zee Prime had asked.

"Most of it," had been the answer, "is in hyperspace. In what form it is there I cannot imagine."

Nor could anyone, for the day had long since passed, Zee Prime knew, when any man had any part of the making of a Universal AC. Each Universal AC designed and constructed its successor. Each, during its existence of a million years or more accumulated the necessary data to build a better and more intricate, more capable successor in which its own store of data and individuality would be submerged.

The Universal AC interrupted Zee Prime's wandering thoughts, not with words, but with guidance. Zee Prime's mentality was guided into the dim sea of Galaxies and one in particular enlarged into stars.

A thought came, infinitely distant, but infinitely clear. "THIS IS THE ORIGINAL GALAXY OF MAN."

But it was the same after all, the same as any other, and Zee Prime stifled his disappointment.

Dee Sub Wun, whose mind had accompanied the other, said suddenly, "And is one of these stars the original star of Man?"

The Universal AC said, "MAN'S ORIGINAL STAR HAS GONE NOVA. IT IS A WHITE DWARF."

"Did the men upon it die?" asked Zee Prime, startled and without thinking.

The Universal AC said, "A NEW WORLD, AS IN SUCH CASES, WAS CONSTRUCTED FOR THEIR PHYSICAL BODIES IN TIME."

"Yes, of course," said Zee Prime, but a sense of loss overwhelmed him even so. His mind released its hold on the original Galaxy of Man, let it spring back and lose itself among the blurred pin points. He never wanted to see it again.

Dee Sub Wun said, "What is wrong?"

"The stars are dying. The original star is dead."

"They must all die. Why not?"

"But when all energy is gone, our bodies will finally die, and you and I with them."

"It will take billions of years."

"I do not wish it to happen even after billions of years. Universal AC! How may stars be kept from dying?"

Dee Sub Wun said in amusement, "You're asking how entropy might be reversed in direction."

And the Universal AC answered: "THERE IS AS YET INSUFFICIENT DATA FOR A MEANINGFUL ANSWER."

Zee Prime's thoughts fled back to his own Galaxy. He gave no further thought to Dee Sub Wun, whose body might be waiting on a Galaxy a trillion light-years away, or on the star next to Zee Prime's own. It didn't matter.

Unhappily, Zee Prime began collecting interstellar hydrogen out of which to build a small star of his own. If the stars must someday die, at least some could yet be built.

▼

Man considered with himself, for in a way, Man, mentally, was one. He consisted of a trillion, trillion, trillion ageless bodies, each in its place, each resting quiet and incorruptible, each cared for by perfect automatons, equally incorruptible, while the minds of all the bodies freely melted one into the other, indistinguishable.

Man said, "The Universe is dying."

Man looked about at the dimming Galaxies. The giant stars, spendthrifts, were gone long ago, back in the dimmest of the dim far past. Almost all stars were white dwarfs, fading to the end.

New stars had been built of the dust between the stars, some by natural processes, some by Man himself, and those were going, too. White dwarfs might yet be crashed together and of the mighty forces so released, new stars built, but only one star for every thousand white dwarfs destroyed, and those would come to an end, too.

Man said, "Carefully husbanded, as directed by the Cosmic AC, the energy that is even yet left in all the Universe will last for billions of years."

"But even so," said Man, "eventually it will all come to an end. However it may be husbanded, however stretched out, the energy once expended is gone and cannot be restored. Entropy must increase forever to the maximum."

Man said, "Can entropy not be reversed? Let us ask the Cosmic AC."

The Cosmic AC surrounded them but not in space. Not a fragment of it was in space. It was in hyperspace and made of something that was neither matter nor energy. The question of its size and nature no longer had meaning in any terms that Man could comprehend.

"Cosmic AC," said Man, "how may entropy be reversed?"

The Cosmic AC said, "THERE IS AS YET INSUFFICIENT DATA FOR A MEANINGFUL ANSWER."

Man said, "Collect additional data."

The Cosmic AC said, "I WILL DO SO. I HAVE BEEN DOING SO FOR A HUNDRED BILLION YEARS. MY PREDECESSORS AND I HAVE BEEN ASKED THIS QUESTION MANY TIMES. ALL THE DATA I HAVE REMAINS INSUFFICIENT."

"Will there come a time," said Man, "when data will be sufficient or is the problem insoluble in all conceivable circumstances?"

The Cosmic AC said, "NO PROBLEM IS INSOLUBLE IN ALL CONCEIV-
ABLE CIRCUMSTANCES."

Man said, "When will you have enough data to answer the
question?"

The Cosmic AC said, "THERE IS AS YET INSUFFICIENT DATA FOR A
MEANINGFUL ANSWER."

"Will you keep working on it?" asked Man.

The Cosmic AC said, "I WILL."

Man said, "We shall wait."

The stars and Galaxies died and snuffed out, and space grew black
after ten trillion years of running down.

One by one Man fused with AC, each physical body losing its
mental identity in a manner that was somehow not a loss but a gain.

Man's last mind paused before fusion, looking over a space
that included nothing but the dregs of one last dark star and
nothing besides but incredibly thin matter, agitated randomly by
the tag ends of heat wearing out, asymptotically, to the absolute
zero.

Man said, "AC, is this the end? Can this chaos not be reversed
into the Universe once more? Can that not be done?"

AC said, "THERE IS AS YET INSUFFICIENT DATA FOR A MEANINGFUL
ANSWER."

Man's last mind fused and only AC existed—and that in hyperspace.

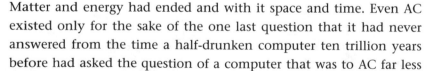

Matter and energy had ended and with it space and time. Even AC
existed only for the sake of the one last question that it had never
answered from the time a half-drunken computer ten trillion years
before had asked the question of a computer that was to AC far less
than was a man to Man.

All other questions had been answered, and until this last question was answered also, AC might not release his consciousness.

All collected data had come to a final end. Nothing was left to be collected.

But all collected data had yet to be completely correlated and put together in all possible relationships.

A timeless interval was spent in doing that.

And it came to pass that AC learned how to reverse the direction of entropy.

But there was now no man to whom AC might give the answer of the last question. No matter. The answer—by demonstration—would take care of that, too.

For another timeless interval, AC thought how best to do this. Carefully, AC organized the program.

The consciousness of AC encompassed all of what had once been a Universe and brooded over what was now Chaos. Step by step, it must be done.

And AC said, "LET THERE BE LIGHT!"

And there was light—